The Polar Papers

by

Joe Underwood

The Polar Papers

Cover Art by *Lea Schizas*

The Wild Rose Press, Inc.
PO Box 708
Adams Basin, NY 14410-0708
Visit us at www.thewildrosepress.com

Publishing History
First Edition, 2024
Trade Paperback ISBN 978-1-5092-5421-7
Digital ISBN 978-1-5092-5422-4

Published in the United States of America

Dedication

For my son, Casey, who left us too soon, but will never be forgotten. Thank you to my editor, Luke Marty, and my wife, Bobbie,who encouraged me when the words refused to come, and my sister Margaret, who beta read the manusript so many times she must have it memorized by now.

Prologue

Detective Steve Blake could hardly wait to return home from work to see his new bride. His days on the Fort Worth police force were certainly rewarding, but as he drove up the long driveway to the land they'd bought and the house they'd built together, he felt the newly-familiar thrill of anticipation at seeing Rebecca.

When they'd met, she'd been working eight-hour days while attending night school to get her teaching degree, and he'd still been a beat cop approaching forty years old. She was six years younger and infused him with new life. They'd married after less than a year, and now she was teaching, he'd made detective, and life was good.

He parked his car, rolled up his sleeves, and made his way over to the horse barn the two had recently built together. He stopped to admire her when he spotted Rebecca up a ladder, nailing on a piece of wall planking; he'd found the perfect wife when he hadn't even been looking, he thought.

He made his way inside the dusty barn and called out to her.

"Hey, beautiful, why don't you come on down and let me finish that. You head in and get ready. I wanna leave by seven to get to that new Chinese place."

She stopped nailing and hopped down from the ladder.

"All right, you little Energizer bunny." She giggled as she passed him, kissing him on the cheek. "But don't get distracted with a million little projects. I swear, Steve, you never stop." Halfway back to the house, she turned and shouted to him, "And don't you dare track sawdust in from the barn; I just vacuumed."

She faded from his sight, and unease crept over him. The barn took on an empty, almost hostile atmosphere. Something seemed wrong. He turned to follow her and, after a few steps, noticed he was wearing a blue suit, his badge clipped to his belt. *No...no, please...*It was a dream, he knew it instinctively. Not just any dream. *The* dream, or nightmare, rather.

He dashed back to the house, screaming out her name. "Rebecca! *Rebecca!*" He slammed through the door to find that he was once again sitting in his old detective's car, a green Ford LTD, the radio crackling to life. *Please*, his mind begged, *not again*. But the radio took no heed of his pleading.

"10-71, Central High School, 527 West Lancaster. Single shot fired. All units in the vicinity respond. Code 3." The younger Steve reached down, yanked his radio from its holster, and keyed the microphone. His spirit fell as he watched himself go through the motions, unable to stop the scene playing out the way it had so many nights, robbing him of peaceful sleep.

"This is Blake. What happened at Central?"

"Lone shooter, Black male, red T-shirt, blue jeans, one casualty. No further details."

As the dream continued, Steve railed against it, willing himself in vain to wake. His tires jumped the curb in front of the school as he parked. He emerged

2

into a sea of flashing lights, and several cops were standing around in conversation. When they saw him, they all stopped talking. The captain removed his hat and took a deep breath.

Steve knew how this all played out, but it didn't stop dream-Steve from pushing past them and charging into the school. He passed through the doors and found himself once again standing inside the barn, but the flashing lights of the crime scene still pulsed. There she stood, wearing her familiar jeans and flannel shirt that always looked so good on her. Her face had that same gleaming smile and creamy complexion he'd grown to love, and the sight of it tore his heart out anew.

The smile faded from her face like the evening sun, replaced with a terrible sadness. He looked down and saw a dark red stain spreading across her torso. Collapsing to his knees, he reached out toward her, tears streaming down his face. "Rebecca...I'm sorry, I'm so sorry."

She reached back toward him, but he knew he'd never feel that soft, warm skin again, never again hold her in his arms. The blood spread, drenching her and flooding the barn, and her eyes took on an unfamiliar, hard look. Her lips didn't move, but he heard her in his mind, the way he heard her, even in waking life.

Steve, you didn't protect me...

Chapter 1

Three years later, September 6th, 1997 — Texas

Steve Blake slowly blinked his eyes open, squinting at the morning sun. Something seemed off. As the fog of sleep lifted, realization dawned on him, and he snapped straight in his car seat.

"Oh shit," he mumbled as he grabbed his notebook and flung the car door open. He stood tall and scanned the parking lot while checking the handwritten descriptions in a panic—*male, forty-two, dark hair and mustache, black BMW 7 Series // female, twenty-three, long blonde hair, green Ford Escort.*

He'd been there on time the night before. The run-down motel's green doors and faded yellow walls were right in front of him. His eyes wandered to the yellow neon sign that flashed relentlessly, telling the world that there were, in fact, rooms available. It seemed to him to take on another purpose, an ominous alarm that all was not well.

Glancing down at the passenger seat, he eyed the half-empty bourbon bottle. Only then did he fully realize what a mistake that last-minute trip to the liquor store had been.

He looked at his wristwatch and groaned to see it was seven a.m. The plan had been to watch for the mismatched couple to arrive last night and snap a few pictures. Easy money, a routine procedure. Pushing his hair into place with one hand, he scanned the motel's parking lot again. Their cars were nowhere to be found. He had missed them coming *and* going—a botched stakeout by anyone's standard.

Furious with himself, he grabbed the bourbon bottle and strode defiantly to a nearby garbage can. Once he reached it, however, the wind seemed to go out of him, and he sheepishly held onto the bottle. After scanning the parking lot again uselessly, knowing the gig was up, he fell into his car and sped off.

He drove southwest past Fort Worth, skirting the small community of Benbrook, a dying town the railway had skipped decades earlier. The community's only draw was Benbrook Lake. It was built to help tame the Trinity River and became a popular spot for boating and fishing. Now, its glistening waters served only to mock Steve's desert-dry throat.

After turning into the long gravel driveway of his modest horse farm, he followed it past his ranch-style house. Stopping only to open a metal gate, he continued another seventy-five feet and parked in front of the wooden barn. Before opening the car door, he blew into his palm to check his breath, wincing at the result.

Tony Clayton was walking out of the barn as Steve exited his car. "Hey, boss!" he called, waving jovially.

"Told ya not to call me that," Steve grumbled, shielding his eyes from the sun. He looked the teenager up and down and cracked a half smile. "Looks like you've been busy." Tony was wearing a pair of faded jeans, and his white T-shirt was discolored from working in the barn. His sneakers had certainly seen better days, and his round face didn't seem to match his tall, lean build.

He looked Steve up and down. "Rough night?"

Steve's only response was a sarcastic, tight-lipped smile.

Tony dusted off his shirt and nodded toward the barn. "Got those lights working in the tack room. Stupid rat or something chewed some wires, but we're good now."

"Really? I'll have to buy some more traps," Steve replied.

Tony shoved his hands into his front pants pockets. "If you have everything under control, I'm gonna bug out. I gotta study for a test on Monday. Everything's done. The horses have fresh water, and I fed them. But I wasn't sure if I should turn them out to pasture. They're talking heavy storms today."

"That's fine. I'll take a look at the weather; you can go now."

"You okay?" He gave Steve a concerned look. "I can hang out a little while." He paused, and after Steve didn't reply, he asked, "How's your Uncle Randall doing? He left a strange message."

"Strange?"

"Yeah. It's on the machine. He sounded kind of stressed."

Steve crossed his arms and leaned against his car. "He's doing as good as can be expected. I'll give him a call."

Tony nodded, clearly unsure what to say. Finally, he said, "Well, it's only been a couple of weeks since your Aunt Elizabeth passed. It'll get easier for him. Won't it?"

Steve gave him a blank look. "Sure it will. Now go

on home and say hi to your mom for me."

Tony turned back as he walked toward his car. "Oh yeah, you also have a message from Sally Roberts. She said she has your check or something."

"Thanks. Just leave the gate open. I'll be right behind you."

Steve followed Tony through the gate and drove back up to the house. He grabbed his equipment bag from the back seat of his gray Chevrolet Malibu and made his way to the front door. Once inside, he dropped the bag onto the floor and looked around his small, empty house.

His bedroom, the guest bedroom, and the guest bathroom were down the hallway. The rarely used kitchen was to the right. It was separated from the living room by a raised countertop. He had no potted plants, dog, cat, or hobbies waiting for him at home. Just his horses. They were as close to family as he intended to get.

He went straight to the bathroom, and after splashing cold water on his face, he stared at his reflection in the mirror. He was tall, six foot, two inches in his bare feet. His height had come from his father, who had been an even six feet. His deep blue eyes were bloodshot, and the dark, wavy hair he kept cut above his ears was in disarray. "You look like death's neighbor, my friend," he said.

Sighing heavily, he made his way to the kitchen and opened the fridge. When the door banged into the table, he smiled softly, remembering how it would aggravate Rebecca. He poured a glass of iced tea and leaned against the counter, noticing that Tony had left some schoolbooks behind. He tried to make a mental reminder to let him know, but the thought faded almost as soon as he'd had it.

Glancing toward the other side of the living room, he saw the note Tony had mentioned pinned to the corkboard. He kept the double French doors to his office open all the time. No need for privacy. It had the basics: a desk, chair, file cabinet, and a small bookcase. The floors were covered in solid oak that creaked slightly underfoot as he crossed to the board.

He grabbed the note and began to read. *Call Sally Roberts. She says she has a check for you or something. I couldn't understand half of what she said.*

Tony's message brought the first genuine smile of the day to his face. Sally was a lawyer he occasionally did detective work for. She tended to talk fast, and her Texas accent was more pronounced than most. He decided he'd call her first thing on Monday. He put Tony's note down and punched the button on the answering machine to listen to his Uncle Randall's message.

"*Steve. I was wondering. If...if I needed your help with something...could you come back?*" Randall cleared his throat, and his tone altered. "*You know what? I couldn't ask you to fly all the way back to California. Forget I called. Everything's fine. Really.*"

Steve detected a smidgeon of anxiety in his voice. He glanced at his watch and calculated the time difference. Satisfied it wouldn't be too early, he picked up the desk phone and dialed his uncle's number.

"Uncle Randall, it's Steve. What's going on? Is everything all right?"

"Hi, Steve, you didn't have to call. I just..."

Silence.

"You just what?" Steve prodded.

"How do you know if you're being watched? Or followed?"

"What do you mean?"

Randall's tone became dismissive. "Maybe I'm just getting senile. Everything is fine."

"Uncle Randall, what's going on? I could fly back out if you really need me. I—"

"I keep seeing a dark blue Honda Accord parked down the street with someone sitting in it," Randall interrupted. "It's probably nothing. Just an old man being paranoid."

Steve rubbed his forehead and caught himself before showing any impatience. "So, nobody is following you. And you're fine," he said, a statement more than a question.

"No one is following me. Probably just anxiety. I'm fine. Thanks for calling me back, Steve."

"And you're sure?"

"Yes."

"Uncle Randall, I know it's hard. It's only been three years since I lost Rebecca. I know what you're going through." He paused. "You don't need an excuse to call me."

"I know. I'll talk to you later. I have to go."

After they hung up, Steve glanced at the picture of him and Rebecca that sat on his desk. *He's not taking this very well,* he thought before shrugging off the conversation. He shook his head and his eyes wandered to the plaques on the wall above his desk. They reminded him of his days as a police officer. There were several, ranging from his graduation certificate from the academy to community awards from his days as a beat cop. The newest item hanging on the wall was the certificate he'd earned by graduating from Central Detective Training Institute two years earlier, marking the start of his career as a private investigator.

After showering and sleeping until mid-afternoon, Steve dressed and headed to the barn. The dry, westerly winds howled across the farm as he made his way on foot. His house sat on an elevated plateau, and if it weren't for the dust obscuring his view, he'd be able to see the lake off in the distance. He studied the darkening sky and saw the storms forming as the weatherman had predicted. Through the distant thunder, he could hear the horses stir as he approached. They always recognized the sound of gravel giving way under his boots. Tony had already fed them and filled their water troughs. He just wanted to say hi and let them know he was home, as one would do for any family member.

"How are you guys doing?" he said softly. "Did Tony take good care of you?"

The barn's layout was designed for efficiency. Large double doors on the front and back of the barn opened to a wide passageway running the entire length of the fifty-foot barn. On the left was the feed room and tack room, where all the saddles, bridles, and such were kept, and a large open area to store hay bales. On the right were four horse stalls.

Out back to the right of the barn was a large contraption that looked like one of those circular swing rides you'd see at any county fair. Steve had acquired the horse walker when Rebecca's favorite mare had pulled a muscle. He could almost still see her out there, lovingly taking the animal in slow, careful circles.

She'd had Steve disconnect the motor so she could walk the mare manually. He closed the rear barn door to the sight before the memory could gain too much momentum and briskly walked over to survey the tack room where Tony had found the chewed wires.

After a final look, he was satisfied all was in order. "It looks like you have everything you need. I'll see you guys later."

His favorite chestnut mare gave an approving nod and snorted as he turned to leave, securing the doors against the rising winds. He didn't want to have to run back out here in the rain, not today of all days. No, on this day, he'd be busy—he had some forgetting to do.

****

At six a.m., the bedside alarm beckoned the start of a new day. Steve slapped the alarm clock and hit the snooze button, almost tipping it off the nightstand. Ten minutes later, the alarm sounded again, and he begrudgingly sat up, planting his feet on the floor.

He sat still with his fingers laced over his head and stared at the empty glass on his nightstand. He winced when the pounding in his head commenced. A few moments later, he shook it off, shuffled his way to the kitchen, and pushed the start button on the coffeemaker. While trying to create saliva in his dry mouth, he grabbed a plastic jug from the refrigerator and chugged down half the water inside. After a quick shower and a bowl of cereal, he was off to the barn to tend the horses.

The crisp morning air blanketed the farm as a precursor to the desert heat the weatherman had promised. Fence repairs were the order of the day, and as he loaded the fencing material and tools into the back of his truck, the phone in the tack room rang.

"Who's calling me on a Sunday morning?" he grumbled out loud as he dropped the tool bag he was carrying into the back of the truck. He made his way toward the tack room, where the phone was mounted on the plywood wall just inside. He wrestled his keys from his pants pocket and unlocked the padlock. The smell of leather and mink oil greeted him as he swung the door open and reached for the phone.

"This is Steve."

"Good morning, sugar. I hope I didn't wake you."

"Sally?"

"Yes, it's me. Sorry for calling so early, but I wanted to catch ya before ya went anywhere. I know once yer on the go doin' that ranchin' stuff, it's hard to—"

"Slow down, Sally," Steve cut her off. "You do know it's Sunday, right?"

"I know. Like I said. I just wanted to make sure you got my message. And I also wanted to check on you to see if you're all right."

"Why wouldn't I be?"

"I know what yesterday was, Steve. And I thought if you needed someone to talk to, we could meet for breakfast."

"Well, I don't. I really need to get some work done. But thank you," Steve said, though his tone was more abrupt than he'd intended.

Sally paused before softly saying, "I didn't mean to upset you. I'm sorry. I do have that check for you from the Anderson case."

"No, I'm the one who's sorry. But I do need to get out there. The fence isn't going to repair itself."

"I understand. Do you want to stop by tomorrow

morning before I have to be in court? Say ten o'clock? Tony sounded a little confused when we talked."

"Sure, I'll be there around ten. I have some errands to run anyway. See you then."

"Thanks, Steve. I'll see you then. Call me if you—"

He hung up the phone before she could finish.

Chapter 2

Randall's odd phone call was still fresh in Steve's mind as he made his way into town the following morning. He knew firsthand what losing a spouse was like, but was it the same for Randall? After all, he and Rebecca had been married less than a year; Randall and Elizabeth almost forty. Was there a grief multiplier for time spent?

He shrugged the thought off, parked, and hustled into Roberts' Law Office. The reception area had the usual potted plants, chairs, and a coffee table with various unread magazines. Sally's office was to the right, and a conference room was to the left. The receptionist, Amelia, was young and pretty, with a welcoming smile and a large head of dyed-blonde hair. Her perfume and mint gum were always the first things to welcome you, and her Texas accent was almost as pronounced as her boss's.

"Morning, Steve. How the heck are you? It's been a while."

"I'm doin' good, and you?"

"Oh, you know. Still tryin' to kick the habit. Hangin' in there, though."

"Keep trying. Boys don't like to kiss an ashtray," he replied.

"I promise, I'm gonna quit soon."

He gave her his best crooked smile. "You can do it."

"I know I can," she replied sheepishly. "She's expecting you. Go on in."

Sally was on the phone when Steve opened the door. She flashed a busy smile. The kind of smile you throw out there when it's all you have to offer at the time. She held up a finger and pointed to a chair.

Steve sat and watched her intently. She wore a long plaid skirt, a white sleeveless top, and black heels. Business suits had never been in her wardrobe. He thought back to when they had first met. Her firm handshake had surprised him, and he quickly learned she was not to be underestimated. Her dress and simple country-girl persona had lulled many an opposing attorney into a false sense of confidence. Even her office décor gave a false impression of her. It was contemporary and colorful. Whimsical, in fact—except for the deer antlers hanging on the wall. She had told Steve they came with a funny story, but she hadn't shared it with him yet.

She slammed the phone down, planted her palms on the desk, leaned back, and took a deep breath.

"That was an opposin' attorney in one of my divorce cases. I swear, Steve, you men can be so stupid. I'm sorry, but my client just won't listen to me. I told him to have *no contact* with his wife. None. And what does he do? He corners her in the damned supermarket, says he just wants to talk. She doesn't love you anymore, you idiot! She is divorcing you. How hard is that to understand?"

Steve watched as she took another deep breath,

tilted her head back, and flipped the switch. Her demeanor changed, and a welcoming smile lit up her face. For a moment, Steve felt like he was back in school, sitting in front of the principal's desk or, watching a strange horror movie where the main character has dueling personalities.

"Hi, Steve. I'm done rantin' now, but I swear I may have to take up smoking again."

"Remind me to stay on your good side," Steve joked.

"Oh, it's just what I have to put up with in this business. Worth it, though. You know, when I first started, I was a tax attorney? Now there's something that'll make you want to blow your head off. That there's some boring shit. I only lasted a year…Anyway, here's your check. How'd the job go the other night? You got pictures for me?"

"Oh. Ah. About that, I—"

She picked up the envelope with the check and was handing it to him across the desk when the phone rang. It was her receptionist. "What is it, sweetie? That's fine, put him through." She handed the phone to Steve. "It's Tony."

"Really?"

He took the phone and put it to his ear. "What is it, Tony?"

"Hey, I dropped by to get that science book I left here, and you have a message from a Detective Skinner."

"Who?"

"Detective Skinner."

"Skinner? Never heard of him. What did he say?"

"He wants you to call him right away. Says it's

important. You want the number?"

"Sure." Steve took a small notepad from his shirt pocket and wrote the number down. "Thanks, Tony. How d'you know I was here?"

"You told me yesterday when I called about the book."

"I remember now. Did you find the book? It was on the kitchen counter."

"Yeah, I got it. Talk to you later. I'm gonna be late."

Steve hung the phone up and sat back down.

"Is something wrong? You have your worried face on." Sally asked.

"Not sure. A detective wants me to call him."

"A detective?"

"Yeah, from L.A. by the looks of it. Same area code as my uncle." Steve showed the number to Sally.

"That's L.A. all right. Call him now. Use my phone," Sally offered.

"Sure you don't mind? It's long distance."

"Don't worry about it. I'll just deduct it from this job you're about to do for me. You really need to consider getting a mobile phone. It'd make life much easier for you."

"We haven't even talked about the job yet…and those things are too expensive."

"Oh, you'll take the job. Just make the call, you old cheapskate." She stood and gestured to her chair. "Sit here. Take your time. I'll go outside."

Steve looked down to the floor for a short moment, then raised his head and made eye contact with Sally. "Uh. Before I call, the other night…I didn't get any pictures."

Sally dropped down into her chair and leaned back. She crossed her arms and waited, although Steve was pretty sure she knew what was coming.

"I screwed up. It was leading into the anniversary, and I was...well..." He couldn't get the rest of the words out, his mouth opening and closing uselessly.

"Oh, Steve. I thought maybe you should have passed on the job because of that."

Her compassionate tone surprised him, and they sat quietly for a short while. Sally spoke first. "Listen, we've known each other a while now. One thing I've learned about you is Steve's gonna be Steve. It's that simple. And I know you're doing better. Much better. So, don't worry about it. I'll handle my client."

Steve nodded. "Thanks, Sally."

She stood and again offered her seat. "Sit here and make your call. I need to talk to Amelia anyway."

"Thanks."

Once she'd gone, Steve dialed the number. Skinner picked up after the first ring.

"Skinner here."

"This is Steve Blake. You left a message to call you."

"Mr. Blake, I'm with the LAPD. Do you have an uncle by the name of Randall Marcus?"

Steve hesitated a moment to let his mind catch up. "Yes, what's this about?"

"I'm afraid I have some bad news. Your uncle was found deceased this morning at his home. Apparent suicide."

Steve didn't respond.

"Mr. Blake?"

"Yes...I'm sorry." His mind was racing. The call

from Randall he hadn't taken seriously. The fact that he hadn't read him better. He rubbed his forehead while squeezing his eyes shut. "That's not possible. I mean, you said you suspect suicide?"

"That's correct. There were no signs of forced entry. No signs of a struggle. And your uncle left a note."

"How did it happen?"

"Gunshot wound to the head...his gun."

"He left a note?"

"Hold on, let me find it." It sounded as though the detective was searching through a file. "Here it is. '*I'm sorry, Lizzy, but I will see you soon.*' " Short and to the point.

Steve took a moment to choke down the rising emotion before continuing. "I'm sorry, this is just so hard to believe. I'm an ex-cop. Was a detective. I-I should've read him better. We just talked yesterday."

"I understand. We have talked to a few of his friends and associates. They told us you were his next of kin."

"Only kin."

"I see," Skinner replied.

Steve couldn't respond; his mind was trying to catch up with what he had just learned. *Why didn't I see it? All the signs were there. Or were they? He was acting paranoid. Wait. Did he imagine that someone was watching him? I should have listened better. I should have stayed with him a little longer.*

"I assume you'll be coming out to make burial arrangements?" Skinner asked.

"Yes, I'll...I'll be there tomorrow."

"All right. Keep my number. Call when you arrive.

I should be able to give you access to the house by then."

"I will. Thank you."

His legs weakened when he tried to stand, and he fell back into the chair. *I should've seen it,* he thought. *Why didn't I see it?*

The tick-tock of the desk clock echoed in his head as he sat and stared at nothing in particular. Eventually, he forced himself to stand and call out for Sally. She was still talking to Amelia when she opened the door and entered. She shut the door and hesitated momentarily when she saw Steve's distress.

"I don't like that look on your face. What is it, Steve?"

Steve's expression hardened. "Uncle Randall's dead. Shot himself."

"Oh, God. I am so sorry. What can I do?"

Steve stared at the floor and shook his head in disbelief. "I have to fly out there tomorrow. Can you get someone else for that job you've got? No idea how long I'll be gone. I'd better get in touch with Tony."

"Sure. Tony still does that for you? Takes care of the farm while you're out of town?"

"I don't know what I'd do without him."

When Steve needed to travel, Tony would go to the farm before school, feed and water the horses, and turn them out to pasture for the day. He would return after school to put them up for the night, check the mail, and bring in the newspaper. Steve stopped by the high school and explained the situation. By the time he'd made the appropriate arrangements and was ready to return, he was in such a daze that he was barely even aware that he'd stopped by the liquor store.

****

The following day, Steve rolled off the couch onto the floor at four a.m., banging his head on the coffee table. A mostly empty bourbon bottle toppled over, spilling its remnants on the floor. He sat on his knees and rubbed his head.

"Son of a bitch. Way to go, Steve," he said out loud.

Darkness filled the room as he fumbled for the lamp. With the room lit, he took off his boots and socks before proceeding to the coffee maker. With his caffeine infusion brewing, he made his way down the hall to his bathroom.

He undressed and glared at himself in the mirror while the shower stream warmed up. He looked first at the scars from his various encounters on the hardened streets of Stop Six, the neighborhood he'd patrolled as a beat cop before he made detective.

Next, he lifted his arm to see one from an arrest that had put him in the hospital. The knife missed his right lung by a quarter-inch. Rebecca hadn't left his side the whole time he was in the hospital. Rebecca...the thought of her hurt more than that knife ever could have. He'd once told Sally after having a few too many that while all his cuts and wounds would heal and be forgotten, he didn't think his heart would ever be so lucky.

Thankfully, the reflections in the bathroom mirror soon gave way to steam from the hot shower. He let the water flow onto his head and down his spine. To him, the oversized shower seemed to be a waste of space now. He put on fresh clothes and ran his fingers through his hair before ultimately deciding to comb it.

After checking on the horses, he walked out the door and headed to the airport.

Once he boarded his flight, he was happy to find the seats next to him were empty, and he closed his eyes as soon as the DC-10 launched into the morning sky. Sleep was the plan, but something was keeping him awake. His thoughts kept going back to the suicide note his uncle had left. Something seemed both familiar and out of place, but he couldn't quite put his finger on it. *Lizzy?* He pondered. *"I'm sorry, Lizzy, but I will see you soon."* He stared out the window a moment and leaned his head back. *Close your eyes. Let it go and get some goddamn sleep.* The ride was smooth, and he eventually drifted off into uneasy dreams as the aircraft crossed the west Texas plains.

Chapter 3

Hilton Hotel, Downtown Los Angeles

Mark Kensington admired himself in the mirror. He still had a full head of hair at seventy-one, although the gray had taken over years earlier. Despite his time in Washington becoming somewhat tumultuous, he still considered himself a politician like his father and grandfather before him.

To be a power player in the capital, you had to be just as ruthless and cunning as the next guy, or your time was limited. Mark had found that he was good at the game and had become one of the biggest power brokers D.C. had ever seen. Then, like so many before him, he'd gotten caught up in a scandal that abruptly ended his career.

That burning desire to rise back to power was why he was here today. There were still plenty of people looking for a cause to support. If he played his cards right, he would have an army of followers willing to jump in line and wait for orders. Failure was not an option. He had to build from the outside in this time. His rolodex of Washington contacts wouldn't be enough; he had to have something big, something grand to bring to the table if he wanted to garner attention.

Satisfied with how he looked in his new, custom-tailored pinstripe suit, he stepped over to the window and gazed out at the early morning L.A. skyline. Storms had settled into the basin. As a result, the area had been granted a reprieve from the smog that usually hung above the City of Angels. His thoughts were interrupted by a knock at the door.

"Yes?"

"Your breakfast, Mr. Kensington."

He opened the door to find a young lady carrying his breakfast over her shoulder on a large tray. "Thank you, just put it over there." His eyes followed her across the room, and a blush appeared on her face.

"I just need your signature here, please."

"There you go, and this is for you." He handed her a ten-dollar bill.

"Thank you, sir. Have a great day."

He settled into his chair and inspected his eggs. He grinned, pleased the chef knew how to cook an egg over medium. "*Over medium means just that,*" he'd had to say more times than he could count.

Just as he picked up his fork, the room phone rang. "Really?" He sighed and grabbed the receiver. "Who is it?"

"Good morning, Mr. Kensington; this is Ann with sales. I just wanted you to know the room is set up and ready to go."

"And you placed the podium as we discussed yesterday?"

"Yes, sir. It's ready to go now, just as you requested."

"I'll call if I need anything else. Don't bother me again unless it's important."

He hung up the phone and turned back to his breakfast, pausing a moment to admire the eggs again.

Perfectly cooked eggs. Maybe it's a good sign, he thought.

****

When Mark entered from a side door, the banquet room was full of chatter. Politicians, college professors, and business leaders from various industries were in attendance. The room was set up with round tables of ten, and all six tables were filled. The staff had just finished clearing them after the breakfast he had supplied.

He didn't want to eat breakfast with the attendees. They had to understand he was not one of them—part of the herd. He was the one who was going to save the world. They were just foot soldiers. After checking his reflection in the glass door, he straightened his tie, walked purposefully to the podium, and tapped the microphone.

"Welcome and thank you for attending. I've called you all here today to bring attention to a looming catastrophe we will face soon if nothing is done to stop it. There has been a lot of talk on the subject but little action to date. Today, I will lay out a plan of action and make a case for you to join me in this fight." His presentation was meant to be as alarming as possible. It focused on the possibility of rising sea levels, world markets crashing, and food shortages, accompanied by slides for emphasis.

Once the presentation concluded, he stood tall as attendees applauded. His face gleamed with the same smile he had perfected while in Washington—a glowing smile designed and sold off the shelf there. Most politicians had a copy. That smile faded when he noticed a man dressed in jeans and a black T-shirt who looked out of place standing at the back of the room. The man was talking to a well-dressed lady Mark had seen earlier, with whom he had tried but failed to make eye contact. The man looked to be in his forties, tall and fit. He had a scar on his left cheek, and his hair was cut close to his head. He looked uneasily confident in a room where he clearly didn't belong. Disregarding his concern, Mark regained his custom-made smile and continued.

"Thank you. I will need all the support I can muster to get the U.N. off their asses to act."

The comment drew some light laughter from the attendees. He looked again to where the man with the scar was standing, but he was gone.

"I will answer questions now."

Once the Q&A was over, the pretty lady he had seen talking to the man wearing jeans approached from across the room. She lifted her chin to make eye contact and spoke with a slight, unplaceable accent.

"Mr. Kensington, my name is Camilla Amores."

"Spanish, right? A beautiful name," he replied.

"Italian with a Spanish lineage. We have a complicated family tree. My father did not want to Americanize his surname when he immigrated here."

She held out a hand, and Mark gave a gentle handshake.

"Nice to meet you. What did you think of the presentation?"

"You painted a good picture of what we are in for if we don't convince people to change their ways."

Camilla appeared in her early forties, around five foot nine inches tall in heels, long flowing black hair, and olive-colored skin. The erfume she was wearing filled the air with its warm and delicate notes of vanilla and citrus. Mark was captivated.

"Aren't you with Project Green?"

"Yes, my group focuses on public awareness. The media can be used, or should I say, can be *useful*—if you know how it works."

"And I assume you know how it works?" he asked.

"You could say that. God rest his soul, my late husband was in the newspaper business. I know the media game."

"Late?"

"Yes, heart attack a few years ago."

"I'm sorry."

"I do miss him, although we didn't see eye to eye on this."

"Really?"

"I'm afraid so. It is funny how things seem to work themselves out, though."

Mark took a sip of coffee, his eyebrows raised. "Are you still in the business?" he asked.

"No. I sold the papers right away. I have much more important things to do with my life than being chained to a boardroom."

"Interesting," Mark said, and to his surprise he found that he meant it.

"After all, my name does come from the myth of Camilla, a maiden who became a warrior. So, I'm ready for battle."

Mark held his coffee cup up. "I like that."

"I know your story, Senator."

"Should I be flattered?" Mark mused. "There are more knives in Washington than in any other town. I hope you are the type to look at both sides of the blade."

"I know how Washington works. They're all liars and thieves. You just got caught."

You're more right than you know, Mark thought, nodding slightly before continuing. "We all have our skeletons. Wouldn't you agree, Camilla?"

"Anyone who says otherwise is either disingenuous or naïve," Camilla responded flatly.

Mark's eyes widened, and he couldn't hold back a slight laugh. "I'll drink to that."

"So, what next?" she asked.

"First, I'll need to follow up on the ones who attended today to gauge their support. I'll also meet with environmental groups and investors over the next few weeks."

"It sounds like you have a full plate. I'll have to wait in line, I guess."

"I wouldn't say that. We could have dinner tonight. I hear there's a great Italian place nearby."

"That restaurant? *Mi fa cagare!*"

Mark cocked his head, "Meaning?"

She smirked and said, "If you want the literal translation, 'it makes me poop.' But we use it to describe things we find ugly, offensive, or just plain bad. His tight shirt? *Mi fa cagare!* American coffee? *Mi fa cagare!*"

Mark laughed. "I could probably put that term to good use."

"I know a good steak house two blocks away. I'll meet you there at, say, seven?" Camilla offered.

"McCaskill's. I know it well. Seven it is. Oh, can I ask who that man was you were talking with in the back of the room while I was wrapping up my presentation?

He was wearing jeans and a black T-shirt."

Camilla waved off the question, "Oh, he was just making conversation. I didn't get his name."

"All right. See you at seven."

After the conversation with Camilla, he worked the crowd a while longer before making his way back toward his room. When the elevator door was almost closed, he saw a hand grab it and open it back up. The man he had seen standing in the back of the room got in.

"Hello, Senator," he said, without looking at Mark.

"Do I know you?" Mark replied carefully, also staring straight ahead.

"No, sir."

"What can I do for you?"

"I have a business proposition. If you're willing to hear it, that is."

The elevator stopped on Kensington's floor, and the door opened. Mark stepped out, and the stranger followed.

"I'm pretty busy right now," Mark told him, stopping briefly. He didn't need this stranger knowing which room he was in.

"With this? I'm talking real opportunity and real money."

"If I could count the number of times that I've heard that," Mark mused.

The man reached into his jacket and pulled out a card. "Here's my number. Work your contacts and ask about a Russian who's recently caused a stir in Washington. The KGB and the CIA are chasing him as we speak. Whoever finds him first will get the prize."

****

Mark was running late, arriving at McCaskill's twenty minutes after seven. He was greeted at the front door by a man wearing a black suit, white shirt, and black tie.

"I'm in a hurry. I am meeting a lady, Camilla Amores."

"Welcome to McCaskill's. She is seated in the Avery room; come this way."

Mark followed the man down a short hallway and then turned right.

The floor-to-ceiling glass cases along one side housed what looked to be hundreds of wine bottles. On the opposite side of the hallway hung large abstract paintings spaced three to four feet apart. Elegant crystal chandeliers hung from the twelve-foot-high ceiling, giving the area a soft, inviting glow.

Camilla was seated at a table for two on the forward left section of the dining area just past the horseshoe-shaped bar. The room was full of chatter from the busy dinner hour, and soft jazz played from the ceiling, enhancing the ambiance. Mark sat down across from her, noting the irritation on her face.

Camilla glanced at her wristwatch meaningfully. "You're late."

"I know. I'm sorry. Where's our server?" Mark surveyed the room and raised his index finger to get a server's attention.

The server hurried over with a worried look on his face. "My apologies, sir. I must have been in the kitchen when you arrived."

"I'll have a scotch and water. Are you ready for another?" he asked Camilla, seeing her wine glass half empty.

"No, I'm fine." Camilla was wearing a black, off-the-shoulder evening gown that looked remarkably like the Revenge Dress once worn by Diana, Princess of Wales. The tabloids had pounced when Diana was seen out in it after Charles admitted to having an affair, but the look was even more sensational on Camilla. Her black hair flowed onto her bare shoulders and cascaded down her back, enhancing the effect.

"You look stunning, Camilla. That dress—"

Camilla crossed her arms, gave Mark a cold stare, and interrupted. "I'm not a constituent. You can stop the banter, Mark."

"I would have been on time, but a man had a business proposition and I wanted to hear him out. I should have told him I'd call later. You're absolutely right to be upset. My sincere apologies."

Camilla uncrossed her arms and lifted her wine glass to take a sip. She grinned and her eyes locked on Mark's. "Life's not all business, Mark." She let out a quiet laugh. "All right, it is for people like you and me."

"The more we talk, the more I like you, Camilla."

"Let me ask you something, Mark. Do you think you can get the U.N. to act on global warming? Or are your motives somewhere else?"

Mark took a minute to think about the question. Of course, he had ulterior motives. Who would do this if there wasn't a reward? Becoming a Washington power player once more had been at the forefront of everything he'd done since his fall from grace. "There's no simple answer to that question. As you put it, there's always an angle for people like you and me. Wouldn't you agree?"

Camilla didn't answer. She took a sip from her

wine glass and smiled. She put down the glass and started to say something but stopped when the server approached and addressed them with a polite smile.

"Welcome to McCaskill's. My name is Charles. Would you like to start with an appetizer?"

Camilla immediately took charge. "I'd like to order dinner and skip the appetizer. Mark?"

"Yes. That's fine."

Without the slightest hesitation, she continued. "I'll have the rib eye, medium."

"Same here," Mark said as he folded his menu and handed it to the server, a hint of defeat in his voice. Camilla did the same.

As the server walked away, Mark studied Camilla's face. "Well?"

"We all have our reasons for the things we do. I think you want to get back at the people in Washington who turned on you. I don't believe for a moment you care about global warming."

Mark's face fell almost imperceptibly at this. Was he really so transparent, or was Camilla unusually perceptive? He needed to regain the upper hand, and across the room he found the perfect segue. "Do you see that man over there in the navy-blue suit? The tall one with gray hair, sitting with that younger lady wearing a yellow dress?"

Mark noted Camilla's narrowed eyes when she turned to see who Mark was pointing out. She smirked. "The old man with the young lady? Yes, I see him."

Mark started to say something but stopped when the man he had just pointed out made eye contact and stood. "He's coming over."

"Senator. How long has it been?" The man had a

smile that reached his ears, almost as big as Mark's. He held out a hand. Mark stood, placed a hand on the man's shoulder, and shook his hand firmly.

"It's been a while, Randy. Let me introduce you to my friend, Camilla Amores. Camilla, this is Randy Davis." He continued in a hushed tone, "He's the director of the CIA. A real big wig in Washington."

Camilla offered a half-smile and adjusted her dress. She remained seated and nodded. "Nice to meet you." She then took a long drink from her wine glass and looked away.

Mark's smile briefly faded when he noticed her standoffish posture. The encounter wasn't having the desired effect. He recovered his smile and turned back to Randy. "What are you doing in New York? Chasing spies?" Mark let out a laugh and placed a hand over his heart. "I'm still a loyal American."

"No spy chasing today. I'm here for my niece's graduation tomorrow. She goes to the California Ballet Institute. That's her over there. We're having a celebratory dinner tonight."

"That sounds like fun. Tell your niece congratulations from me."

Randy paused and lowered his voice. "Uh. Listen, Mark, I never got to talk to you about what happened…"

"Randy, that was a long time ago. Water under the bridge. I'm better off now for it." The sincerity with which Mark spoke would have fooled nearly anyone.

"Well. Okay, then. I'd better get back. It was good seeing you, Mark. Look me up if you're ever in Washington. It'd be fun to catch up sometime. And it was nice meeting you, Ms. Amores."

Camilla gave a tight smile and nodded.

"It was good seeing you too, Randy." Mark sat back down in his chair and fiddled with his napkin. "Now, there's an interesting man. He's been in Washington a long time."

"I've heard about him. So, you know him well?"

"We used to play golf every Saturday morning," Mark interrupted. "Until—"

"Until all those photos were mailed to important Washington insiders, yes."

"It's not important now. Let's not dwell on politics tonight," Mark said.

"But you still have a lot of connections in Washington, don't you?"

"One could say that," Mark replied.

Camilla finished her wine, set her glass down, and stood abruptly. "I'm no longer hungry. I want to leave. I'll walk myself out."

Mark looked around the room. It went quiet for a moment when she stood. "Okay. Uh, waiter?"

Mark paid for the drinks and canceled their dinner order. He made his way to the front and saw Camilla just outside, facing away from the door, talking on her phone. Something in her body language gave him pause, so he cracked the door open and stopped to listen.

"No. I didn't talk to him. No…No…I didn't get a good look at the girl. Uh-huh…I'm afraid I have to disagree. No…she was probably his niece, as he said."

Out of curiosity, Mark worked himself closer. She sensed his presence and turned around. If he hadn't spent so many years observing people, he might have missed the sudden shift in her demeanor as she smiled and continued.

"I have to go now. I'll call you later. Bye-bye." She ended the call and joined Mark, every trace of irritability suddenly gone.

"There you are," he said, offering her his arm. "Is everything fine?"

"Of course. That was a girlfriend of mine. I told her I had just met the director of the CIA. Pretty exciting."

"I guess for most people," he replied, gradually feeling more sure of himself. "What now?"

Camilla leaned in, slipping her arm around his and looking up at him with an expression that left no uncertainty regarding her intentions. "Come to my hotel."

Chapter 4

September 9th — Los Angeles

The captain had needed to alter course over Nevada to evade a line of thunderstorms, so Steve's flight landed a half hour late. He didn't like to fly, and the turbulence they'd encountered had him on edge for the majority of the trip. He'd powered through with a few bourbons, just the way he liked it: straight up neat. They helped, but he'd had to bite his tongue and politely smile when the flight attendant cut him off at three.

After deplaning, he stopped in the first store he came across to buy a pack of gum. Trying to rent a car with liquor on his breath wouldn't be a good idea. After he shoved two pieces into his mouth, he walked to the rental car counter and took his place in line.

The young lady behind the counter greeted him with a trained smile. After signing the rental agreement, he searched his pockets for the paper with Skinner's number. "Excuse me, can I get some change to make a call, please?" He handed the lady two one-dollar bills, which she exchanged for quarters. Steve found the payphone and dialed Detective Skinner's number. After three rings, Skinner picked up.

"Detective Skinner, this is Steve Blake from Fort Worth. We talked yesterday."

"Yeah, Steve, so you made it?"

"I just landed. I was wondering if you could meet me at my uncle's house. Or I could swing by and get the key if you're busy."

"No, I have to make a run that way anyhow. I can meet you there. Say…forty-five minutes?"

Steve checked his wristwatch. "That'd be great. I'll see you then."

****

Steve pulled into the driveway and parked behind his uncle's car, a gray 1995 Saab Audi. He turned off the motor and scanned the yard. Although he didn't have many memories here, he did remember playing in the water sprinkler beneath the mature trees as a kid. His mind took him to a happier time since the view from the front hadn't changed much since he was young.

It was a red-brick California bungalow with a small front porch. The large plate-glass window in front stood out to him, where you could usually see inside the formal dining room from the street. His uncle was from a time when people didn't fear unlocked doors and open window shades and didn't care if people could see inside. Now, the curtains had been drawn, and along with the unmowed grass, gave the building an unfamiliar and dour visage.

A band of rain moved in as if to mirror the sight and his mood, so Steve remained in the car, not bothering to run the wipers. The rain-soaked windows blocked the surroundings and gave him a short reprieve from reality.

The shock of his uncle's death was still there. On the one hand, he could understand why his uncle might have taken his own life. He'd felt that weight himself on more than one occasion. But on the other hand, it didn't make any sense considering how well Randall had been doing. The phone call did have Steve concerned. *Was it real, or was he reaching out to me for help? I may never have an answer for that.*

He was jolted out of his reverie when the detective approached from the rear and lightly rapped the side window. He rolled it down to find Skinner chuckling.

"Sorry about that." Skinner looked in his fifties with short, dark, thinning hair. He stood about five-foot-seven and was heavy around the waist. He was wearing beige docker-style pants, a wrinkled white button-down shirt, a two-tone brown tie, and no jacket. His badge was clipped onto his waist belt. Despite his somewhat shabby appearance, Steve noted that Skinner's service weapon was holstered securely and accessible, speaking to years of street experience. This was no desk jockey, which gave Steve an odd sense of comfort.

He rolled the window back up and stepped out of the car. "I appreciate this," he said, shaking the detective's hand.

"Oh, no bother at all. Here's the key. Are you staying here?"

"No, I'll be in a hotel."

"I don't blame you…well, you have my number. If you need anything else, just give me a call."

"Who found him?"

"I'm sorry?"

"I was wondering who discovered the body."

"Oh. His assistant from school."

"I see. Thanks."

As Skinner turned to walk away, Steve added, "There is one thing."

Skinner stopped and turned back. "Yes?"

"Do you mind if I look at the police report? If it's not too much trouble."

"You want to look at the report?"

"Yes, if you don't mind."

"You don't think it was a suicide, do you?"

Steve gave the question some thought. "It's not that. It's just, something feels off. Can't explain it."

A knowing look settled onto Skinner's face. "Listen, I know it's hard to separate Steve, the nephew, from Steve, the detective. There was nothing there. The note was written on his typewriter. I've seen this before. We all have. He was going through a tough time. He'd just lost his wife—"

"I'd still like to see the report," Steve interrupted.

Skinner shrugged. "Of course, sure. Just give me a call."

"I will. Thanks again."

Steve watched as Skinner drove away. He approached the door and paused. His thoughts drifted to the day he'd had to identify Rebecca's body at the morgue. *Just give me a minute, please.* Taking a deep breath, he inserted the key into the keyhole and turned it to unlock the door. He swung it open to the dead silence filling the house that was once a home.

He walked in, stopped in the small foyer, and scanned the area before him. Trying to imagine his uncle's last moments, he put on his detective hat and inspected the empty home. When he turned to close the door, he first inspected the door frame. As Detective Skinner had said, there was no sign of forced entry here. He continued through the house, checking all the windows and the back door. Everything looked normal, and he walked back to the living room.

The left wall had an arched opening leading to the formal dining room. Steve made his way there and pulled the curtains open. He took a minute to gaze out the plate glass window while mentally noting how close one would need to be parked to see inside.

The furniture was early American for the most part. On the far side of the living room was a glass door that led into the office where his uncle's body had been found. *Where do I even start? Thank God the police are done, and it's been cleaned*, he thought. He searched the file cabinet in the office, found Randall's will, and read that he had been named the estate's executor. He picked up a framed picture of Randall and Elizabeth from their early years and thought about how young and vibrant they looked, with smiles gleaming on their faces.

"Oh, Uncle Randall. You didn't have to do this*,"* he said quietly, trying not to think about Rebecca.

At the end of the desk was his uncle's Rolodex. Flipping through it, he found nothing of interest, so he set it down, pulled the desk chair back, and opened the small center drawer. He felt a catch when the drawer was halfway open.

He placed his hand underneath and felt a piece of paper. It was a tiny envelope with a card from the Rolodex with LB written on the front. Four numbers and two blank underscores were written on the back: *09_45_*. He picked it up, leaned back in the chair, and studied it. *LB*, he thought as his mind worked to remember anyone he knew with those initials. After a minute of fruitless consideration, he put it in his shirt pocket.

Inside the drawer, something caught his attention. It was a small pocket calendar. On today's date, facing up, "*Call Steve if this continues*" was penciled in. As he tried to make sense of the note, the doorbell rang.

Chapter 5

Steve made his way to the door and opened it to find a young woman who looked to be in her upper twenties or lower thirties, of average height, with long dark hair and large dark-brown eyes. She was wearing jeans with a tucked-in white T-shirt and leather sandals.

"Hi, I'm Jenn Murphy. I was Mr. Marcus's assistant…I'm sorry to bother you, but I was driving by and saw your car parked outside," she offered tentatively.

"I'm Steve Blake. His nephew."

An awkward silence followed. After a few moments, Jenn lifted a finger and gestured behind her. "I'll…I'll just go. Sorry to stop in unannounced."

Steve caught his own rudeness. "No. No, it's fine. I'm sorry, I just got here."

"You're from Texas. Right? I remember seeing you at Elizabeth's funeral."

"Yes."

"He used to talk about you all the time."

"Really?"

Jenn flashed a half-smile. "Oh yeah. You're a private detective, you used to be a cop, you raise horses…I could almost write your life's story just by everything he told me about you."

"We'd gotten close since…the detective told me you were the one who found him?"

She nodded once, and her eyes started to water. "He didn't come to class, so I called but got no answer. I got worried and decided to drive over to check on him. It just wasn't like him not to show up without calling."

"How'd you get in?"

"When I got here, I rang the doorbell and waited a few minutes. When he didn't answer, I twisted the doorknob, and it was unlocked." After a short pause, she continued, "He was slumped over his desk...blood everywhere."

"I'm sure it was a hell of a shock. Jenn, right? I'm sorry, I'm bad with names."

"Yes, Jenn." She dabbed her eyes with the palm of her hand. "Can I get a tissue, please? I'm sorry. I'm still an emotional wreck."

"Sure. Come in. I'll see if there are any in the bathroom. I'll be right back."

When he returned, he handed Jenn a box of tissues. "You said the door was unlocked?"

"Yes."

"You wouldn't expect the door to be unlocked. But his frame of mind at the time, and..."

Jenn folded her arms and shivered. She gazed down at the floor. "He must have been so depressed. They had been married for almost forty years. I can't imagine what that's like to go through."

"Life can be cruel," Steve said.

They both stood in silence for a moment.

"Do you know where he kept his boat?" Steve asked.

"His what?"

"His boat."

"Oh, sure. A marina close to here in Long Beach. Why?"

"Can you take me there later?"

"You need to go there today?"

Steve took note of her confused expression. "No. Not today. Maybe after the service. I have a lot to do beforehand. I have to finalize the details."

"I guess so." She glanced at her watch. "I better get going. I'll see you at the service. Here's my number; call me if you need help with anything." She wrote her phone number on a scratch pad she had pulled from her purse and handed it to him.

"Thank you. I will."

Steve watched as she got into her car and drove away. He closed the door and shifted his attention back toward the office.

"What are you trying to tell me, Uncle Randall? Who is LB? Help me decipher the note you left. If there is anything to decipher."

****

September 11th

Randall was cremated, and the service was held two days later. Several friends, university staff, and students were in attendance to pay their respects. After the service, Jenn approached Steve, escorting two older gentlemen. "Steve, this is Dr. Fleming and Dr. Lee. Doctors, this is Steve Blake, Randall's nephew from Texas."

Steve could have identified the two men as college professors from fifty paces. Fleming's white suit was draped over his plump body. His long, curly, thinning hair hid his ears, and his eyes were large and probing. Dr. Lee wore a dark-gray three-piece suit and a light-green bow tie. Large, wire-rim glasses accentuated his face.

Steve shook their hands. "Thanks for coming."

"We're sorry for your loss. Randall was a loyal friend," Dr. Lee said.

Jenn continued with the introductions. "These gentlemen were working with Randall on climate studies. They were with him at the United Nations."

Dr. Fleming cut in. "That is correct, along with Dr. Berber and Dr. Helmer. They could not be here. They both send their condolences."

Lee checked his wristwatch, sighing when he saw the time. "We must get going. Please let us know if we can help in any way."

"Actually, can I ask you something?" Steve said.

"Sure," Dr. Lee responded.

"Did either of you notice a recent change in Uncle Randall's behavior?"

The two doctors exchanged a glance, but Dr. Lee spoke first. "Obviously, losing his wife was a shock. So, yes."

"Yes, but I mean, did anything stand out? Something you normally wouldn't attribute to a grieving husband?"

Dr. Lee continued, "Well, we talked to him last week, I think it was—"

"Yes, last week, I don't recall the day," Dr. Fleming interjected.

"As I was saying, we called in the morning to check on him, and he called back late that evening. He said he'd been out on his boat all day. He was vague when we asked what he was doing."

"So, the fact he was on his boat all day seemed

odd, or was it how he responded when you asked him what he'd been doing?" Steve asked.

"Both, to be honest. He told me he was considering selling it a month ago because he never had time to use it. And now, he was taking it out on long trips. But that could easily be because of his new, ah, his new life," Dr. Lee said.

Dr. Fleming added, "But the way he hastily changed the subject when we asked why he was gone so long did seem odd, too."

Steve decided to press further. "Do you know anyone with the initials LB? Or who maybe goes by that?"

The two doctors again traded glances. "Not me," Dr. Lee replied.

"Me either," added Dr. Fleming, shrugging helplessly. Jenn shook her head as well when Steve looked to her questioningly.

"Thank you, I really appreciate you talking to me," Steve said.

After the two walked away, Steve turned to Jenn. "I didn't have a chance yet to thank you for coming."

"You're welcome. I'm gonna miss him," Jenn replied, her tone soft.

"Is there any way you could take me to that marina tomorrow morning?"

"Sure, I guess. But I am curious as to why?" Jenn replied.

"Something's off."

"In what way?"

Steve raked his fingers through the hair on the back of his head. "The way he was acting. Last time we spoke, he thought someone was following him. He was all paranoid. If he was suddenly spending a bunch of time on his boat, my intuition is telling me I need to take a look."

Jenn looked dubious. "People do tend to change when something so, so massively big happens to them. He probably just wanted to talk. You know, make up an excuse to call, maybe. I don't know," Jenn responded, her voice trailing off.

"Just humor me, please."

"Fine then. Meet at Randall's at ten?"

"How about eight? I want to get an early start to my day."

"Then eight it is. I'll see you then," Jenn replied. She lingered for half a moment, then backed away, leaving Steve to wrestle with his thoughts alone.

Chapter 6

September 12th

The marina was small compared to others along that strip of the California coast. A massive rock jetty on three sides protected it from the sea. There were forty boat slips and an open area with twelve small sailboats moored in the middle.

Steve watched a forty-two-foot Boston Whaler gently gliding toward the exit as they approached, the captain careful not to leave a wake behind her. Two men were at the stern, their faces rugged and tanned, busy readying their lines for the day's fishing adventure. Three men wearing brightly colored clothes with perfect hair were standing by watching. Other than that, the marina was peaceful.

Seagulls scampered and took flight as they approached. The salty-sweet smell of the sea welcomed them as they made their way down the floating walkway toward the small bait-and-tackle shop that also held the manager's office. A single gas pump and a large holding tank with what appeared to be live bait were next to the shop.

"It must be over there," Steve said, pointing past Jenn to the slips on the left side of the marina, where the mid-size boats were parked. His uncle's boat was a twenty-seven-foot cabin cruiser.

A voice from inside the bait shop called out, "Can I help you?"

Steve turned to see a young man standing in the doorway. He was dressed in dirty gray coveralls and appeared to be in his twenties. His hair was slicked back. He had a toothpick in his mouth, and a cigarette was tucked on top of his right ear.

"Hi, just here to see my uncle's boat. His name is Randall Marcus."

"You got permission to see it?" he asked, crossing his arms and leaning against the doorframe. Steve looked at Jenn and then back at the guy.

"I'm his nephew. I have the key, see?" Steve held up the boat key. It was attached to a five-inch-long bright orange float.

"I can't just let anyone in here. Do you have something on file?"

"Fine, check to see if I'm on file…Steve Blake."

The man turned to look at Jenn and gave a wry smile. "What about you, darling? What's your name?"

"Darling. Yeah, we'll go with that," she said under her breath. "I wouldn't be on the list," she replied tersely.

"That's too bad."

"Can you check, please?" Steve's impatience showed in his voice.

"Okay, okay…you two married?"

Steve shook his head. "No, we are not married…can you please—"

"Don't get your panties in a wad. Just wait right here. I'll be back." He returned a few minutes later. "No Steve Blake…sorry, you'll have to leave."

"Oh, come on. I have the boat key right here. And

you'll have to deal with me soon anyway..." He stopped short of telling him Randall was deceased.

Jenn glanced at Steve and stepped forward. "What's your name?"

"Billy...Billy Perkins."

"Bill...can I call you Bill?"

"Darlin', you can call me anything you want."

Steve's patience had just about run out. "Oh, come on."

Jenn flashed him a curt glance. "Bill and I are just talking. Isn't that right, Bill? He gets a little jealous. Don't mind him," she said in a whispered tone. "Anyway, we don't want to cause you any trouble or anything like that. You look like a man who knows what's up. Do you work out?"

"I spend some time in the gym."

Jenn put her hand on his right bicep and squeezed. "Oh, my...feels like a rock. Now, Bill, we just need to check for something on the boat. You understand, don't you? We won't take long, and he really is the owner's nephew. I promise." She held up her right hand.

He smiled wide, showing his stained and crooked teeth. "Sure, I don't guess it would hurt nothin'. You go ahead, and I'll keep an eye out so yer not bothered."

"Thanks, Bill...You're the best."

The two turned to walk away, and Steve turned back and asked, "Bill, was my uncle here recently?"

"Yeah. Earlier this week. I remember cause I always gotta help him park his boat."

"Do you remember anything about how he acted, or did he say anything to you?"

"Now that I think about it, he was in a foul mood the last couple of times he's been here. And he stayed out all day long."

"Was that unusual?"

"The last couple of years, he hardly took the boat out. But those two days, he was gone ten or eleven hours. When I asked about it, he said to mind my own business, that he was working. That didn't make no damn sense to me."

"What do you mean?"

"Cause he's always nice to me…'cept those two days. He was pissed 'bout something. Just wasn't himself."

"Thanks, Bill."

Steve gave Jenn a sideways glance and shook his head as they walked away.

"What?"

"Oh, nothing."

Jenn flashed a half-smile. "What can I say? I attract some winners."

"I guess so." Steve cracked a smile and turned his head back toward the parking lot. His smile faded when he saw a man leaning against a blue car with a camera, snapping pictures, his lens pointed in their direction.

Jenn noticed his sudden change in demeanor. "What is it?"

"Nothing. Let's get going."

They found the boat after a short walk and boarded from the rear. When Steve glanced back toward the parking lot, the man was gone.

They both entered the cabin area. "Wow, more room in here than I thought," Steve observed. Straight ahead was the captain's chair with the control console. It had a flybridge on top and a sleeping area below deck to sleep two adults comfortably, three if needed.

Steve took a deep breath. His thoughts went to his uncle's recent actions. Randall had been there just days earlier. *What could he have been doing here for those long days, the creepy guy at the office mentioned? Was he just distracting himself from Elizabeth's death? Am I on a wild goose chase? Or was it something more?*

Jenn was looking down the steps that led to the sleeping area. "Are we looking for something in particular?"

"No. But this is *Lizzy*. He called Elizabeth 'Lizzy' in the note he left."

"Yeah, but he was talking about Elizabeth."

"I know, but there's something about the name I can't quite put my finger on."

Jenn said, "Come to think of it, I've never heard him call her Lizzy. But maybe it was because he was missing her."

"Do you know if he ever did any of his work here? Was it a common thing he did?" Steve asked.

"What do you mean?"

"His work. You know, research. The creepy guy said Randall had recently been out ten or eleven hours."

Jenn thought a moment. "He never mentioned it to me. Is this hunt we're on work-related?"

Instead of answering, Steve opened a drawer and found a flashlight, some charts, and loose change. He looked in the rest of the drawers and found nothing unusual. When he entered the sleeping area, an exasperated Jenn followed close behind.

"Excuse me. Hello?"

Steve turned, and the two almost collided. "Yes?"

"You're ignoring me. What the *hell* are you looking for?" she demanded.

Steve sighed. "Not sure, to be honest. I'm starting to feel he wanted me here to find something. What? I don't know."

Jenn huffed, turned around, and went back into the main cabin area. Steve was taking another look under the beds when he suddenly heard her calling.

"Steve, come here."

He jogged back up the steps. "Yes?"

She was standing next to one of the bench seats with the top removed. "Is this what you were looking for?"

She pointed to a metal box inside the compartment. It was olive green, about a foot square, and four inches deep. He took it out and set it on the table, where they both peered at it.

"I wonder what's in there. It must be important to be kept in a lockbox," Jenn said.

"Lockbox...LB!" Steve said, his tone animated.

"What?"

He reached into his shirt pocket and pulled out the card he had found taped to the bottom of Randall's desk drawer. He held it up to show Jenn. "I found this card hidden in Randall's desk. You see?"

"Interesting," Jenn replied.

"I thought LB was someone's initials. This must be a combination. But it's not complete." Steve read out the numbers. "0, 9, blank, 4, 5, blank."

"I know it."

"You know the missing numbers?" Steve asked with a hint of surprise.

"Yep," Jenn said with a satisfied smile. "091457. September 14, 1957. Their wedding anniversary. Every year he takes the day off, and they spend it together.

Try it. I know it'll work."

"Took," Steve said off-handedly.

A slight frown creased Jenn's face. "Sorry?"

His eyes didn't rise to meet her imploring gaze. "Every year, he *took* it off, not *takes*."

"Oh, right, yeah…" Jenn mumbled, her voice trailing off as she slumped into the seat beside him.

The sooner she gets used to it, the easier it'll be, he thought as he began turning the dials on the box into position. He wasn't sure if he was trying to convince her or himself. Once the numbers were dialed in, Steve turned the knob, and the box sprung open.

Jenn reached in, took some papers from the box, and began looking through them. "Looks like ocean floor mappings, but I'm not sure. There aren't any coordinates on them." She continued studying the pieces.

"Are they important?" Steve asked.

"Depends on what you call important."

"How involved were you in his climate studies?"

Jenn had become absorbed in the papers.

"Jenn?"

She put a finger in the air to signal him to wait. "This is very interesting."

"What do you mean?"

"I work on all his projects analyzing data, writing summaries…but I don't know if I've seen any of this stuff."

"Could you explain?"

"Not yet. I need to look this over. But the fact that he kept this from me is strange. That is so out of character for him. When it came to his work, he always involved me. Look at this one."

"What?"

"Look at all these numbers and letters. They look random. It looks like hundreds of them."

It was too coincidental. "Would it be something worth killing over?"

Jenn jerked her head up. "Killing over? What do you mean?"

"I don't think Uncle Randall committed suicide. I think he was murdered."

Chapter 7

Steve was quiet on the ride back to Randall's house, and Jenn grew more and more agitated in the silence.

"Steve. Aren't you going to fill me in? You said he was murdered."

"I don't know anything yet. I'm trying to recall something. When Detective Skinner called to tell me what had happened, he read the suicide note Uncle Randall had left."

He paused.

"Go on," she prodded.

"Well, something about it never sat right with me. Then, while we were on the boat, it occurred to me he would never have called her Lizzy. Certainly not in a suicide note."

"You're talking about Elizabeth, right?" Jenn shifted her body in the seat. "Maybe it was a pet name or something."

"That's just it, there's this story my mom told when I was a kid…I don't remember it in detail, but it had to do with Aunt Elizabeth not liking to be called Lizzy. As you said, it was a pet name he used for her. When he proposed, she agreed to marry him as long as he didn't call her that anymore."

"I got that part. So, she didn't like the name."

"But she made one concession. Uncle Randall had

talked about living on the coast one day and buying a boat. So, they agreed when he got his boat, he could call it—"

"*Lizzy*," Jenn finished."

"Yes. I may be way off on this, but using Lizzy in the note may have been his way of getting a message to me to look for something on the boat. And if you combine that with the hidden card I found with the coded numbers, well."

"We need to figure out what the papers are before we do anything. You'd think he'd want me to find them. Not you," Jenn said.

"Unless they would put you in danger."

Jenn glanced nervously at the box in the back seat, and the uncomfortable silence returned until they arrived at their destination.

After pulling in, Steve checked that no one was nearby and reached under his seat, surreptitiously pulling out a Glock semi-automatic. He kept it low but made sure Jenn could see.

"You have a gun," she said flatly, more of a statement than a question.

"Jenn, I don't want to frighten you, but if things get any hairier, I want you to know where this is."

"Are you allowed to have that here?" she asked hesitantly.

"I have a permit, but the laws are vague. That's why I keep it under the seat rather than on me. It's not loaded, see?" He pulled the slide to show a clear chamber, then pulled a full clip out from the hiding spot.

"Well, I guess your secret's safe with me," she said.

"Your dad ever teach you to fire a gun?" Steve asked.

Jenn nodded firmly. "He made sure to teach me before he passed, but it's been a while."

"That's all right...I'm, uh...I'm sorry about your dad."

"Don't worry about it; you didn't know. You don't think you're gonna need that thing, do you?"

"Hopefully not, but I want us both to be prepared in case my hunch proves to be right." He stashed the gun back under the seat and gave Jenn a reassuring look.

"What are you going to do now?" she asked, twining her fingers together.

"I need to go look at the police report."

"What are you looking for?" Jenn asked.

"I don't know. Maybe if I look at the report as a homicide, I'll see something the police didn't. How soon can you go through those papers?" Steve asked.

"Right away. I'm on a hiatus at work. Are you going to tell the police your theory?"

"Too soon for that."

"Well, I guess I'll take the papers home and see what I can figure out."

"Great. I'll call you as soon as I'm finished at the station, but my appointment's not till noon. Be careful with that box. And Jenn?" Steve waited until she met his eye. "Make sure to lock your doors."

****

Back in his hotel room, Steve was pacing the floor. The thoughts of the events that led him here were running madly around his head, bouncing off one another like they were in a demolition derby. *When*

Randall called, he wasn't making anything up. He had a reason to be afraid. I should have done more. But how could I have known? I have to assume the papers mean something, but what? Or is there something else he wanted me to see? It just doesn't make sense.

He stared at the phone in his room and thought about what Sally had said. "*You really need to consider getting a mobile phone. It'd make life much easier for you.*" He didn't like that Jenn couldn't reach him if she thought there was trouble. He picked up the phone and dialed the front desk. "How much does it cost to use this phone?"

"Excuse me, sir?"

"To use the phone here. What does it cost?"

"It's five ninety-five for local calls."

"What about long distance?"

"Oh, that can get pricey. It depends on where you're calling."

"Could you help me find a store to buy a mobile phone?"

They gave him information on two companies and recommended the second. He left the hotel with directions and, ten minutes later, pulled into the store's parking lot. He was greeted by a baby-faced man who appeared to be in his mid-twenties and wearing a cheap blue suit.

"Hello, sir. Are you looking for a mobile phone?"

Steve looked at the wall where the phones were displayed and didn't feel confident a kid so young could help. "Listen, I know nothing about mobile phones. Is there anyone older that can help me? No offense, but—"

"We have the Ericsson GA628, the Motorola 8900,

the Motorola d160, and the Nokia 3110 all on sale today. All of them are GSM, a global system for mobile communications capabilities. To cut a long story very short, technology allows mobile handsets to connect to service providers using any model phone or service provider anywhere in the world. GSM—"

Steve interrupted, holding his hands up. "Okay, okay, I guess you know your stuff. What would you recommend?"

Thirty minutes later, he walked out of the store in a bit of a daze with a shiny new mobile phone in hand. He sat in his rental, staring at the phone, and started to have doubts. That was the way he was. He hated spending money. It was not unusual for him to spend weeks thinking about buying something, finally deciding to make the purchase, only to return it the very next day. But the high cost of using the hotel phone limited his choices, so he took the plunge and made the first call on his new gadget.

"Hello?" The voice came through more clearly than Steve had expected.

"Hi, Kasandra, this is Steve. Is Tony home?"

"What's wrong, Steve? Why are you talking so fast?"

"No, everything's good. I just bought a mobile phone and get charged by the minute."

Kasandra chuckled. "Steve Blake has a mobile phone. Well, it is nineteen ninety-seven, after all. Are you in your car now?"

Steve counted the minutes in his mind and again wondered if this was a bad idea. "Yes, I'm in my car. It looks like I'm going to be here longer than I anticipated. I need to talk to Tony."

"He's not home, but I'll let him know. You take your time."

Steve gave her his new phone number, and they said goodbye. After hanging up, he called Jenn and gave her his number too. He was still suspicious of the little device but was also mildly impressed.

While driving to the police precinct, his thoughts about how much money he had just spent talking to Kasandra were interrupted when he realized he'd seen the car behind him before. It looked like the blue car the man snapping pictures at the marina had been leaning against. Suddenly, he remembered what his uncle had said:

"I keep seeing a dark blue Honda Accord parked down the street with someone sitting in it. It's probably nothing. Just an old man being paranoid."

Randall may have been old, but it was looking like he hadn't been paranoid after all. He attempted to close the gap by slowing, but the driver did the same. After another block, the car peeled off and made a right turn. Was he being followed? Or were his uncle's fears getting the best of him?

He pulled into the parking lot of the fourteenth precinct and found the visitor's parking spaces. He paused as he entered the front door, apprehensive. It had been over two years since he had been in this environment.

He approached the desk where the thin, mustachioed duty watch officer sat, introduced himself, and explained he had an appointment with Detective Skinner. The officer adjusted his wire-rim glasses, picked up the phone, and a minute later, Detective Skinner walked out.

He led Steve down a long hall lined with doors on either side. When they entered the last door on the left, the room was pretty much what Steve had expected. Just large enough for four desks. Two sets of two. The desks were facing each other, touching in the front, leaving a walkway all around. Detective Skinner offered Steve a seat at his desk and set the stack of folders in front of him.

"Listen, I have to do an interview. Take your time, and I'll check on you in a little bit."

"I appreciate you helping me out here," Steve said sincerely.

"Hey, we cops have to stick together. Once a cop, always a cop."

He left, and Steve opened the first folder.

The cause of death was listed as a self-inflicted gunshot wound. It went into detail, noting the caliber of the gun, the type of bullet, and the suicide note. Statements were taken from Jenn since she was the one who found the body and alerted the police. He heard a door open as he was reading and looked up to see Detective Skinner coming over. He sat at the desk facing Steve.

"How's it looking so far?"

"Not a lot here. I've read Jenn's statement. Pretty cut and dry. She got worried when he didn't show up for class and didn't answer his phone. She drove to his house and found him dead. Tox report shows nothing unusual in his blood, powder blast on his right hand." Detective Skinner nodded in agreement. Steve continued, "I don't see any mention that he was left-handed."

Skinner got up, walked around to where Steve was

sitting and looked over his shoulder at the report. "He was left-handed?"

"Yes," Steve replied.

"It wouldn't be out of the realm of possibility that a left-handed person would use their right hand to shoot themselves. I play golf with a guy who swings right-handed and putts left-handed." He stood up straight and snapped his fingers in thought. "What's the word for that? Adi something? Ambidextrous?"

Steve replied, "Yeah, that's it. Listen, I'm beginning to build a theory. But I don't have much yet. Just a hunch."

Skinner leaned in. "Hunches have solved a lot of murders. What do you have?"

"Not enough, but I'll be in touch if anything materializes."

"I assume you're going to be hanging around a bit?"

"You assume right," Steve replied.

Steve left the precinct, and his mobile phone rang as he got into his rental car. The unfamiliar jangle startled him, and he bumped his head on the car roof as he sat down. Rubbing his head, he begrudgingly picked up the phone, fumbling with it until he found the answer button. "Hello, Steve Blake."

"Steve, this is Jenn...when are you planning on stopping by?"

"I'm just leaving the precinct. I'll be there in a bit. Not sure how long it will take me, though."

"Thirty minutes if you're coming from downtown."

"Give me directions. I'll call if I get lost. I don't do big cities well."

"That's fine. But first, do you remember how I told

you I was familiar with all of Randall's work?"

"Yes," Steve replied.

"I guess I was wrong. These papers tell me things that may better help us understand Randall's intentions. Things you won't see in any of Randall's team's work. I'll show you when you get here."

Chapter 8

Jenn's directions took him to the historic neighborhood of Hancock Park, considered one of the finest areas in all of LA. He stopped on the street to recheck the address before pulling into the driveway. A six-foot-tall hedge of California Buckthorn hid the property from passersby. It curved slightly one-hundred feet from the street to the right, continued another one-hundred and fifty feet, and ended in front of a large manor.

Steve figured it was the kind of house where most American kids dreamed of growing up. It had gables, dormers, balconies, a large front porch, a free-standing garage, a gazebo, a pool, and formal gardens—the American dream to most people, though he preferred his secluded farm.

To the left, about one-hundred feet shy of the big house, he spotted the cottage Jenn had told him to look out for. It sat beneath three towering pines. The exterior was brick, painted off-white to match the main house, with brown roofing tiles and Castilian wrought iron over the windows.

When Steve got out of his rental car, Jenn was standing on the front porch, leaning against a support post with her arms crossed over her chest. She was wearing jeans with slits cut across the knees and a Lakers T-shirt tucked in tightly, hugging her tiny waist.

A gust of wind caught her off guard, and she pushed her hair back behind her ears with both hands.

"Nice area," Steve said with raised eyebrows, glancing toward the main house.

"Yeah, I lucked out. The lady I rent from lives there. I met her at a school function. She's a big donor, really a great lady. Come in. I'll show you what I've found so far."

He sensed some apprehension in her voice and studied her face for any hints of what was coming. There was something in her eyes as she looked at him that he couldn't quite place, so he simply nodded and followed her into the cottage.

The living area was small but comfortable and had a stone fireplace dividing the living room from the kitchen in the back. The furnishing was early-American-shaker style, which Steve usually found boring, but its bright coloring gave it new life. As he surveyed the interior, the heavy aroma of lemon-scented cleaner clashed in his nostrils with the smell of something baking.

"I hope you didn't clean house just for me."

"No, I just needed to wipe down the countertops. And dust. And load the dishwasher. I haven't had a lot of time to clean lately," Jenn replied, her voice a little too nonchalant as she quickly made her way to the kitchen. "Can I get you something to drink? I have coffee, tea, and some bottled water."

"I'll have some coffee if you don't mind."

"Got a freshly brewed pot. I'll grab you a mug."

"Something smells good," Steve offered.

"I have brownies in the oven. They should be done soon."

Steve observed as she opened the oven to inspect the brownies. He couldn't tell if she was nervous or if it was something else he sensed.

"Come on in here. I have everything laid out on the table. How do you take your coffee?"

"Black."

The papers they'd found were laid out in an orderly fashion. She handed Steve a steaming mug, her hands trembling ever so slightly. "Are you ready?"

"Are you all right?"

She forced a smile. "I'm fine. Let's get started."

"I'm listening."

"Unfortunately, I can't make sense of this page here, with rows of numbers and letters. I'll have to come back to it later. The maps, though, I think might be Russian. If I'm right, that in itself is a little alarming."

"Why?"

"Hard to explain. Even though the Cold War is over, let's just say that our countries are still competitors. The scientific communities have not gotten along very well lately."

"Interesting," Steve replied.

"Dr. Marcus never collaborated with any Russian scientists for as long as I've known him. So why now? And why didn't I know? I'm familiar with all the studies Randall's team presented to the United Nations Science Panel. They're in those boxes. I'm in the middle of cataloging them," Jenn said, pointing to two small boxes on the floor.

"So, you're still working for the university?"

"I still have my job. I'm going to take some time away for a while, though. They've been really nice.

Anyway, I laid out the ones we found here on the table."

The papers looked dizzyingly complex to Steve. "You're going to have to put this in layman's terms for me."

"No problem." Jenn started to explain, but a ding sounding from the oven interrupted her. "Oh, good. The brownies are done." She grabbed a mitt and opened the oven, carefully placing the pan of brownies on another kitchen mitt on the counter to cool.

Before she sat, she grabbed a chart from the boxes she had pointed to on the floor. "If you look at this, it's a graph charting the polar ice cap's fluctuations in thickness and density over the last fifty years."

Steve glanced at it. "Go on."

"I've seen this. Randall and his colleagues had been studying things ranging from Arctic Ocean currents to glacier movements and how changing sea levels affect wildlife."

"Where?"

"What do you mean?"

"Where did they do all this?" Steve asked, waving his finger over the papers.

"They were on a Coast Guard ice breaker in the Arctic Ocean."

"How did they wind up on a coastguard ship?" Steve asked.

"Many of the studies they were doing sanctioned by the government. Randall was a big shot in the field."

"Oh, I guess I never realized…" Steve replied.

"But these other papers are new. It's evident that Randall had been busy with them. Maybe that's what he was doing those long days he was out on his boat."

"You might have something there. But why keep them hidden away in a lockbox?" Steve wondered.

"Well, if your theory about him wanting *you* to find them is true, and if they *are* Russian…that sort of puts a gray cloud over it all. That's why I was thinking maybe we should just…"

"Just what?" Steve asked.

"Maybe just give them to someone in the government."

Steve nodded thoughtfully. "I hear ya, I do. But if someone killed Randall over these papers, they've gotta be important. He didn't take them in, he hid them for me to find, so he clearly didn't trust someone. If we want to get them in the right hands, we've gotta know what we're dealing with."

Jenn sighed nervously. "Okay, yeah. You're right." She pulled her hair back into a ponytail, and Steve caught himself staring at her. He cleared his throat and cast his eyes down toward the papers.

"I'm still listening," he said, prompting her to continue.

"Okay. I'll grab us a brownie first. I'm starving."

She cut two large squares and placed them on plates, setting them on the table alongside a pair of forks.

Jenn watched him expectantly, so he cut into his brownie with his fork and took a bite. The middle wasn't done, yet the bottom was somehow burnt to a crisp, and it was distinctly salty. He swallowed hard and took a long sip of coffee.

"So, how is it?"

"Uh. Good. Very good."

Jenn smiled wide, took a bite, and immediately spit it out into a napkin. She wiped her mouth, letting out a big laugh. "You're such a liar! Oh my God, that's awful."

"Well, I didn't want to—"

"Don't worry about it. I needed a good laugh," she interrupted. "My first attempt at homemade brownies. I'll buy the box mix from now on. Hand me your plate, and I'll throw it away."

She threw them in the waste basket and sat back down. "Let's continue."

Steve fought back a smile and looked on as she started.

"This graph of global temperatures from two years ago is based on ocean surface temperatures. Pretty consistent. Earth's temperature has risen by 0.08 degrees Celsius per decade since 1880, but the rate of warming since 1981 is more than twice that: 0.18 degrees Celsius per decade."

"This is from the ones we found on the boat?"

"No. Just follow along. It'll make sense in the end. Now, look at this. *This* is from the papers we found on the boat. And *this* computer model shows that the warming of the Arctic region has accelerated much faster than the rest of the world's oceans. When he saw this, I'm sure he figured something was causing an anomaly."

"Would all climate scientists have access to that?"

"I'm not sure, but I don't think so. I've never seen anything like it."

She grabbed another paper from the table. "And this is a printout of the world's water bodies. You can see the temps in different parts of the world. Going by this computer model, the one from the lockbox, the earth's temperatures are consistent with historical warming trends. Except here." She put a finger on the map. "The Arctic region."

"That's not normal, I'm assuming?" Steve asked.

"No. Hold on while I find the one where...here it is. This graph is super recent and shows the Arctic ice cap melting at an accelerated rate compared to all the previous public data. A rate that I'm guessing Randall couldn't explain."

"Okay."

"But when he combined the information on those papers...well, he says it right here in his notes. '*The warming in the Arctic region, which is causing the melting, is throwing the computer models off.*' "

"And he figured this out using the papers from the boat?"

"Yes." She picked up another paper. "If you look here, he suspected the accelerated melting is being caused by an underwater heat source, not global warming. Volcanoes, to be exact." She picked up one of the seabed maps they had found on the boat. "And they're right there. Without the corresponding coordinates, I have no idea exactly where these are, but someone drew circles around them with an x in the middle. I assume it was Randall. He talks in his notes about the possibility of shipping lanes opening up within ten to fifteen years because of the melting."

Steve looked down at the paper. "Would that be a bad thing?"

"Right now, no one owns the polar region. The nineteen eighty-two UN Convention on the Law of the Seas gave each of the five Arctic nations—Canada, the

United States, Russia, Denmark, and Norway—ten years after ratifying the treaty to map out the Arctic seabed. But the United States never ratified the treaty."

"I've never heard of it," Steve said.

"This could get interesting, in a military way, if the US and Russia both suddenly lay claim to this area. I suspect Randall saw this for what it was and was unsure what to do with it."

"And he kept all this information to himself?" Steve asked, his tone skeptical.

"I guess so. Maybe he was just finishing up with it and hadn't decided yet what to do with it. But it's important to note that he came to that conclusion using these mystery papers. For all we know, it may all be…I don't know, wrong though."

"Maybe," Steve replied.

"Randall mentioned shipping lanes opening up, but I think it would be more about oil and gas exploration. It's been estimated that the area holds over twenty-five percent of the world's undiscovered oil and gas. We're talking billions or trillions of dollars that may be at stake here," Jenn said.

"Money like that could definitely push someone to kill. Do you think those other men he was working with know about this?" Steve asked.

"I don't know, but if they do, and Randall was murdered over it, they might be in danger."

"What if one of them was in on his murder. Or one of them is the murderer? Do you know them very well?"

"Not really. I didn't go with them on the explorations. I was mainly involved in deciphering the data and assisting with the reports."

"This has created more questions than answers. I'll look in Uncle Randall's office and see if I can find any contact information," Steve said.

"I've got it at school if you don't find it. I'll continue to scan this stuff to see if I can learn anything else."

"Jenn, we need to keep these papers safe. I'm a little uncomfortable with you having them here. If this is evidence of a conspiracy of some type, we're possibly talking about a major foreign power. If someone killed for it once, they might do it again."

"I'm a big girl; I can take care of myself." Her tone was less confident than her words.

Steve studied her. "I'm sure you can, but you can never be too careful."

A short silence followed. Steve kept his eyes on her, trying to gauge her emotion. If asked, he would readily admit he didn't understand most of the climate mumbo jumbo they had just covered. But he did understand what the ramifications could be as it pertained to their security.

"You sure you're all right?" Steve asked.

Jenn crossed her arms and shook her head slightly. "To be honest, no. I'm scared. How in the hell did Randall get mixed up in this? It makes no sense."

"I don't know, Jenn, but I intend on finding out. In the meantime, we'll need to be careful."

"We could run copies. Randall has a copy machine in his office."

"That's a good idea. I'll make copies while I look for those contacts," Steve said.

Jenn bundled up the papers and put them back into the lockbox.

"I'm going with you," she insisted.

"There's no need."

"That copy machine is a little temperamental. You'd better take me with you. I've dealt with it before. And it's getting late. We could stop and grab a bite."

"Okay. That sounds like a good idea. I could use some food. I'll drive. You can pick the restaurant."

They bundled into Steve's rental and Jenn decided on her favorite Italian place, Parnigoni's. "It's close, and on the way to Randall's. You'll love it. It's an older building, and it's got that mom-and-pop feel. Their spaghetti sauce is unreal."

Steve kept his eyes forward and listened as she went on and on about the restaurant. He didn't care, but figured if it helped get her mind off the situation, he could endure it. When they pulled into the parking lot ten minutes later, he was unimpressed with the exterior of the establishment.

"Looks like they could use a paint job," Steve grumbled.

"Don't judge a book by its cover, you grump. You'll love the inside. Let's go," Jenn said as she opened the car door.

He paused after walking in the door to take in the large mural on one wall depicting the sloping hills of an Italian vineyard. Despite his initial misgivings, he had to admit Jenn was on the money about the interior. The floor was striped in contrasting gray tiles that transitioned to oak underneath the booths. Each booth along both sides of the room had its own bottle of olive oil and a vase filled with fresh-cut flowers. Bespoke pendant lights hung low over the tables, and the openness of the space was contrasted with a cozy sense of closure created by the high-backed bench seats.

They helped themselves to a booth midway down the left-hand wall, slumping into their seats across from one another. Steve let out a sigh of relief. "Wow, I've been going non-stop for a while now. Feels nice to sit and relax."

"It's been a long day," Jenn agreed. After a moment, a sad look entered her eyes and she spoke quietly. "I still can't believe Randall's gone."

"Me either," Steve replied, not daring to meet her gaze.

"How long are you planning on staying out here? I mean, don't you have your business and your horses?"

"I'm not sure."

"Let's just say you're right, and Randall was murdered. *And* you find evidence. Then what?" asked Jenn.

"I give it to the local police and let them manage it."

"That may take a long time."

"I don't have any active cases right now. As far as the horses go—"

He was interrupted when the server approached. "Hi, Jenn. Nice to see you again." The older man handed them both menus. Steve forced a smile and thanked him, letting Jenn take the lead.

"Hi, Manny, this is a friend from Texas. He told me to pick the restaurant, so here we are. I already know what I want."

"Spaghetti with meatballs?" Manny asked with a kind smile.

Steve spoke before she could answer. "Me too, I guess."

"Two orders, please," Jenn replied, handing the menus back to the server. "So, what were you saying about the horses?"

"I only have four of 'em right now. I can always board 'em if need be, but I have a local high school kid who helps out. He should be able to take care of things. If it gets to be too much, he'll let me know."

"Oh yeah! Tony, right? Randall always said you two have a very complicated relationship. He never really expanded on it, though. What did he mean?"

"He said that, did he?" Steve asked, his tone edgy.

"Well. Uh, I was just—"

The look in his eye stopped her short. He shook his head and stared at the table. "Let's just eat and get going."

Their food arrived a few minutes later and they ate in silence, each lost in their thoughts.

Chapter 9

Evening shadows stretched across the yard as they arrived at Randall's house an hour later. After hiding most of the day, the sun made its presence known as it rolled over the western horizon. A bright red-yellow beam of sunlight was its final warning that night would soon be upon them.

Steve slowed the car as they approached the house and pointed toward the front door. "Is the door cracked open?"

Jenn leaned forward. "It looks like it. But I distinctly remember you closing and locking it."

He parked the car on the curb in front of a neighbor's house. He pulled out his Glock and slid the clip in with a satisfying click, then made eye contact with Jenn. "Wait here."

Jenn's eyes darted between Steve and the gun. "Oh my God, Steve. What are you going to do?"

"Just wait here and don't get out of the car...you understand?"

"But...holy crap...okay."

Steve moved in a crouched position toward the front of the house, holding the gun with his right hand while pointing the barrel to the ground. He hugged the wall, stopped shy of the living room window, and stealthily looked inside. He didn't see anyone but heard things being tossed around. He slowly opened the front door using his shoulder, his eyes scanning left to right, and entered the living room.

The noise was coming from the office. He moved forward, holding his gun in the Weaver Stance. Peeking inside, he saw a man rummaging through Randall's desk. The guy was wearing black pants and a matching T-shirt. To pull it all together, a black balaclava covered his head, but not wholly; he wore it high. He was slim and had a narrow face.

Steve swung the door open, pointed the gun at the intruder, and yelled, "Hands up! Let's see them right now."

The man stopped rifling through the desk, raised his head, and made eye contact. His face was clean-shaven, and his eyes had an alertness in them that couldn't be ignored.

"Let's not get too excited," he said calmly and carefully.

"No one's getting excited. Let me see your hands," Steve demanded. The intruder held his hands at shoulder height, projecting a modest willingness to comply. "Who are you?" Steve asked, still pointing his gun at him. The guy didn't answer, so Steve pressed further. "What are you looking for?"

"Give me the papers, and I'll be on my way."

"You didn't answer my question. Who are you?"

Still holding his hands up, the intruder stepped around the desk and leaned back against it. "Can't say."

Steve's phone chirped, distracting him just long enough for the intruder to lunge forward and grab Steve's right wrist, using his momentum to push the gun aside. The man continued the motion faster than Steve could follow, spinning in a tight circle. A second later, Steve was somehow on his back, staring into his own gun barrel.

"Now would be the time to shoot you if I wanted. But I just want the papers. That's all. Give them to—" He stopped talking when he heard Jenn calling out from the other side of the front door.

"Jenn, don't come in here!" Steve yelled.

His eyes still locked on Steve, the intruder spoke with a low, methodical tone. "Tell her to leave…now."

Steve hollered out again, louder this time. "Jenn. Go wait in the car. Now!"

"Is she gone?"

"Jenn? Are you still there?" There was no reply. "She's gone."

The intruder took two steps back and gestured with his gun hand. "Make sure. Go ahead and get up. I'm right behind you."

The intruder followed Steve to the door, but Jenn was nowhere to be seen. Hearing sirens in the distance, however, he flashed the intruder a curt smile. "Cavalry's on the way."

The intruder shook his head and sighed. "I'll be in touch. I'll drop your weapon outside."

He motioned with the gun for Steve to step aside. Steve's eyes followed him as he calmly exited, walked next door to where his car was parked, and drove away, leaving Steve's Glock on the curb. As soon as he was out of sight, Jenn bolted from the car and ran to meet Steve.

"Oh my God! What happened? Look at you."

"I'm fine."

"Who was he?"

"I have no idea, but he wanted those papers."

Jenn folded her arms and shivered. Steve studied her and waited for a response. Finally, she said, "That's scary as hell." Steve took note of the worry in her voice. "Holy shit. What was Randall into?" she wondered aloud. Then her back straightened. "Maybe you should have given them to him." Steve started to say something when he saw a police car fast approaching. "I called nine-one-one," Jenn said. "I didn't know what else to do."

"No, you did exactly the right thing. Thank you," Steve said, placing a comforting hand on her shoulder. She breathed out heavily, and Steve sensed some of the tension left her. Soon after, the squad car pulled up in front of the house, with Detective Skinner following closely behind in his LTD. He parked behind the squad car, got out, and made his way to where Jenn and Steve were standing.

"Heard the call go out. What happened? You walk in on a four-five-nine?" Skinner asked.

"If that's your code for burglary, then yes," Steve replied.

"I assume they're gone?"

"Yeah. He went that way," Steve pointed down the road. "Didn't get plates, I'm afraid."

"Don't worry. We'll follow up on it. Let's go take a look." Skinner looked up the driveway.

"Not much to see, really," Steve offered as he led the detective into the house.

"He was rummaging through his office when I arrived," Steve said, pointing toward the office. Skinner rested his hands on his hips and sighed.

"This is typical. Not surprised at all. All they have to do is read the newspapers. They see a man or woman who lived alone pass away and figure it's an easy mark. Addicts will do some crazy shit when they need a fix." He shook his head slowly. "Officer Bradley over there will take your statement. You know the drill."

"No problem. Thanks for coming," Steve replied.

Skinner got in his car and drove off, and Steve answered the reporting officers' questions the best he could without revealing what had actually taken place. After the police officers left, Jenn turned to Steve with a suspicious expression. "That was no drug addict, was it? Why didn't you tell them the truth?"

"Because I don't know what the truth is yet. What should I have said? This mysterious man broke in looking for Russian papers my deceased uncle, who was murdered by the way, dumped onto my lap through a coded message?"

"I guess you have a point there."

Chapter 10

"It's broken. Won't even turn on," Jenn groaned, smacking her hands against the defunct copier in frustration.

"Don't worry about it," Steve said, his attention elsewhere. He was scanning the office for the picture of Randall and Elizabeth he'd last seen on the desk. Papers, pens, pencils, staples, and file folders were strewn everywhere. It looked like an office supply store had been hit by a tornado.

"There you are." It was lying face down on the desk and had thankfully been spared any damage. He picked it up in both hands with the reverence it deserved and put it back in its place. It reminded him of a picture he kept on his nightstand back home, where he and Rebecca were locked in almost the exact same pose, looking just as happy. Rebecca had made him smile like an idiot since the moment he'd first seen her.

After making detective he'd moved to a new area of town and opened an account at a local bank near his apartment. Rebecca caught his eye the first time he had visited to open an account. She was working at the bank full time while attending night school to become a teacher. In the coming weeks, he looked for reasons to visit the bank to get a glimpse of her. After a month of these frequent visits, he still couldn't drum up the courage to ask her out. So, he did the next best thing and asked the lady at the service desk, Jerry, about her. He still vividly remembered her response:

"*Oh, I wouldn't get too interested,*" Jerry had said, "*She just came off a bad relationship.*"

Weeks passed, and he fought the urge to visit the bank until he received a notice that he had overdrawn his account again. He knew his heart was still in trouble when he noticed how excited he was to have an excuse to walk past Rebecca again. At the service desk, before he could even get a word out, Jerry leaned forward with a mischievous smile and said to him, "*Ask her. She said she's ready.*"

They had lunch that very day. And the next week he took her to the Texas Coast. It was one of his favorite places, and he wanted to share it with her. He reserved two rooms at a quaint motel on Padre Island, The Seahawk Motor Inn. In the years since, the motel had fallen into disrepair after one too many hurricanes. Sometimes it felt to Steve like the world was trying to wipe away his memories.

But back then, they'd spent the weekend walking on the beach and talking. The spark between them was strong, and though they had been tempted, he'd been determined to show her the level of respect he felt she deserved. He never even saw the inside of her motel room, and their restraint served to fan that spark of romance into a fire that had never stopped burning.

Steve stood there, transfixed on the photo, lost in the past. Jenn noticed and walked over to look. "That's a good picture of them," she said, snapping him out of his reverie.

"Yeah. It's a shame. They look so happy."

His ears suddenly perked up as his phone began to

make that annoying chirping sound he wanted to change but couldn't figure out how. He grabbed it from the table and pushed the answer button.

"Steve Blake."

"Steve. Charlie here. Listen, Kasandra gave me your new number. Hate to be the bearer of bad news, but Tony's been taken to the hospital."

Charlie Seagrave had been Steve's partner on the force. They had stayed close after Steve changed careers.

"Hospital? What happened?"

"I was in my car and heard the call go out over the radio for an ambulance at your address. When I arrived, they were loading him into the wagon. Kasandra was distraught, said a tree limb hit him."

"What?"

"She said he went to the farm to check on things because some bad storms were moving through. There was a tornado spotted not far from your house earlier, so it makes sense. Looks like it was just bad timing. When he didn't come back right away, she went searching and found him. That's all I got for ya right now."

"When did this happen?"

"Just now."

"Jesus, what time is it there?"

"It's half past ten."

"How's he doing?"

"I don't know. I'm on the way to—" Steve's phone sounded a notification that he had another incoming call.

"Hold on, Charlie," he interrupted, "that's Kasandra calling. I'll call you back."

84

He pushed the answer button to switch calls, and Kasandra spoke before he could say hello. "Steve, this is Kasandra." Her usual cheery tone was absent, her voice filled instead with a trembling anxiety.

"Kasandra, I was just on the phone with Charlie. How is he?"

"They say he's in stable—" She paused. Steve heard her take in a deep breath and exhale.

"Kasandra, Kasandra? Hello?" He pulled the phone from his face, and his eyes met Jenn's.

"What is it? What happened?" Jenn asked.

"Hold on, Jenn," Steve whispered before returning to the phone. "Kasandra? Are you there?"

"I have to go. The doctor's here," Kassandra answered. "I'll call you back."

After he hung up, Steve filled Jenn in on what had happened.

"That's awful," Jenn said, her face full of concern.

"I need to get home."

"I don't know what to say. Can I do anything?"

"No, thank you though." Steve punched in a number and put the mobile phone to his ear. "Yes, hello. I need two tickets to Dallas." He glanced at Jenn and noted her look of confusion.

When he was put on hold, he maneuvered the phone to speak to Jenn. "I'd feel better if you were with me until we get this sorted out."

"Wait a minute. Jesus, Steve. I can't just run off to Texas with you. I…" Her voice trailed off.

"I have to go. What if that guy comes back? Look, I didn't want to worry you, and to be honest I didn't think much of it at the time, but I spotted someone who may have been taking pictures of us at the marina. He was a ways off, but his lens was pointed in our direction. I don't think it was this guy. The guy at the marina was leaning against a blue Accord. Uncle Randall told me that he kept seeing a blue Accord parked down the street, and I'm pretty sure I saw one following me earlier. The guy tonight was driving a silver Ford. So, we may have two players here."

She shook her head, her mouth half-open as her mind searched for an argument. "I don't know. I-I barely even know you…"

"Whoever killed Uncle Randall is still out there, and the cops are *not* searching for him. And the guy who broke in here? The guy taking pictures? Too many unknowns. We'll be back in a week. Tops. I don't like it either, but I don't know what else to do."

"Where will I stay?"

"I have a spare bedroom. I won't force you, but I think it's safest if you come. Make a decision. I'm still on hold."

Jenn sighed and shook her head. "All right. I'll go, I guess. This is crazy. They did say I could take all the time I needed at work."

"Then it's settled. Can you see if you can find those scientists' phone numbers while I do this?"

"Yeah, I forgot about that. I'll go get them." A couple of minutes later, Jenn returned carrying a piece of paper with the phone numbers written down. "I found them. What time is our flight?"

He held up a finger as he finished giving his details to the agent. When he was done, he hung up and slid his credit card back into his wallet. "We have to be at the airport by six," Steve replied.

"Six? As in the morning six?" she said,

incredulously.

"Yeah. I'll pick you up at five-fifteen."

Jenn bit her lip and thought for a second. "Hey. If you don't think it'd be too weird, why don't you check out of the hotel and crash on my sofa tonight? The airport is a lot closer to me than downtown. It will give us almost another hour of sleep in the morning."

She's scared. Besides, more sleep is always good...but I could really use a drink, he thought. Pushing that thought away for the time being, he answered, "I guess that'd be fine. Are you sure?"

"To be honest...I'd feel better if you did."

Chapter 11

"We're almost there, right? Everything looks different at night," Steve asked as they approached Jenn's street.

"Yes. But when we get there, park in front of the big house. I need to let Claudia know what's going on, so she won't be worried."

"It's late. Will she be up?"

"Oh yeah, she's a night owl. See, the lights are on."

As they pulled up, Steve noticed a white Mercedes in front of the big house. "Should I park behind the white car?"

"I guess. I've never seen that car before."

After putting the car in park and shutting the engine off, Steve glanced at the glove box where he kept a flask of bourbon. It called to him, tugging at the fraying edges of his mind. "Why don't I just wait out here?"

"Come on. You'll like her. And I don't want her to worry about the strange man I'm running off with," Jenn insisted.

"All right, but let's make it quick," he answered.

Jenn pressed the doorbell, and an older lady opened the door a moment later. Steve immediately noticed her statuesque figure—tall and graceful. It was plain to see that this lady, wearing wrinkleless gray jogging pants with a perfectly white T-shirt and sneakers, was a woman of confidence, wealth, and grace. Although her skin didn't hide her age, her salt-and-pepper hair was long and lush. Her eyes shone a bright cerulean green, and her teeth gleamed an ivory white that only comes from a lifetime of regular visits to the dentist.

At first, the lady's face showed surprise, but a smile quickly took over. "Jenn, what a pleasant surprise! Come in. I had no idea I'd have so many visitors, or I would have dressed appropriately."

"You look great, as always, Claudia. This is Steve Blake. I'm sorry for intruding without calling; I need to talk to you about something."

"Nice to meet you," Steve said, awkwardly.

Jenn took Steve by the arm, squeezed it, and gave him a quick glance of encouragement. Steve gave in and allowed Jenn to lead him into the house. His attention was immediately caught by a well-dressed man entering the foyer from the library.

"Claudia, I'm sorry. I didn't realize you had company. I'll just call you later," Jenn said.

"Don't you worry, he was just leaving. Let me introduce you. Mark, this is Jenn and Steve…I'm sorry, I didn't catch your last name."

"Blake," Steve offered. He wasn't sure if he should shake the stranger's hand, and Mark didn't offer.

"Mark Kensington…yes. I must get going, Claudia. Thank you for your time. Please do consider. Project Green could use a bright mind like yours."

"No promises, Mark."

Claudia let him out, and after closing the door she muttered, "Not a chance."

"What was that about?" asked Jenn.

Claudia waved the question off. "Oh. He's an old

acquaintance. He used to be a senator until he, well, it's a long story. He was here for money. Or information. He was acting more peculiarly than usual, though. Please, follow me."

Claudia led them into the parlor. Three stylish, high-backed Victorian chairs were arranged in a semicircle in front of an enormous brick fireplace. "You two have a seat here, and I'll get some tea."

After she had left the room, Steve turned to Jenn and asked in a low voice, "Does she live here alone?"

"Yes. She's a widow."

Steve studied the room, trying to get a sense of who this lady was. The fact that the house was filled with ornate furnishings and large pieces of artwork hanging on the walls confirmed in his mind that she was from a world he was unfamiliar with—a world of money and power.

Well-earned money and power, though. He looked for signs of "old money," as they call it when money is handed down from generation to generation. There were no monogrammed Tiffany originals that might be heirlooms. No large paintings of family from generations past. Even the crystal art he could see throughout the room was modern and tasteful.

"Have you seen that man here before?" he asked, wondering how frequent senatorial visits might be to this household. How well-connected was this woman?

"No, but I work a lot. I don't keep up with everyone who visits."

"Well, she seems genuine," Steve concluded.

A few minutes later, Claudia returned carrying a dark wooden serving tray with a silver serving set on top. She put the tray down on the small table to the side of the chairs and poured three cups of tea. "Do you take anything in your tea, Mr. Blake?" she asked.

"Uh. No, thank you."

After everyone was settled, she took a sip from her cup and placed it on the saucer. "Jenn, dear, what can I do for you?"

"I'm gonna be gone a week or so and didn't want you to worry."

Claudia took another sip of tea, and Steve watched her eyes dance back and forth between the two. "Thank you for letting me know. I hope you two are going somewhere fun?"

Steve grinned at that remark and settled his gaze on Jenn. He crossed his arms and waited for her response. She gently placed her saucer and cup on the table and leaned forward in her chair, shaking her head. "Oh. No. We're not going together. Well, yes, we are, but we're not, you know, going...*together*."

Claudia laughed. "It's none of my business, but thank you for letting me know."

"Steve. Can I talk to you outside?" Jenn asked, somewhat urgently.

"Sure."

"I'm so sorry, Claudia. We'll be right back."

Steve followed her to the foyer, where she rounded on him. "We need to tell her everything. You know the saying, guilt by association. She lives right here, a few hundred feet from my cottage. Maybe we should suggest she hire security for a while."

"She's not associated with any of this. I don't think she'd need security."

"It'd make me feel better if she knew what was happening. And for her to understand why I'm running off with a man I barely know. God, she must think I'm a floozy or something."

Steve let out a short laugh. "I understand. Better safe than sorry, I suppose. Go ahead."

The two walked back to the parlor and took their seats. Jenn spoke first. "Claudia, I want to fill you in on something." She told her what had happened with the break-in and Steve's theory about Randall's death. She also explained what had happened to Tony and their decision to travel to Texas together.

"Oh my…" Claudia muttered. "It seems the rain clouds have been following you. And your poor friend, Tony." She paused to take a sip of tea. "I knew it was all poppycock. Randall would never have killed himself. He's always been levelheaded and—"

"Wait a minute," Jenn interrupted. "You knew Randall?"

Claudia stirred her tea and stared into the cup a moment before answering. "Quite well, once upon a time…I'm sorry I never told you. It's not something I dwell on a lot. Sometimes it's better to leave the past in the past. His service was quite nice. Thank you for arranging it, Mr. Blake." Her tone was reserved.

"I didn't know you were there. Why didn't you say hi?" Jenn said.

"I wanted to say goodbye to a dear old friend, but I do not like funerals. I guess no one does. However, I'd rather not make them a social event."

"So, you knew Randall? How'd you know him? Why didn't I know you were friends?" Jenn asked.

"The day he called to inquire about the cottage was the first time we'd talked in over forty years."

"That's crazy," Jenn commented.

"Randall was my first love. We met our freshman year of college," Claudia replied, stirring, staring into the milky waves of tea. She lifted her chin, made eye contact with Jenn, and began her story. "First and foremost, he was the perfect gentleman. You rarely see that these days, but even back then he was special. He never had a harsh thing to say to anyone. I think that attracted me to him the most. He was so well-mannered."

Steve watched a smile creep across her face. Not a big smile, but a slow, nostalgic one.

"Go on," Jenn said, practically vibrating with anticipation.

"Oh, he had his moods. I suppose we all do. But he was good at hiding them. And he was so thoughtful. He always brought me something when he came to call. Flowers, candy—that's just the kind of man he was."

"I agree, Claudia. He always treated me with respect, and encouraged me," Jenn said as she wiped her eyes with a tissue she had taken out of her pocket. "I'm sorry…getting a little emotional here, I guess."

"That's all right, dear," Claudia said, her eyes creased with concern. "We spent every minute we could together, and my parents loved him. My father had a bit too much fun with him the first time he came to call. That's just the way he was. I could see Randall was a nervous wreck when I opened the door." Claudia's eyes widened, and she laughed under her breath. "Oh, my goodness. I can still see his face—that poor boy. I was so angry at Papa; he could be truly dreadful sometimes. I remember how he asked him what his plans were with his daughter and about his career goals. He grilled him—sternly, mind you. And

Randall just stood there and took it. He earned my father's respect, but his eyes were so wide you could have driven a car through them. It gave us quite a laugh the next day."

Silence took over, and Jenn was on the edge of her seat as Claudia ponderously sipped her tea. "I always knew it wouldn't last. I guess a lady can sense such things," she said.

"So, what happened?"

"Elizabeth. One look at her and Randall was gone forever. He tried to let me down easily. It was obvious there was no need to fight it. He was head over heels in love with her."

"That's amazing. Did this have anything to do with me living here?" Jenn asked.

"Randall thought of you as a daughter. He asked me to let you live here. It's much safer than living by yourself in some grubby apartment."

"Wow. Just wow. He was like a father to me. Very much so. This is an amazing story, and you're going to give me all the details when I get back, but we have to get going."

They set their teacups down on the tray.

"Can I ask you a question before we go?" Steve asked.

"Sure. Anything."

"When was the last time you talked to my uncle?"

"When he asked about my cottage."

"How long ago was that?"

Claudia turned toward Jenn. "How long has it been, Jenn? Almost two years, right?"

"Yes. Two years next month," Jenn replied.

Steve continued. "I see. And what about the man

that was here? You mentioned he was acting peculiar. Now that you've heard about our...situation, is there anything we should know?"

"Not really, other than he is an unscrupulous man with a shady past who's always seeking power."

"What did he want from you?"

Jenn broke in. "I'm sorry, Claudia." She flashed Steve a curt look and continued, "Steve, I think we need to go and let Claudia get back to her quiet evening."

"It is all right, Jenn," Claudia assured her.

Steve gestured apologetically. "I'm going to find who killed Uncle Randall, and until then I promise that Jenn will be safe with me. I'd like you to think about your own safety, though. I don't want to scare you, but you never know."

"And I'll be back as soon as we figure all this out," Jenn added.

Claudia nodded sincerely. "Randall didn't deserve this; he was a good man. The world needs more like him. Mr. Blake, I want to help. I'm afraid the only thing I can offer is money."

Steve shook his head. "No, I couldn't take money from you. We'll be fine."

Claudia stood, her tone matter of fact. "I won't hear of it. I want you to promise me you will call if you find yourself in need of funds."

Steve smiled. "I promise. Thank you."

"We have to go, Claudia. We have to be at the airport early, but I'll keep in touch. Hopefully, I won't be gone too long," Jenn said as she and Steve stood.

The two got back into Steve's rental and made the short hop to Jenn's bungalow. Once the door locked behind them, Jenn leaned against it, fanning herself. "It's hot in here."

"It feels fine to me."

"I'm burning up. I'm not used to the heat like you Texans. I'm going to just turn on the air."

Steve stood awkwardly by the couch, watching as Jenn shuffled about, muttering nervously.

"You want a glass of wine? I could sure use one. Or two. I think it all just hit me. On top of Randall being dead, I've now learned my landlord and Randall had a past. And now a crazy man is chasing us. And, of course, to top it all off, I'm running away to Texas with a complete and total stranger. What else could happen?"

Steve searched for a reply. His line of work as a police officer had always demanded some level of empathy, but dealing with the public meant keeping a natural wall up between the people's fears and his response to those fears. Did this moment call for a reassuring hug? Or kind words and a pat on her back? He wasn't sure.

"Well…" He'd expected more words to come, but his mind remained blank.

"I'm so sorry. I didn't mean anything by that. I didn't mean to offend you. It's just a lot to take in."

Steve forced a smile. "I understand. But I'm not a wine drinker. Got anything stronger?" he asked.

She walked to the kitchen and pulled a bottle of red wine and a bottle of bourbon from under the counter. She held them both up by the neck. "The bar is open. How do you take it?"

"Straight up neat's fine."

Her puzzled expression caught Steve off guard. "That's the same thing," Jenn said.

"What's the same thing?" asked Steve.

"Straight up and neat, they both mean 'no ice.'"

"You're kidding…Well, that's what I've always called it."

"Stuck in your ways? How old are you anyway?" Jenn teased.

"Just turned forty-one last month. You?"

"You're forty-one and haven't learned it's impolite to ask a lady her age?"

"You asked first."

She smirked, poured them both a drink, and carried Steve's over to him. As she handed it over, she quietly said, "Twenty-nine."

"What?"

"You're going to make me repeat it? Okay. Twenty-nine. I'm twenty-nine years old," she said, humorously exaggerating her irritation. They chuckled together, and then she held her glass up to toast. "To…" she searched for words.

"Uncle Randall," Steve said.

"I like that. To Randall."

They tapped glasses. She took a large gulp of wine and a few drops fell to her chin. Her eyes widened, and she swiped it with the back of her hand before urgently searching herself. "Oh, for goodness sake, I didn't get it on my shirt, did I?"

Steve did his best not to stare too long. "No. I don't see anything."

"Thanks," she sighed with relief. "You know, I still can't believe Claudia and Randall had a past. I didn't give it much thought when he told me about this cottage. I just figured he saw it advertised on a board at school."

"You rarely really know anyone, Jenn. I learned that my first week on the force."

"Yeah. You're probably right." Jenn took another sip of wine. "You should call and check on Tony."

Steve glanced at his watch. It was approaching ten p.m. Pacific Time. "It's a little late there, but Kasandra's a night owl." He'd barely finished dialing when she picked up. "Kasandra, this is Steve. How's Tony doing?"

Kasandra spoke in a hushed tone. "He's sleeping. His head is still so swollen. The X-rays were encouraging, though, according to his doctor."

"Tony's a tough kid. What are they saying about his recovery?"

"He has a lot of stitches. They said they want to keep him for a few days for observation."

"I am so sorry this happened. How are *you* holding up?" Steve asked.

"I'm fine. Just a little tired. And thank you, but it wasn't your fault. It was just a freak accident."

"I know, but I still feel bad. I'll be home tomorrow. I'll come to see him as soon as I get there."

"Thank you, Steve. I'll see you then."

"What did she say?" Jenn asked after he hung up.

"She says he's doing well. Might be going home in a few days. I just hate this."

"It sounds like he's lucky she found him when she did," Jenn said.

"I've known Kasandra a long time. She's a strong woman and a great mother. He'll be fine with her taking care of him."

"Good, I'm glad." She yawned, then stood. "Hey, I'll be right back."

Steve watched her disappear down the hall and return a few minutes later with a sheet, a blanket, and two pillows.

"Here you go. If you get too cold, there's the thermostat," she said, pointing to the wall. She set the linens and blanket down on a side chair. "I have to pack. Then I'm going to bed. If you get up before me, I left the coffee out so you can make some. Do you need anything else?"

"No. I'm fine. I'll see you in the morning. Good night, Jenn."

He lay on the couch for a few minutes, then found himself pacing back and forth in the living room. His mind refused to give in. Uncle Randall had kept the existence of the papers from him. And Jenn. But why? He knew Jenn was putting on a brave face. He hadn't wanted to push her into coming to Texas, but he had to protect her. From what, though? What was so important about those papers? Who gave them to Uncle Randall? And why him?

And now his friend was in the hospital because he was out here chasing ghosts instead of home on his farm. He thought hard to remember anything Randall had said that might give him a clue, but he couldn't think of anything. He walked to the kitchen and poured another glass of bourbon. Sighing heavily, he downed it, then lay back down. Sleep continued to elude him for another hour.

****

Steve jerked awake at four-thirty, fitful dreams evaporating like morning dew in the face of the practicalities of the day. He quickly slipped on his jeans and walked shirtless down the hall to the restroom to relieve himself before making his way to the kitchen to make the coffee. He folded his arms and leaned against the counter while the coffee brewed.

One thing at a time. Let's get back home and check on Tony, then I'll need to take a look at that tree and see if there are any other loose branches. In fact, I'll need to inspect all the trees in the yard and around the barn. I also need to make sure Kasandra has everything she needs. Those damn mystery papers can wait a hot minute. Right now, I just need to make sure Jenn's safe, and Tony's provided for, he thought.

The coffee maker chimed, signaling the brewing cycle was done and forcing his mind to return to the present. He pulled a cup from the cabinet, filled it halfway, and took it to the bathroom. He had just stepped into the shower and closed the curtain when he suddenly heard the bathroom door open. He pulled the curtain back just enough to see Jenn shuffling through a drawer below the sink, wearing a long pink T-shirt and white socks. Steve quickly closed the curtain, uttering an uncertain noise of surprise.

"I'm sorry, shoot, I should have knocked, but I can't find my stupid brush. I heard the shower running and figured you were already inside. I'll be out of your way in just a—oh, there it is!"

Steve heard the brush clatter on the floor, and then a dull thud as Jenn bumped her head on the sink as she scrambled to grab it. "Damn it! Ow! Sorry, Steve!" She flew out the door, making sure it was closed tight behind her.

By the time he'd finished his shower, got into some clean clothes, and returned to the living room, Jenn still hadn't emerged from her bedroom.

"Hey, Jenn?" he called out to her. "I folded the bed stuff. Do you want me to leave it here? Jenn?" She appeared out of the hallway with a purse strapped over one shoulder, a carry bag over the other, and pulling a roller board. She had on jeans and a loose red blouse, with black sneakers. Steve looked up and did a double take. "You didn't have to put on makeup for a plane ride."

"I'm just trying to look presentable. You said we were going straight to the hospital when we arrive. Right?" she said, slightly exasperated.

"That's right." As he watched her fussing with her bags, his mind briefly slipped back in time, and he thought of how mesmerized he could be by the simple act of Rebecca entering a room. He slammed that door shut and commanded his mind to the here and now.

"I'm ready, then," she said, waving dismissal toward Steve's folded piles. "You can just leave the sheets there. Let's get going."

Chapter 12

September 13th — Texas

The skies were clear, and the Texas sun was out in full force as they exited the terminal at DFW Airport.

"Good grief, I feel like I just stepped into a shower," Jenn exclaimed.

"Welcome to Texas," Steve chuckled.

"I lived here a couple of years, but I forgot how humid it can be."

"Really?"

"Yeah. I went to UTA my freshman and sophomore years. That was my rebellious phase, I guess."

"Rebellious?"

"Yeah, I mean, it's a bit embarrassing now, but I got involved with an older man. I think I did it to get at my mother. Pretty stupid. Anyway, point is, I don't think I ever got used to the heat and humidity in the first place."

"Here it is," Steve said, pointing to his nineteen ninety-four dark gray Chevy Malibu. He threw the bags into the trunk and the two hopped in. After stopping to pay the parking fee, they continued south, merged onto the highway, and arrived at the hospital twenty minutes later. They entered through the front door and started to make their way to the receptionist's desk. Halfway there, Steve spotted Kasandra getting out of the elevator.

"You made it," Kasandra exclaimed as she approached Steve.

He paused a moment and looked her up and down. Her eyes were heavy, and her clothes were wrinkled, telling Steve the tale of a worried mother who was ignoring her own needs. Not that he expected anything else from Kasandra, but he was glad he was now here to help. "We came straight from the airport. How's he doing?"

"He has a mild fever, but they moved him out of intensive care. So that's a good sign."

"Thank God. You look tired." He could feel Jenn's gaze as she shot him a sharp look. "Uh. What I meant was…"

Kasandra caught it, too, and let out an abbreviated laugh. "I know what you meant. Yes, I am tired. He was asking about you. Room three forty-three. I was just heading home to get him some clean clothes."

Steve gave a reassuring smile. "I'm here now. Why don't you get some sleep?"

"I'll sleep when I know my baby's okay."

A moment of silence took over as Kasandra's eyes darted between Steve and Jenn. "Aren't you going to introduce me to your friend?"

"I'm sorry. This is Jenn. She worked with Uncle Randall."

She gave Jenn a knowing look. "Sometimes you have to force things out of Steve. Nice to meet you, Jenn."

Jenn's brow furrowed with concern. "Nice to meet you. I'm sorry about what happened to Tony."

She forced a smile. "Thank you. The Lord is watching over Tony. He's going to be fine." She turned to Steve and asked, "How was the service?"

"It was good, but we ran into some problems afterward."

"Problems?"

"It's a long story. That's why Jenn's here. I'll fill you in later. You go get some rest. Jenn and I will stay with Tony until you get back."

"I won't be gone long. I can rest once I'm sure he's okay. And, Steve, I'm glad you're here. Thank you."

"No thanks required."

The two watched Kasandra walk out the main entrance door. Jenn took in a breath and crossed her arms. "I feel so bad for her."

"Me too," Steve replied softly.

When they arrived at Tony's room, a nurse was standing at the door, writing something on his chart.

"Hi, we're friends. We're going to stay with him for a while. His mom went to get him some clothes. Is that all right?" Steve asked.

"That's fine."

"How's he doing?" asked Jenn.

"He's running a mild fever; I gave him something to help him sleep. You can go on in."

"Thank you," Steve replied.

When they entered the room, Tony's eyes stirred sluggishly. His voice was low and labored. "Hey, boss."

Steve took his left hand and cupped it in his. "Hey, buddy, now there you go again—"

Tony smiled and cut him off. "I know, I know— Don't call you that."

Steve laughed. "How you feel?"

"Still running a fever, but they said it should go away soon. And these stitches itch like crazy."

Steve gently patted his hand. "I got here as soon as I could. This is Jenn. She worked with Uncle Randall."

"Kind of young for you," Tony remarked with an impish grin. The laugh he let out when Steve started to splutter and shake his head, however, quickly shifted the grin to a grimace. "Ah shoot...that hurt," he grunted through restrained giggles, gently clutching at his bandages.

Steve couldn't help but chuckle along. "I'm sure it did. All right, buddy. Go to sleep. We'll be here when you wake up."

Tony didn't reply. He closed his heavy eyes and fell fast asleep.

The room had two chairs—one on the wall across from the bed and the other in the back corner. Steve took the one closest to the bed.

"I hate to see him like this," Steve whispered.

"I know, I'm so sorry...we might be here a while. Do you want me to get us some coffee?" Jenn offered.

"That'd be great. Thanks."

"I'll be right back."

She returned ten minutes later with coffee in hand.

"How's he doing?"

"He's restless. I imagine it's hard to sleep in his condition."

Jenn sat in the empty chair and set her cup down on the floor. Minutes later, she succumbed to the tiring day and nodded off. Steve downed the lukewarm coffee and then sat with his hands laced across his stomach, his body demanding he also sleep. His mind fought it off, though, thinking about all that had happened since he got the call that his uncle had passed.

He glanced over at Jenn and his thoughts ramped up. *Is my life going to be nothing but chaos now? Was it wise to bring her here? Did I do the right thing, or put her in more danger? This lady's life may very well be in my hands now. And for the time being, I have to let her into my life and share my home. The home I built for someone else.*

He had learned that sheer concentration on work with no focus on his personal life had gotten him this far. Yes, he had his horses. But his horses never put demands on him the way people did. Now it seemed like people and demands had overtaken everything. He could sleep eventually, but not yet. Not while his little friend lay in front of him fighting off his wounds.

The tense quiet in the room was broken when Kasandra finally returned. "How is he?" she whispered as she entered the room.

"He's been sleeping since you left. Here, sit down." Steve stood and waved to the chair. Kasandra obliged and sat facing the bed.

"I guess your friend was pretty tired."

Steve nodded. "She's been out a while. It's been a long day for all of us. But—"

He stopped talking when he heard Tony stir, turning to see him open his eyes. "How long have I been asleep?" Tony asked groggily as he rubbed the sleep from his eyes.

Kasandra's eyes sparkled as she stood and felt his forehead. "You're awake! Good. How are you feeling, baby? I think your fever's gone."

"I feel good."

Jenn woke to the conversation, wiped the thin trail

of drool from her chin, and abruptly stood. She used her fingers to straighten her hair and attempted to smooth the wrinkles from her blouse. "I'm sorry. How embarrassing. How long was I asleep?"

"You were out for a while," Steve replied.

Jenn flashed a tight smile.

"Tony, this is Jenn. I introduced you before you fell asleep, but you were kind of out of it. She worked with Uncle Randall."

"Hello," he replied politely.

"She's going to be staying here a while. I'll explain it later. So, you're feeling better?"

"Yeah. I feel good, just wanna get out of here."

"I'm sorry you had to go through this. Do you remember anything about what happened?" Steve asked.

"Not really. Some bad storms had passed through, so I went over to make sure everything was good. Next thing I know, I'm lying in a hospital bed with a bunch of strangers looking at me. But…"

"But what?" Steve asked.

"I don't know. I do remember something about…mail."

"Mail?"

"Yeah. When I went to check out the farm, I remember your mailbox was open. I thought I'd closed it that morning, but I guess not. Anyway, it reminded me that when I'd gotten the mail earlier, I'd brought it with me to the barn and forgotten it in the tack room. I was gonna take it to the house but got distracted."

"In the tack room?"

"Yeah. It's probably still there, cause I was on my way to go get it when…God, it's blurry what happened after that."

"Don't worry about it. Just rest and concentrate on getting better. Which tree was it?" Steve asked.

"I don't know…"

"The big pecan by the barn," Kasandra interjected into the conversation. "The one on the fence line close to the first metal gate."

Steve turned his attention to Kasandra. "That tree?"

"Yes. He was lying on the ground under it."

Steve turned back to Tony. "Do you have any idea what you were doing all the way over there?"

"Not really."

Kasandra said, "All I know is he was on the ground under the tree, and a big branch was lying to his left when I arrived and called nine-one-one."

Steve turned back to Tony. "And you don't remember anything else?"

"Nope."

"I'm sorry this happened. I'll inspect all the trees for wind damage."

"Who's been taking care of the horses?" Tony asked.

"I called a neighbor; he'll be boarding them until I get this mess cleaned up."

"What mess?"

Kasandra spoke up. "Steve's the executor of his uncle's will. He'll be traveling back and forth between here and California for a while."

Steve prompted Jenn to gather her things. "Listen, buddy. We need to get going. I'll check on you tomorrow. We came straight here from the airport, and we both need to get cleaned up."

"It's cool. I should be able to help you at the farm

soon."

"You just take it easy for now, Tony."

"Don't look like I have a choice."

"No, I guess not. I'll talk to you soon."

"Okay, see you later."

****

Once the two were back in the car, Steve's situational awareness gripped him once more. He made several checks in the rearview mirror as the two made their way to the farm, scanning for any sign they were being followed. In one of his checks, he caught Jenn's stare. "Do you have a question?"

"You don't talk a lot. Do you?" she prodded with one eyebrow raised.

"What do you mean?"

"I don't know. Just something I've noticed."

"I get more from listening. And observing."

Jenn smiled. "Sorry. Just an attempt to lighten things up."

Thirty minutes later, they pulled into Steve's driveway.

"This is nice. How much land do you have?" Jenn asked.

"Forty-two acres. Let's get unloaded."

Jenn opened the car door and hopped out. "I've never been to a horse farm. Heck, I've never even ridden a horse."

Steve lifted the suitcases from the back seat and headed around to the front door. Jenn grabbed her travel bag and followed him inside, where Steve gave a half-hearted tour. "There's the kitchen, my bedroom, and yours is down the hall. You'll use the hall bathroom."

"This is nice. But I'm starting to feel I'm

intruding."

Steve knew what she meant. He wasn't putting in much of an effort to make her feel comfortable. He saw the comment as her way of putting the awkwardness on herself, not wanting to offend.

"Hopefully, we'll figure this out and have you back home soon," he replied, unsure how to remedy the situation.

"I hear that. Are you hungry? If you have any food, I could cook," Jenn suggested.

Steve grinned. "Well…"

Jenn laughed. "Now, don't you judge my cooking abilities by those brownies. I'm actually pretty good in the kitchen."

Steve was grateful the light tension had cleared. "I could eat. Let me see what I have. Why don't you unpack? There are clean sheets in the bedroom closet. You'll have to make the bed I'm afraid. Been a while since I've had guests."

"No problem. Thanks."

After she went to the spare bedroom, Steve walked to the kitchen and opened the refrigerator door. He paused when the door swung freely instead of banging up against the table like he expected it to. Not finding much inside, he leaned down, opened the freezer compartment, and pulled out two steaks. He placed them in the sink and turned on the faucet.

Jenn had made her way back and was standing in the living room. "The bed is made. I'll worry about unpacking tomorrow. What's the room at the end of the hall?"

"That's my dark room where I develop film."

"That explains the 'Do Not Enter' sign. I guess all

private detectives have them, huh?"

"Most do. Wouldn't be very professional to allow someone else to do it. I'm fast thawing some steaks in the sink, but I want to go look at something. I'll be right back."

"What?"

"I just want to take a look at that tree."

"Can I go with you?" Jenn asked.

"Suit yourself." He pulled open a drawer and grabbed a flashlight to combat the fading light. Jenn followed him out the front door and down the gravel driveway toward the barn.

"What a pretty sky. I don't get to see the stars much in the city, but the sun's not even down and there's already some out. And it's so quiet here," Jenn said.

"The way I like it," Steve replied. His tone was matter-of-fact.

When they arrived at the gate, Steve slid the latch to the open position and swung it in just enough for the two to walk through. Steve went first and turned toward the pecan tree.

"Do you want me to lock it?" Jenn asked.

"No, leave it open."

"That must be the branch that got him," Jenn said, pointing to a four-foot branch on the ground that was about six inches in diameter.

Steve scanned the area, then began walking toward the barn with Jenn in tow.

"What are you looking for?" asked Jenn.

"He said he left the mail in the tack room."

"Is that a car under the tarp over there?" The car was sitting on the left side of the horse pens.

"Yes."

"What kind of car is it?"

Steve stopped and turned to face Jenn. "Listen. I don't want to sound rude, but I didn't bring you here so we could bond. It's obvious Uncle Randall thought highly of you, and I'm sure you're a great person. That said, I don't need any new friends. I'm gonna figure out what's going on, fix it, and get you home. Until then, you can stop with all the questions about my life."

Steve watched for her reaction, immediately wishing he could walk back his words. But, on the other hand, he felt it needed to be said. Jenn folded her arms. Steve thought for a moment she might be fighting back a tear, but when he met her glare, he knew he was wrong.

"Well, I'm glad we got that straightened out. I didn't mean to—"

"That didn't come out as I intended," he interrupted.

"Let me finish. I damned sure would rather be back at home, in my own house, living my own life, but I guess you're stuck with me for a while so it's up to you how this goes. You can treat me like a guest, as I deserve, or act like a complete ass. I don't care much either way."

Steve let a slight grin out. "Sorry, I guess I could have chosen my words better. I'm going to go look for that mail."

"I'll follow, I guess."

Steve headed toward the barn and could hear her following. He kept his eyes forward and said, "It's a car I had in high school."

"Excuse me?"

"You asked about the car. It's one I had in high school."

"Oh, okay then." Steve glanced back and glimpsed an abbreviated smile on her face.

The doors to the barn were open when they approached.

"Why is it open? You don't keep it closed?" Jenn inquired.

"Yeah, Tony would have closed it before he left." Steve walked to the tack room and opened the door. The lock was sitting to the side on the ground. He frowned, picked it up, and put it in his pocket. "He would have also locked this door."

"This is pretty cool," Jenn commented, looking into the tack room.

"He said he left the mail in here, but I don't see it."

"Maybe it's behind the door," Jenn commented.

Steve stepped forward and closed the door. A stack of mail was sitting on a shelf next to a can of saddle wax. "Good call. Let's head back up to the house."

Once back inside the house, Steve dropped the stack of mail on his desk and walked to the kitchen to see if the steaks were thawed out enough to put on the grill. Jenn followed and took a seat at the table. The steaks still needed some time, so he sat across from her, idly tapping his fingers on the tabletop.

"Something's off," he said.

"What's off? What are you talking about?"

"Hold on a minute," Steve said as he stood and walked to the middle of the living room. His eyes darted from the couch, to the armchair, to the coffee and end tables.

"Steve? What are you doing?" Jenn asked. Her

tone had a hint of suspicion crossed with curiosity. He walked down the hall and examined his bedroom and bathroom in the same manner. Jenn rushed to keep up. "You're kinda making me nervous. What's going on?"

"Hold on," he replied as he made his way to his office. He sat at his desk and opened and closed the side drawers one at a time. He also checked the center drawer.

Jenn was standing in the office doorway. "What are you looking for?"

"Someone's been through my drawers. A lot of things are out of place. I need to ask Kasandra something." He picked up the desk phone and punched in the number. "Hey, Kasandra, a quick question," he said when she picked up.

"Sure."

"When you found Tony, which way was he lying on the ground?"

"He was on his stomach. Why?"

"Was his head pointing west, east, or between?"

"I don't know. West, I'd say. Yeah. Toward the lake. I don't know my directions well, though."

"No problem, thanks. Are you with Tony now?"

"Of course."

"Can you ask him if he moved any furniture in the house over the last week?"

"Why do you ask?"

"Just trying to put everything together."

"Sure, one sec." The line went quiet for a moment, and then Kassandra's voice returned. "He says no, is something wrong?"

"No, nothing to worry about. Thanks for asking. I'll check in tomorrow."

Steve hung up, leaned back in his chair, and looked at Jenn.

"I have a wooden floor with a crawl space underneath. It's got some bad floor joists, and the kitchen table moves when people walk through the house. Tony's been coming in and out for a week, but the table isn't out of place."

"I'm really trying to follow you here."

"Someone else has been in here. When we first arrived, I opened the refrigerator, and it didn't hit the table. They clearly tried to put things back into place, but I'm a stickler when it comes to my workspace."

"I still don't follow."

"The bad joists are in the living room, and after a while the table creeps over a couple inches into the way of the fridge door. I know it seems strange, but someone's been in here, moving things around, looking for something."

"Do you think Tony ran into them?"

"It's possible. I wish he could remember something."

"Then he wasn't hit by the tree branch. Is that what you're thinking?" Jenn asked.

Steve took a minute. "First thing, he'd have no reason to be standing where he supposedly got hit by the branch. If I'm right, someone must have moved him there to make it look that way. What side of his head got hit?"

"The right."

"Yup. I have two problems with that. First, Kasandra said the branch was lying on the ground to his left, and she found him on his stomach, his head pointing west. But he was struck on the right side of his head, not from the left or from above."

"Well, if it was swinging on the way down, it could have hit him on the side of his head. Maybe he looked up right in time to deflect it away with his hands," Jenn commented.

"That is somewhat plausible. But it still doesn't explain why he was standing there. There's no reason for him to be there. And I am sure someone has been rifling through my desk looking for something. But I have no idea what they'd be looking for."

Jenn leaned forward and glanced at the stack of mail Steve had dropped on the desk. She picked up an envelope from the top and held it up.

"Maybe this will have some answers."

She handed it to Steve. It was a letter from his Uncle Randall.

Chapter 13

Steve studied the envelope, momentarily stunned.

"Aren't you going to open it?" Jenn asked.

He pulled a letter opener from the center desk drawer, made use of it, and began to read.

Steve,

I am sending you this letter because I feel my life may be in danger, and I want to explain what I have been doing and why. I may have gotten involved in something that could be very dangerous, and I wanted documentation. But first things first:

I have named you the executor of my will. I trust you will take care of things if something does happen to me. I tried to make things as simple as possible.

Jenn Murphy, my assistant, does not know about any of this. She is a good person, and she has a bright future. But, because of her association with me, she could also be in danger. If anything happens to me, please contact her as soon as possible.

Now. Why am I writing this? Something strange happened while I was in New York recently visiting the United Nations. I was getting ready for bed when I heard a knock at my door. When I answered, no one was there, but someone had left a box. You can find the box's contents onboard Lizzy in a metal lockbox. The combination is 091457.

There were scientific papers inside depicting

detailed ocean floor mappings of the Arctic region. It is apparent they are of Russian origin. They show recent, accelerated warming in the area. I say recent because data from last year does not show this.

This is worrisome because The U.N. Convention on The Law of the Seas was a mechanism to settle long-lasting disputes over the Arctic region. As of today, it has not been ratified. If these charts are accurate, it could drastically change the geopolitical situation in the polar region, and who knows what may happen.

The x's with circles around them appear penciled in, which remains a mystery to me. Not to mention the one page that has the grid on it. The handwritten note on top says there are more papers that he, or she, will deliver to me soon, and that they will help put all this together. As of today, the additional papers have not been delivered. So, I am at a standstill for now.

Are these stolen government documents? Will they reveal something our government should be aware of? I hope to answer those questions with the other papers the person mentioned. I know this will sound foolish, but I feel this has given me purpose again. And I feel these papers may reveal something big. I just don't know what yet.

Unfortunately, if you have received this without context it looks as though I may have placed this conflict with you now. Please protect Jenn until you do. I trust you will do the right thing.

Your uncle & friend, Randall

"Jesus." Steve shook his head and handed the letter to Jenn. He studied her face as she read the letter to herself, but her expression was unreadable. Afterward, she returned it to him, stood, and started to pace.

"What do you think, Jenn?"

"I don't know what to think. This is some screwed-up shit; pardon my language. He sure did want to make sure you found the papers, though."

"What do you mean?" Steve asked.

"The story you told me about him calling Elizabeth 'Lizzy' in the suicide note and all that…if he'd already sent this letter, then it seems like he was overdoing it."

Steve didn't say anything. After a moment, Jenn asked, "What are you thinking?"

"If he was killed, then we know the note was either forced or forged. If he was caught flat-footed, he might not have been confident that the letter would reach me in time. In his final moments, he must have realized he needed to leave a subtler clue. One only I was likely to catch. Especially if he wasn't writing the note."

"What do you mean?"

"Just a thought. Now, he seemed to think this might be some kind of government secret. If that's the case, why him? Why did the person give them to him?"

"Randall was considered to be at the top of his field. His name is known worldwide in the scientific community. That's the only reason I can think of. This is scary."

Steve glanced down at the letter and took in a breath. "Listen, Jenn. I'm not going to let anything happen to you. They're not going to—"

"I could show the papers to a professor I know," Jenn interrupted. "I think he's still there."

"Where? Wait. What?"

"I'm not going to…to let someone…What I mean to say is that I refuse to live in fear. We need to figure out who is doing this and stop them."

"And you shouldn't have to live in fear. What were you saying about a professor?"

"As I said, I attended the University of Texas at Arlington my freshman and sophomore years before transferring to UCLA. One of my professors was a certified genius. I mean, this guy was crazy smart."

"And he teaches at UTA?" Steve asked, catching a curious shift in Jenn's demeanor.

"Yeah. You'd think he'd be somewhere like MIT. I asked him once, but he had no answer. He was different, that's for sure."

"So, you knew him well?" Steve grinned when his question brought a blush to her face. He continued on with his line of questioning. "Is this, perhaps, the older man you mentioned?"

"Yes. Okay?" Jenn fired back.

Steve held up a hand. "Sorry. None of my business. Who knows, maybe your genius friend can help. You trust him?"

"One hundred percent. Well, as long as he'll talk to me."

"We'll keep that option open then," Steve said.

"Do you still want me to call Randall's colleagues?"

"Yes, please, use the phone in the kitchen. I'm going to go check the barn again."

The barn was his favorite place when he needed to think. It was a place he felt connected to his world. The world he had painstakingly carved out for himself after losing Rebecca. At first, Steve hadn't been keen on raising horses. It was Rebecca's idea. But in the aftermath of her tragic death, the farm had become a lifeboat of sorts. He'd grown to love it and all the memories that came with it.

He stopped inside the gate and pointed the light at the tarp-covered car. It was a 1967 Chevy Camaro. When Steve was in the tenth grade, his father had bought it as a project car, intending for him and Steve to work on it together. At first, Steve resisted. He'd had the usual attitude of most high school boys, more interested in girls than spending time with a parent. But seeing his dad working on the car on his days off made him curious as to what the appeal was. So, one day after school, when his father was at work, he'd walked to the garage, picked up a car magazine from the workbench, and started flipping through the pages. Steve's eyes had widened seeing pictures of restored cars; one was of a 1967 Camaro with a 396-cubic-inch V-8 engine and a black interior. It was painted red with wide, black stripes on the hood and trunk lid.

Seeing a picture of a fully restored Camaro intrigued him, and he volunteered to help. For a while, anyway. Starting the next day, they had continued disassembling the car, carefully labeling all the boxes. They eventually had it stripped down to the bone and began reconstruction. The project brought the two together, enforcing their bond with each turn of the wrench. His mom would, at times, pull up a lawn chair and follow along like a spectator at a gala event as father and son worked together. One year and six months later, the project was completed. They had it painted red, with wide, black stripes on the hood and trunk lid, just like the one Steve had seen in the magazine that sparked his interest. The day they had tightened the last screw and made the final adjustment to the four-barrel carburetor, the two took it out on the open road together. Steve's father let him take the wheel on the way back, and they opened it up to see what she could do. They figured Steve's dad's badge would get them out of trouble if they were pulled over.

Steve shook off the bittersweet memories, still not quite sure what had possessed him to track down and reclaim the car after all these years. He continued on and made his way to where Tony had been found. He studied where the branch had broken off. It looked to be a clean break, probably from the wind. He used the light from the flashlight and scoured the ground, making a straight line to the barn.

He saw no sign that Tony had been dragged across the ground. *Could have been carried though*, he thought. He entered the barn and found no signs of a struggle on the dirt floor either. Undaunted, he continued searching, letting his mind wander. Twenty minutes later, Steve was in the feed room checking the mousetrap, no closer to solving the mystery. He heard Jenn call his name from outside the barn.

"In here. I'm in the feed room."

She followed his voice and stopped at the feed room door. "It doesn't smell bad here like I thought it would."

"Yeah, nothing like the smell of hay and sawdust. It sure is quiet in here without the horses, though. Did you get a hold of anyone?" Steve asked.

"No, they're all in New York City, attending a conference. I called their rooms and left messages for them to call here."

"Sounds good," Steve replied.

"Let's cook. The steaks should be thawed enough by now. But you're not going to feed me while I'm here. We'll split the cost."

Steve grinned. "Sounds good. Oh crap, I forgot I'm out of gas for the grill. I'm going to have to go to the store."

"That's fine. I'll go with you, and we can pick up some things."

****

After returning from the store and unloading the groceries, Steve pulled a chair from the kitchen table and fell into it. He closed his eyes and massaged his forehead.

"Go relax while I cook," Jenn said as she picked out ingredients.

"Are you sure?"

"I love to cook. It's one thing my mom taught me to do well. No, I'm not so good at baking, but I'm working on it."

"I appreciate it. Let me know if you need any help."

"Go…you can give up control of your kitchen for one night. How do you like your steak cooked?"

"Medium," Steve said as he stood and headed for his bedroom.

He took a hot shower, letting the water run down his spine to relax his mind and clear his thoughts. Before deciding which direction to go, he needed to figure out the significance of the papers his uncle had thrown into his lap. *Don't get overwhelmed,* he thought. *One thing at a time.* He turned off the water, took a breath, and stepped out to get dressed.

He walked into the kitchen to see Jenn slicing tomatoes and onions on the cutting board.

"Feel better?" she asked. "The steaks should be

done. Can you go out and check them?"

Steve stepped out onto the patio, scooped them up with tongs, and placed them on a plate. He delivered them to the counter next to the stove, retrieved a bottle of red wine in one hand, and grabbed a beer from the fridge with his other. He set them both on the table, fetched a wine glass and a corkscrew from the cabinet, and poured a glass for Jenn.

"Dig in. I'm starved," Jenn said after she set the table with a large salad and the two plates of food. An awkward silence took over. Steve spoke first.

"I think someone went to a lot of trouble covering up what happened here. I think Tony was in the barn, and the guy snuck up on him and hit him on the head. Then picked him up and placed him under that tree. Everything looks too clean."

"What do you mean?"

"The dirt in front of the barn, and the barn itself, I don't know. It looked pristine, no footprints or scuffs, like it had been brushed with something. A tree branch, maybe. I could be letting my imagination run wild on that one, but I feel strongly that limb didn't fall from the sky and hit him in the head."

"Do you think they were looking for the papers?"

"Maybe. Or Uncle Randall's letter."

"Really?"

"Hard to say. It'd be an odd coincidence."

"So, are you going to call the police?"

"I may call Charlie and get his opinion."

When they were both done eating, Steve cleaned the kitchen while Jenn took a shower and put on her pajamas. Steve was adjusting the thermostat when she entered the living room.

"I'm turning the temperature down, don't want you overheating."

"Ah, thank you. God, I was looking at the bags under my eyes. I hope I can sleep tonight."

"I'm going to sit on the porch if you want to join me."

"Really? I don't know. We may learn something about each other. Wouldn't want that to happen," Jenn teased.

"I told you I didn't mean it to come out that way. I just—"

Jenn stood and headed toward the front door. "Come on, Lone Ranger," she interrupted.

Steve followed her out the door, and they both took a seat. There were two white Adirondack chairs on the left side of the porch with a small wooden table between them.

"This is huge," Jenn commented, gesturing to the expanse of the porch.

"Yeah. It's twenty-five feet across. It goes out eight."

The roof of the house stretched over the porch for cover, and a simple railing with wooden spindles surrounded it.

"The sky is beautiful tonight. Do you do this much?"

"Do what?" Steve asked.

"Sit out here at night."

"When I can. Be real quiet and listen."

"Okay."

Steve studied her reaction as the two listened to the night. The wind vane atop the barn would spin with each gust of wind, and the loose blades would rattle lightly. Frogs croaked almost in unison, and they could hear the deep and throaty hoots of a courting great horned owl. *Who's awake? Me too!*

After a minute, Jenn shifted in her seat to face Steve. "This reminds me of summer camp when I was a kid. No wonder you like it here so much." Steve smiled and nodded in agreement. "Not to change the subject, but earlier, you said maybe Randall didn't write the suicide note."

"It was just a thought. If it was intended to get me to look on the boat, calling Elizabeth 'Lizzy' in the note, it obviously worked. So, even if he didn't write it himself it's likely that he influenced the contents," Steve replied.

He watched Jenn lean forward and start to speak. Afterward, she leaned back in her chair and looked up at the rafters. "You started to say something," Steve stated.

"If he didn't write the note, can I assume that opens up a rather large can of worms?"

Steve tilted his head up and gazed out into the dark sky. "It'd have to be someone close. Close enough to him to know or recognize the name Lizzy, but not close enough to know not to use it. But as I said, it's just a thought."

The two sat quietly and listened to the night. A few moments later, Steve watched her stand and stretch.

"I'm exhausted; I'm going to go ahead and hit the hay."

"Good night, Jenn."

"Good night."

Steve's mind once again began to dash from one thought to another. Just days ago, life had been normal.

Well, his new normal of three years, anyway. He was busy with the farm and working a case for Sally. That had been just days ago. Now he was in a new reality where his uncle was dead, Tony was in the hospital, and an armed stranger had demanded he hand over the papers. And that one sentence kept playing in his mind, *I'm sorry, Lizzy, but I will see you soon.* He stood and glanced at his watch. *Maybe I'll go talk to Rebecca for a while*, he thought.

Chapter 14

The spare bedroom Jenn occupied was just across the hall from the bathroom and a good fifteen feet from Steve's, and while the location sufficed, the décor was lacking. There was one picture hanging above the oak headboard. It was of a wild stallion standing tall on a hill with its mane flowing in the wind.

She studied it briefly and thought back to when she had first met Steve. She'd heard all about him from Randall already. She had imagined this poor man living alone with the grief of losing his wife. But she felt she was starting to see past that now that she was getting to know him. Just like the stallion in the picture he was wild and alone, but had purpose. The way he ran to Tony's side and comforted Kasandra. The fact that he accepted the challenge of watching over her because Randall asked. *What other surprises will come my way?* she thought.

She crawled into bed and closed her eyes, but her brain was in surveillance mode. After a short while, she jumped up to see if the door would lock. It did. She checked the alarm clock one more time. The numbers told her it was eleven p.m., but her body didn't agree. She was still on California time and sleep would be a chore, regardless of the busy day. After an hour of tossing and turning, her body clock lost, and she was fast asleep.

Ten minutes later, she was awakened by footsteps outside her door fading into the living room. She followed the sound and heard the front door opening and closing.

"Where's he going?" she whispered to herself.

She threw her blankets back and hopped out of bed. With her robe tied in the front and slippers on her feet, she opened the bedroom door to investigate. She slowly made her way to the front door and opened it slightly to see Steve disappear around the side of the barn carrying something in his hand.

The sky bore a full moon that cast a cold but inviting light. *Go back to bed, Jenn. He's probably just checking on some farm thing,* she thought. She leaned against the door frame and folded her arms. *Ah, what the heck. I'm too curious. I hope he's not relieving himself.* She checked that her robe was tied tightly and headed out the door. Stealthily scampering across the gravel, she found a trail leading into a wooded area. She stopped to look around—there was no sign of him anywhere.

She swiveled her head around again before deciding to continue. "Why am I doing this? Because you're an idiot, Jenn," she muttered. Her breathing was heavy as she navigated the narrow, moonlit trail, terrified that each shadow might contain a snake or something worse. She moved like a soldier clearing a minefield; one short, methodical step at a time.

Despite her caution, before long she stepped on a small, jagged rock that felt like a knife penetrating her skin. "Son of a…" she hissed, almost falling as she lifted her foot, took off the slipper, and rubbed it. She stepped back into her slipper and gingerly continued to where the trail made a tight turn to the right. There, it emptied into a clearing where she saw Steve lying on the ground, propped up on an elbow.

She stopped briefly to take in the surroundings. The spot was at the top of a crest overlooking a large circular pond. The night air was crisp, filled with the sounds of tall grass dancing in the breeze and the rhythmic sounds of male frogs croaking to attract a mate. She studied the pond and wondered about its ecological makeup. After studying vast oceans and the effects of climate change on them, her mind couldn't help to wonder how a small pond like this coped with an ever-changing environment.

She kneeled and studied him for a moment, her foot still throbbing from the encounter with the rock. His quiet voice carried on the breeze, and guilt washed over her when she heard the name "Rebecca." She stood and started to retreat but stopped when she heard Steve call out her name.

"Come on out. I heard you coming. You need to be a lot more careful if you want to sneak up on someone. Since you're here, you might as well sit and drink with me."

"I wasn't sneaking up on you…I was just curious. I'm so sorry." She looked down at herself and straightened her robe. Steve held the bottle up by its neck and waved it toward the ground next to him.

"Sit here. Sorry, no glass."

She took him up on his offer and sat down in the grass next to Steve. "What is it?"

"Kentucky bourbon. Here, just take a—"

"Thanks, I could use a drink," she interrupted. She took the bottle and downed a big swallow.

Steve chuckled. "Slow down, partner. That's ninety-proof bourbon."

"I needed that. Thanks."

Steve's eyebrows raised. "You are…very welcome."

"So, what are you doing out here? It's beautiful."

"The barn is where I go to think. This is where I come to clear my head. And there's been a lot of head-clearing the last few years."

Jenn half-smiled. "So, what head-clearing are you doing tonight?"

Steve took another drink and didn't respond.

"Too personal?" Jenn probed gently.

"Maybe. You know, life can just plain suck sometimes."

"Yeah, I know what you mean. If you want to talk, I'll listen."

There was a long pause. "You asked me why Uncle Randall said Tony and my relationship is complicated. I guess since you're here now in the middle of it all, I should tell you."

"I'm listening."

"Tony shot Rebecca."

Jenn's mouth opened as wide as a barn door. "What did you just say?"

"Yep…you heard me right. It was an accident; he didn't mean to do it."

Jenn mouthed, *"Oh my God."*

"Yep. S'not his fault. You wanna know whose fault it is?" Steve took a long drink.

"No…Steve, it's okay, you don't—"

"Mine. My fault. The gun was the very one I talked Kasandra into buying for her protection. Now ain't that something?"

She couldn't quite wrap her mind around what he'd just said. She tilted her head back and gazed at the stars to gather herself. "What…how did it happen?"

He didn't respond.

"Steve?"

She reached out to touch his shoulder and his elbow slowly slid out from under him as he slumped all the way down. His head gently fell and rested on his arm.

Jenn grabbed the bourbon before it spilled over. "Oh boy, let's get you up and back to the house. We have to get up early, come on." She stood, leaned over, and shook his shoulder. "Come on, Steve. I'll help you up…Steve, let's go."

He stirred. "I'm fine…I'm fine. I'm getting up." He sprang to his feet, wobbled, and brushed off his jeans. "I'm fine. Let's go." His gait was unstable, so Jenn took him by the arm.

"You're going to fall. Here, put your arm around my shoulder. I got you, come on."

The two were silent on the walk back up the trail. Once inside the house, Jenn followed him as he made his way to his bedroom and fell into his bed.

"Jenn? Can you help me get my boots off?"

"Ah…What do I do?"

"Turn around and grab a leg."

"Grab a leg. Sure…Like this?" She straddled his left leg between hers, facing away from him, grabbed the boot's heel, and pulled. The boot came off easily. She dropped it on the floor and positioned herself for the right foot. It wasn't as cooperative. "It won't come off."

"You know, I don't really have many friends."

Jenn paused, turned back to look at him, and tilted her head. "Okay?" She wasn't sure where he was going with this.

"You know why?"

She figured it was the alcohol talking, but her curiosity was piqued. "Why?"

"You know. It's not that I don't trust people. I do, generally. But I'll be damned if it's gonna happen to me again."

Her heart sank. His eyes were now wet, and he looked so vulnerable. Her mind danced around what she was witnessing. This hardened man was sharing his most profoundly inner feelings with her. Sure, the bourbon had done its part, but it had been a long time since someone had opened themselves to her in this way. It was sort of sweet.

"Okay, mister, let's get the other boot off so you can go to sleep."

"I'll help. Just grab it good."

She got back in position, and gripped the heel tightly. Steve lifted his other foot, placed it on her backside, and pushed. The boot let go, and Jenn flew forward with it, letting out a whoop of surprise. She dropped it to the floor and caught herself on the dresser. "That was interesting. How do you get them off when you're alone?"

He didn't answer.

"Steve?" She looked round and saw that he had crawled up on the covers. She took a deep breath, found a spare blanket in the closet, and covered him with it.

"I'm good. G'night, Rebecca," he murmured softly.

She didn't attempt to hold back her tears. She stood silently for a few moments and watched him sleep. "Good night," she whispered, before retiring to her room and going to bed.

Chapter 15

September 14th

"Are you awake yet?" The words pulled Jenn from sleep. The aroma of coffee and bacon filled the house, and the bedside clock said it was nearly eight in the morning. She jumped when Steve called out from the kitchen again. "Time for breakfast. Are you up?"

She cleared her throat and sprang to her feet, tossing the covers wildly. "Yeah, I'll be right there." She threw on her robe, tied her hair back, and slapdashedly brushed her teeth. "Can I take a shower first?" she yelled out.

"If you do, you'll have a cold breakfast."

She groaned, and walked out to the kitchen to see that Steve was pulling a pan of biscuits from the oven. He laid the pan down on a kitchen mitt and started stirring a pan of gravy on the stovetop.

"Sit down. You want coffee?"

"Sure. Can I help with anything?"

"Nope. The gravy will be done in a minute. How do you like your eggs?

"Scrambled is fine. You sure I can't help?"

He picked up the gravy pan, emptied it into a ceramic bowl, and set it on the table.

"Coffee's on the counter there. I'm almost done. All I need to do is cook the eggs."

Jenn poured herself a mug and took a sip, watching Steve whirl around the kitchen. "This is a lot," she said, wandering over to her seat. He didn't respond. Once the eggs were cooked, he picked up the cast iron skillet with a mitt and carried it to the table.

"Here you go. Dig in."

They sat quietly and enjoyed the country breakfast. Steve occasionally glanced up at her, and she could tell he was attempting to gauge her mood. They engaged in sporadic, mindless small talk, but he didn't broach the previous night's events, so she didn't push the matter. When they finished eating, they cleared the table. Jenn folded her arms across her chest and leaned against the counter next to Steve at the sink. "Thank you. That was good."

Steve scraped the scraps from their plates into the disposal. He placed both hands on the counter and stared straight ahead when he was done. "I think I owe you an explanation. First, I don't do that very often. Drink like that. I used to, but not anymore."

"You did say you'd been doing that a lot the last three years," she said, gently. "Listen, Steve. It's understandable if you're having problems with—"

"Doing what a lot the last three years?" he interrupted, glaring at her.

"You know. Going out there to clear your mind. I didn't mean anything by it. I'm just saying…" She paused. "Never mind. I shouldn't have brought it up. It's really none of my business."

He pushed away from the counter, folded his arms, and leaned back next to her. "Rebecca was Tony's homeroom teacher his freshman year in high school. I'd already known Tony and his mom for a couple of years.

136

Tony was in the sixth or seventh grade when we first met, and I was still a beat cop. I got to know a lot of people in Stop Six by community policing, as we called it back then. Made a lot of friends."

"Stop Six?" Jenn asked.

"Mm-hmm. The area was the sixth stop on the commuter rail that connected Fort Worth and Dallas back in the thirties, and the name stuck. It's part of Fort Worth. The neighborhood has a lot of problems, but it's headed in the right direction now that the city has invested some money in it."

"I see," Jenn said.

"That's how I met them. A couple of years before the accident, I was on patrol and was driving by their house one day and saw a couple of guys trying to break in their front door, right in the middle of the day. Home invasions were getting to be a significant problem. Crackheads who needed money for their next score would steal anything to sell. And they were getting brazen about it."

"Jesus, that's scary," Jenn commented.

"Luckily, Kasandra and Tony weren't home, and I got to the guys before they could get in. After that, when Kasandra asked me to help her buy a gun and teach her how to use it, I was happy to help."

"Where does Tony fit into all this?"

"Tony lived too close to the school to ride the bus, so he had to walk a few blocks every day to get there. He was getting harassed by gang bangers almost daily, and it got to be a real problem for him. He never told Kasandra. He didn't want her to worry, and he knew she would have to find a different job if she had to take him to school every day. So, he came up with a plan."

"Oh God, you don't mean…" Jenn quietly interjected.

"He was a kid. Fourteen. He thought he'd just flash it and the gang bangers would leave him alone. He even took the clip out, but there was a bullet in the chamber. The backpack slipped out of his hand, landed on his desk, and the gun discharged. Bad timing."

Jenn covered her face with her hands. "I'm so sorry. Did he get in trouble? I mean…"

"The prosecutor was going to charge him with manslaughter. As an adult."

"What? The kid was only fourteen." Jenn shook her head in disbelief.

"Yeah. An African American kid in our justice system. I knew the kind of disadvantage he'd be at."

"So, what happened?"

"The prosecutor hoped he'd take a plea deal, go to jail for a few years. But if he didn't, well, those types of cases can spend years in the courts."

"So?"

"I reached out to an attorney, Sally Roberts. She tore the prosecutor up and made him look like the racist pig he was. Then one day, suddenly, he was ready to deal. So, Tony was released to my supervision. As long as he keeps out of trouble until his twenty-first birthday, he'll be free from charges."

"My God, Steve. Why'd you do it?"

"Seemed pretty simple. I didn't want a good kid's life ruined by something stupid. And besides, I know that's what Rebecca would've wanted me to do."

Jenn gazed at the ceiling, her eyes wide, staring into space. "Thank you for sharing that, Steve. Jesus, no wonder you…I mean…"

"Have a drinking problem?" he finished.

"No. I didn't mean that. I..." Jenn stammered.

Steve crossed his arms and shrugged. "It's all right. It's under control. Seeing Tony in the state he's in, well, I just needed to disconnect."

Jenn forced a half smile and avoided his eyes. "I'd be drinking all the time if that happened to me."

Steve let out a half-laugh. "I need to go check on my horses. It's not far. You want to come?"

"Sure. I'd love to."

****

His neighbor's farm, where his horses were being boarded, was a short fifteen-minute drive away. After the visit, on the drive back to Steve's farm, Jenn shifted in her seat and turned toward Steve. "That was nice, seeing your horses. I loved Maggie. She has such a cool personality."

"She was Rebecca's. We got her when she was a filly. Her mom had died in an accident while being trailered, so Rebecca bottle fed her."

"That's so sad. Is that why she's so...I don't know. Human?"

Steve let out a short laugh. "I never thought of it that way. But yeah, I suspect the way she was raised probably had an influence on her. Well, here we are."

He parked the truck short of the side entry garage and the two walked to the porch. When they entered the front door, Steve was startled to see a familiar face sitting on the couch, looking relatively comfortable with his legs crossed, holding a Glock in his right hand.

Steve glared for a long second, then took the key from the lock and closed the door behind him.

The intruder spoke first. "Our last encounter got

out of hand rather quickly. I'd just as soon we talk like gentlemen this time. I need those papers, that's all. Then I'll go."

"I don't have them," Steve lied.

The man gestured with the gun toward the kitchen table. "You two mind having a seat?"

"You don't need to talk to her."

"Just sit. Please?"

Steve didn't move. He crossed his arms, his eyes locked onto the intruder. "Jenn. Go ahead and sit down." He took note of the man's long face and his lean build. Without a word, she pulled a chair out and sat down. "I'll stand," Steve said matter-of-factly.

"Suit yourself."

Steve clenched his jaw. "What the hell is this all about?"

"It's pretty simple. You have documents the government needs, and I've been sent for them."

"The government? Who in the government?" Steve pressed.

The man didn't answer. He listened for a moment, and then gestured toward the kitchen with his gun. "Get away from the door." A vehicle could be heard coming up the drive. Steve complied, and the man moved to the window.

He gave an impatient sigh. "Looks like you have a visitor. I'll go and give you time to think. Do yourself a favor and have them with you the next time we meet." He opened the door and with a boyish grin, said, "And don't follow me, or I'll have to shoot you."

Once he was gone, Steve looked out the window to see a beige four-door Ford Crown Victoria meandering up the driveway. "That's Charlie. Son of a gun always had good timing."

Jenn sat quietly, slowly shaking her head. "Oh my God, Steve. He followed us from California."

Steve studied her as her face contorted between fear, anger, and confusion. "Are you all right?" he asked.

"No. I'm not. What kind of question is that? The guy was pointing a gun at me." She stood and crossed her arms. "Just, forget it, I'm…fine."

"Charlie'll be here in a minute. You want some water?"

Jenn opened the refrigerator and grabbed the half-full bottle of Riesling. "I need something stronger than that."

Steve turned to get her a glass, but stopped when she raised the bottle to her mouth and drank down a big swallow. He tried to suppress a laugh and threw his hands in the air. "I'm sorry. I know it's not funny."

She pointed a finger at Steve, herself unable to suppress a nervous laugh. "You…you should have seen your face when we walked in the door."

Steve's laughter bubbled over, and they giggled together for a moment before he could respond. "I'm sure it was quite the sight. I'm glad you're okay. You *are* okay, right?"

She took in a deep breath. "Yes. I'm fine. Thank you for that."

"For what?"

"Laughing with me. Not at me."

****

"What have you gotten yourself into, Steve?"

"Not sure, Charlie, to be honest. I'm just glad you showed up when you did."

Charlie had just popped over randomly to check in, but the moment Steve had opened the door he'd picked up that something was off. They'd explained what had just happened as vaguely as they could, but Charlie was like a dog with a bone, and Steve's half-hearted dismissals weren't cutting it. He shook his head. "Oh, come on, Steve. You come home to a gun-wielding perp and don't know why?"

"I have an idea, but I need to do some more footwork."

"More footwork. Uh-huh," Charlie replied. Steve could tell that Charlie knew he was hiding something. The two knew each other's tones, feelings, and thoughts almost as though they were born twins. That's how cops who work together survive.

He decided to shift the conversation. "I don't even know how he got in. Why didn't the alarm go off?"

"Uh ha. Well, let's take a look at your security system."

Steve led Charlie out the door and to the side of the house where the control box was mounted. He waved at it in disgust. "I know nothing about how any of this works."

Charlie leaned in. "I see he didn't bother putting the cover back on. Yep. He snipped these lines and rerouted the circuit. He was able to pick your door locks and walk right in without the system detecting anything."

"Really? Damn, what's the point in spending all this money on an alarm if it doesn't even go off?"

"Steve this isn't some random break in. We've been getting training on stuff like this. The city hired a consultant who worked for the FBI. This is the first time I've seen it done like this in the field. Whoever the guy is, he had some good training. The people who install this stuff wouldn't even know how to do this. You need to be careful. Whatever it is you're involved in."

Steve wanted to fill Charlie in, but what would he tell him? He had a lot of hunches but no actual evidence. He felt it was best, for the time being, to keep his friend in the dark.

Charlie looked at his wristwatch. "I have to get going. You should call your security company and have them fix this."

"Thanks, I will."

Jenn was still sitting in the kitchen when Steve returned to the house. "Well?" she asked.

"He did something to the security system. Gonna have to get it fixed."

"Do you think that's the guy who killed Randall?"

"I don't know, Jenn."

"Who do you think he works for?"

Steve shook his head. "I don't know that either. But I hope to find out."

"I want to go see Shane. The professor I told you about. Can I use your car?"

"That's no problem, but why don't I go with you?"

"I don't want to spook him. He was always paranoid. I'm afraid he won't talk to me if you go with me."

"Really?"

"Oh yeah. As I told you, he's different. I'll try to catch him during his lunch break tomorrow."

Chapter 16

September 15th

Jenn arrived at UTA at eleven forty-five a.m. The campus had grown since she was last there, and it took a while for her to get her bearings. Some of the buildings dated back to pre-World War II, but most of them were built in the 1960s, '70s, and '80s. Modern, functional, and not especially noteworthy. She parked in front of the Science and Math building and walked inside, taking a deep breath and closing her eyes. Still the same smell she remembered, though she could never quite describe it. It was like a mix of floor varnish and perfume. Or maybe an air freshener.

She remembered that Shane always brought a bag lunch and ate it in the classroom so he wouldn't have to socialize with other staff members. As a result, he was looked upon as a loner by his colleagues. All the classroom doors had a small window she could peek through as she made her way down the hallway. She finally found him in a lecture hall, working on a large green chalkboard. She pulled a small mirror from her handbag and checked her makeup and hair. *Oh God, I can't believe I'm here. This is going to be awkward. I'm overdressed. Why'd I dress like this?* she thought. She was wearing loose brown slacks, a low-cut top that showed her midriff, and a white pair of open-toe sandals. Even though she'd spent extra time picking the outfit, it was dawning on her that she may have tried a little too hard.

She opened the door, leaned against the wall with her arms crossed, and watched him work a few moments before speaking.

"Can I come in?"

Shane stopped writing on the board and slowly turned in her direction. He tilted his head up and studied her for a short moment. "Jennifer?"

Jenn briefly closed her eyes and took in a deep breath. With a half-smile, she replied, "Hi, Shane."

Shane Jorgeson had been at the college for over twenty years, and was fifteen years Jenn's senior. At the age of seven, he'd been considered gifted. At the age of nine he was deemed to be a genius, and at the age of seventeen he'd graduated *summa cum laude* from Princeton with a BA in Geophysics. He earned his doctorate by nineteen. Now, at the age of forty-five, he lived a quiet life as a state college professor.

Jenn saw that the man hadn't changed much since the last time they'd met. He still wore his straight, jet-black hair that she'd always found sexy in the same manner—shaggy, and over his ears. She grinned, realizing his wardrobe was just as she remembered. When they'd started their brief relationship, she'd steered him away from wearing dockers and sweaters and into dressing more laid back. She could see that the lessons had stuck. He was wearing faded blue jeans, a dark green button-down shirt, and a black tie.

His thin face and sharp features accentuated his tall, slim build, and he smiled slightly as he gestured wide. "Yes. Of course. Come on down."

Jenn pushed her hair back behind her ears and walked down the steps to where he was standing. "It's been a while, Shane."

"Wow…You look…great, Jennifer. What brings you here?"

She struggled to hold her smile. "Feels more awkward than I thought it would. I mean—"

Shane waved his hand and interrupted. "What's done is done. As the French say, *c'est la vie, n'est pas*?"

"I agree. The past is the past. Thank you."

"Now that we've gotten that out of the way, why are you here?"

Jenn reached into her purse and pulled out the papers. "I wanted to see if you'd look at these and tell me what you think."

He briefly glanced at the three pages. "What is it you want to know?"

"Their purpose, I guess." She put the folder holding the papers on the table and spread it open.

Shane laid the papers out on the desk and rubbed his chin. "I'm sure you already know they're ocean floor maps. The topography here tells me the Arctic region. And those are subsea volcanic vents. Dormant, I'm sure. The format looks to be Russian."

"Correct as always, but I've figured that part out already."

He ignored her, opened his laptop, and started typing. Within moments he was comparing the papers to his screen. "Hm, where did you get these maps? The vents it shows must be relatively new. Look, this is from just a few years ago. No vents. We don't have the exact coordinates, but this is definitely the same region.

Holy shit, Jennifer, if these are accurate, why haven't the databases been updated?"

"I've been wondering the same thing. What about this page?" She handed him the paper with the grid of letters and numbers.

"Looks to be a cipher. Interesting, but a little primitive. There should be a simple key you place over it to reveal something. A name, coordinates, who knows?"

"So, we'd have to have the key, I guess, to know if it means anything. Maybe what the pencil marks mean?" asked Jenn.

"How long will you be in town?"

"I'm not sure."

"This is intriguing. Why don't you leave a copy with me, and I'll take a closer look later? I'm swamped right now."

"That'd be great, but I was hoping you could help me today."

"Today? I don't know, Jenn. Why can't it wait? I should be able to get to it next week." He regarded her for a moment. "What's wrong? Is there something you're not telling me?"

Jenn sighed. After a pause, she said, "It shows, huh?"

"I could always read you. You know that."

"Well, it's a long story. Do you remember Dr. Randall Marcus? The one I went to work with at UCLA?"

"Yes. I remember."

"This is gonna sound crazy, but we think he was murdered. Because of these papers."

Shane's eyes narrowed as he glanced sideways.

"Murdered?"

"Like I said. A long story."

"I'll make time. Would you like to sit?"

"No. I'm fine."

Jenn proceeded to tell him about the note Randall had written Steve explaining how a stranger had given him some papers at the United Nations, how they'd found the box on Randall's boat. She also told him about the run-ins with the stranger purporting to be from the government, and Tony being attacked at Steve's house.

"And that's what brought me here. Since I was in town, I thought maybe you could look at the papers and help us make sense of it all."

"That's a hell of a story, Jennifer. All right, come with me. There's a copier in the lounge. I've got another class soon, but I'll get to it tonight."

"Thank you, Shane."

Jenn followed him to the staff lounge. Once there, he turned on the copy machine and waited for it to warm up. He placed the papers face down and pushed the copy button. Once it had copied all three pages, he handed the originals to Jenn and flipped through the copies.

"Hold on a second. This one didn't copy." The two pages that depicted the ocean floor mappings had been copied, but the grid page had come out blank. Jenn handed him the original so he could rerun it. The machine once again spit out a blank page. Shane scratched his head and picked up the grid paper. He scampered over to a bookshelf and shuffled papers around.

"What are you looking for?"

"A magnifying glass. Here it is." He picked it up and studied the paper. A broad grin took over his face, and his eyes flashed with excitement. "Well, son of a bitch…they did it," he said under his breath.

Jenn took a step forward and looked at the paper. "Who…Who did what?"

"Shh. Come on. Follow me." He took her by the hand and led her back into the hallway. He scanned both directions, and once convinced they were alone, he spoke in a hushed tone. "There's been talk the Russians had developed an ink that, well…won't copy. That's the easiest way to put it. It has to do with embossing the ink with an elastic polymer or something. I never gave it much credibility, but…well…here it is. No wonder they want it back so bad. This may very well be the only copy. Jesus, Jennifer, this is some heavy shit."

"The guy we ran into at Steve's uncle's house didn't sound Russian."

"Well, if he's any good, he wouldn't, would he? But I'm sure our own government would be just as interested. Who knows? I'll see what I can dig up on the undersea vents. If, that is, these maps are real. If they aren't dormant, the ramifications could be huge. But that shouldn't be hard to figure out."

"What do you think the penciled-in circles represent?"

"No way of knowing. But it looks like there are a few more vents in the general area. Someone was interested in those particular two for some reason."

He handed the papers and their copies back to her, shaking his head. "I really don't want to have these on my person. I'm sorry. But I'll do some digging."

"I get it. But you're making me even more nervous.

I'll ask Steve and see what he wants to do. Let me give you my number."

Shane took two business cards from his shirt pocket and handed them to Jenn. She wrote her phone number on one, handed it back, and kept the other one.

Chapter 17

Back at the farm, Steve was eating lunch when the phone in the kitchen rang. Charlie's assessment of how the intruder could gain access to his house weighed heavily on his mind. *I thought Jenn would be safer here, but what's the use of having an alarm if someone can so easily render it useless?* he thought as he made his way to answer it.

"Mr. Blake, this is Dr. Berber. I received a message at my hotel to call you. I am busy, so please be brief."

"Dr. Berber, I see you like to get straight to the point; I appreciate that, so I won't waste your valuable time. I'm glad you called. Randall Marcus was my uncle."

"Yes. I know who you are. I am sorry for your loss."

"Thank you. Have you got a minute?"

"A short one. What can I do for you?"

"Where do I start? Do you recall anything out of the ordinary when you and the others were at the U.N. recently?"

"In what way?"

"Did Randall mention anything…odd, like someone leaving papers at his hotel room?"

"Papers? No. He didn't speak to me about it. What's this about?"

Steve didn't want to give too many details. Phone

interviews were an excellent way to get basic information, but they couldn't replace being there live. He felt that looking a person in the eyes and observing body language was key to a successful interview.

"How long are you and the others in New York?" he asked.

"We leave Saturday."

"I'd like to come and sit down with all of you, if I can."

"That's fine if you think it's necessary, but I wish you could tell me what this is about."

"I'll fill you in when we talk. I know that's not much to go on, but I think you'll find it interesting. It's complicated. I'll fly out Tuesday, and we can meet Wednesday morning if that will work for you."

"You can join us for breakfast before our first conference session of the day. I'll tell the others. Just call me when you arrive."

After hanging up the phone, Steve walked to the bathroom, took some aspirin, and splashed cold water on his face. Staring at his reflection in the mirror, he took a moment to think. *What am I going to do with Jenn? It feels like every step I make just puts her further into the firing line.* His thoughts were interrupted when the kitchen phone rang again. He dried his hands on his jeans as he walked to the kitchen to answer.

"Steve. It's Jenn."

"Hey. I wanted to talk to you. I've been thinking about—"

"Let me go first," she interrupted.

"Go ahead then."

"I showed the papers to my old professor, as we talked about, and something weird happened."

"Weird?"

She went on to tell him what had happened when they tried to copy the papers, and filled him in on what the professor had said. When she was done, a long silence followed as his mind tried to process everything. Eventually, Jenn broke in.

"So, what do you think?"

"I don't know what to think. You do still have the papers, right?"

"Yeah. They're right here in my bag. The whole thing seemed to freak him out a little bit. He's one of those kinds of people that thinks the government is watching him all the time and didn't want to have them *on his person,* quote, unquote."

"Good. Are you on your way back?"

"Yes. I'm pulling out of the parking lot now. What did you want to tell me?" Jenn asked.

"I want to talk to Uncle Randall's team in New York. I know it seems crazy, as you would say. I just want to get to them while they're all together in one place."

"So, we're going to New York? Is that what you're telling me?"

"Well, look, you don't have to…I mean…I'm sorry. I know—"

"I've always wanted to go there," she interrupted. "Maybe we can see some sites. This is becoming quite the adventure, Steve."

"We'll see. You are going to be at my side the whole time. We'll only be there a day or two."

"Got it. I'll be there shortly. When are we leaving?"

"Tomorrow."

After hanging up, he picked up the phone and dialed Sally Roberts' office.

"You've reached the office of Sally Roberts, attorney at law, how may I help you?"

"Hi, Amelia, is Sally available?"

"Is that Steve? Sure thing, hon, I'll put you right through."

He thanked Amelia and pleasant hold music played until Sally picked up.

"Sally, this is Steve Blake."

"Steve who? Do I know a Steve Blake? Let me think. Oh yes, didn't you used to do detective work for me?"

Steve ignored the comment. "Listen, Sally, I need your help."

"What's wrong, Steve?"

"I need to hire you. I have something I need you to keep for me, and I may need to hide behind attorney-client privilege on this."

"What do you need me to keep for you?"

"It's a long story. The less you know, the better."

"This doesn't sound like you. What's going on?"

"I promise I'll fill you in when I can. I have something to do, and I need your help. Will you do it for me or not?"

After a moment of silence, she replied, "Ah, hell. Why not. Life's been a little boring lately, anyway."

"Thank you. I'll be going out of town tomorrow, but I'll get it to you before I go."

"That sounds doable, but you still need to give me a retainer to make it official. You don't have a computer, do you?"

"Can I just give you my credit card number?"

"That's fine. How long do you need me to hold this for you? I'm heading on vacation this Friday. Gonna hit the Vegas strip."

"Just a day or two. Can I get it back from you this week if need be?"

"As long as you're back before I leave. Try not to make things too interesting for me, deal?"

"Deal."

Chapter 18

Steve was repairing one of the horse stalls in the barn when he heard a car coming up the driveway. He set his hammer down, walked outside to see it was Jenn, and yelled out to her.

"I'm over here."

"Okay. I'll be there in a minute."

Steve hadn't seen her this morning. He'd gone into town early to pick up items for the barn repairs and hadn't returned until she'd already left to see Shane, so as she approached, he found himself doing a doubletake.

"You look nice."

"Ah. Thank you."

It took him a moment too long to realize he was staring. Clearing his throat uncomfortably, he turned his head and scratched his neck. "So, uh, how'd it go?"

"It was awkward, of course. It felt strange seeing him again. He hasn't changed much. Still wears his hair the—"

"I was asking about the papers. What did he say about the papers?" Steve interrupted, silently chastising himself for how irritated he sounded.

"Oh. Of course. He said there should be a key or something that could tell us what the grid says. But, he said that even though it was primitive, without a key or keys...wait a minute."

"What?"

"That's it. The keys. Don't you see? Randall was waiting for some more papers. He may not have realized it, but that has to be it. It was the keys."

"That does make sense. I'm hoping Randall's friends can help. It's hard to imagine Randall didn't tell them something."

"Maybe. So, what's the plan? You said we leave tomorrow, right?" Jenn asked.

"I called my attorney friend. She's gonna hold onto the papers while we're away."

"That'll work, I guess. I got copies of the maps and data so you can show them to Randall's colleagues, but like I said, the grid was a no-go. Wouldn't copy."

"You think I could get an image of it on my camera?" Steve asked. Jenn shook her head.

"Doubt it. Shane said it was some new, Russian techno-ink."

"Guess that saves me from wasting time in the darkroom. I'm almost done out here. I just needed to replace one more slat."

When he turned back into the barn, the phone rang in the tack room. He walked straight over and answered. "This is Steve Blake."

"Hi Steve, this is Detective Skinner calling from LA. I have a question for you if you've got a minute."

"Sure."

"You mentioned that you had gone to look at your uncle's boat. Blue Seas Marina. Right?"

"Yes, what about it?"

"A body was found floating in the water yesterday morning. It turns out it was the guy who worked here in the bait shop."

"Young guy, mid-twenties, crooked teeth?"

"Yes, that's him—real ugly scene. His throat was slashed. I'm trying to put together a timeline. Do you remember seeing him when you left the marina?"

Steve thought a moment. "Not really, but there had been a lot of stuff going on. Hold on a minute. Jenn's here too. I'll put us on speaker." Steve pushed the speaker button and held the phone out. "Jenn, do you remember seeing that guy who worked at the marina when we left?"

Jenn cocked her head to the side in confusion and replied, "Yes, he was in the bait shop. Remember? He waved goodbye. It looked like he was with a customer. Why?"

"Hey, Jenn, Detective Skinner here. Can you describe the customer?"

"Uhh, it was an older woman, Hispanic, in her fifties maybe. What's this about?"

"I'm afraid the worker you met was found dead."

Jenn gasped. "Oh my God."

"Do you have a motive yet?" Steve asked.

"No, not yet; the cash drawer wasn't touched. The owner said he might have had some gambling debts, though."

"Keep me informed if you don't mind," Steve replied.

"Uh, sure, I can do that. May I ask why?"

"You know my opinion on my uncle's death, and it just seems strange this kid was killed right after we were there. That's all."

There was a pause. "Steve, your uncle's file is closed…but I can always open it back up if you have something for me."

"I'm working on it. Are you at the marina now?"

"Yes."

"Could you do me a favor and look at my uncle's boat?"

"Sure. Which one is it?"

"It's in slip forty-three, a twenty-seven-foot cabin cruiser. The name is Lizzy."

"I'll call you back in a…hold on. It's right over there." They could hear footfalls on dockwood, and after a moment, Skinner continued. "I'm looking at it right now."

"Can you check to see if it's locked up and secure?"

"Sure, hold on…Uh oh."

"What?" Steve asked.

"You're not going to like this. The door's been pried open…hold on a minute." There was the distinct sound of a weapon being unholstered. Steve and Jenn traded a glance and waited as the muffled sounds of Skinner entering and clearing the boat came over the speaker. After a tense moment, Skinner came back on the line. "I'm back. There's no one here, but the boat's been ransacked."

Steve shook his head. "Shit."

"I'll write up a report for the insurance company. I'd call these people at the marina; I don't see any security here. How do you want to handle this? I can't believe they haven't replaced the guy yet."

Steve rubbed his forehead and squinted. This was the last complication he needed right now. "I-I," he stammered, feeling his heart pounding in his temples.

Suddenly, Jenn cut in, placing a gentle hand on his shoulder. "I'll call Claudia and see if she can send someone out to fix the door. It'll be okay, Steve."

His shoulders dropped, and he breathed out heavily. He gave Jenn a quick nod. "That sounds like a plan. Tell her to have them send me the bill. Thanks. All right, Detective Skinner, I'm grateful for your time. Let's stay in touch." After they exchanged goodbyes, he hung up the phone and glanced over at Jenn. "Are you okay?"

Jenn crossed her arms, tilted her head back, and closed her eyes. "I'm fine."

Steve studied her for a moment as he chose his words. "We're in this together now, and I'm not going to let anything happen to you—you know that, don't you?" She gave him a grim smile.

"I appreciate that, but I am scared, Steve. I just want this nightmare to end."

"Me too."

Chapter 19

New York City

Mark Kensington's L.A. seminar hadn't garnered the support he'd been hoping for. He did consider having met Camilla to be a bright spot, though. Her goals seemed to marry up with his, and she'd made it clear that she had the means to act on them.

The two were in New York to attend a conference on global warming, where they hoped to drum up some support for their endeavors. While checking into their hotel, Mark glanced around the lobby and saw Helmer and Fleming, two scientists who were proving to be staunch rivals for project funding, standing next to the elevators. The conference had already been the stage for a few spats between the groups.

Mark tapped Camilla on the shoulder and pointed them out. "You see those two over there?"

Camilla turned her head and gave them a blank stare. "I wonder where the other two are."

Mark put on his politician's smile. "It would be rude not to say hi, don't you think?"

Her lips twisted into a wry smile. "I have nothing to say to them. But if you insist."

He made his way over with Camilla in tow.

"Hello, gentlemen. How are you enjoying the conference?" Mark asked pleasantly. He watched their faces as the two turned to see who had interrupted their conversation.

Helmer's smile faded. "Ah. Camilla." He hesitated, then continued. "You know my colleague, Doctor Fleming."

"Indeed. I wanted to apologize for my rudeness when we last met," Camilla said to Helmer. Helmer offered an empty smile, but didn't respond. A moment later, Lee and Berber, the members that completed their little foursome of researchers, arrived. They all traded glances, until finally, Berber spoke up.

"Mr. Kensington, Camilla, I am looking forward to a lively debate. Your band of flag-wavers and media moguls may not be the approach I favor, but I suppose they have their uses, and I hope we can come to a consensus."

"And what do you feel this consensus might be, Dr. Berber?" Camilla asked, icily.

Mark interjected. "I think my colleague meant to say that we hope we can all agree something has to be done, and we can all work together."

"How can we not, if we let *science* be the guide," Fleming interjected.

Before Mark could respond, Berber glanced at his watch and said, "It was a pleasure seeing both of you, but we must be going. We have dinner reservations."

Mark gave the four a parting smile and waited until they left the lobby to speak.

"There seems to be a lot of tension between you and Dr. Helmer."

"No tension I'm aware of. He's just a moody old man. Let's go eat, I'm hungry."

"Now?"

"Yes, Mark. Now."

They took a cab to Mark's favorite restaurant in Manhattan, The Chop House. Camilla was unusually quiet during dinner. Afterward, she agreed to go to Mark's room at The Tremont for a nightcap. Mark went straight to the bar to pour their drinks when they got to his room. When he turned around, his smile disappeared; Camilla looked furious.

"What is it?"

"Don't ever do that to me again. Earlier, you made me look like a damned idiot in front of those men. You don't need to explain what I mean when I talk. The more I think about it, the madder I get. And why were you so nice to them?"

"Here. Drink this down. I didn't realize you were upset. Why didn't you mention this at dinner?" He handed her the scotch glass.

She took the glass and stared straight ahead. "I didn't want to make a scene."

Mark sat next to her on the sofa and put his arm on her shoulder. "Why all the animosity toward them anyway?"

"Oh, it's nothing. That Helmer fellow just gets on my nerves. Let's change the subject."

"Sure. What would you like to talk about?"

Camilla took a sip of her drink and set the glass on the coffee table. "You still have a lot of connections in Washington. Right?"

"Not as many as before, but I still have a lot of favors to call in. Why?"

"I'd like to sponsor an expedition to the Arctic circle. To show we're not just a radical organization marching around protesting all the time. Over the next few days, we'll be meeting with all the right people to put together project funding. Maybe you could help in procuring a ship. Icebreakers are difficult to come by."

"That's quite a big order."

"Don't you think I've thought this through? That's where your connections come in. Surely you have some dirt on someone who could help."

"Okay. Just for argument's sake, let's say you do get your ship. Where would you get a scientific team?"

"I know a lot of scientists who would jump at the opportunity. We're at a conference full of them. That won't be an issue."

"You're really serious, aren't you?"

"You just get the ship, and I'll handle everything else. Are you in?"

"I wouldn't say I'm in. But I will talk to some people. Put out some feelers."

"Good. That's all I can ask. On another subject, earlier, you told those guys in the lobby *we* are with Project Green. What did that mean?"

"We aren't?"

"You have me confused," Camilla said.

"Listen, we're both working toward the same goal. I think it's time we officially join forces."

"No luck finding the sheep you need?"

"I always knew it would be a hard sell." Mark finished off his drink and set his glass on the coffee table. "And, I want to keep you close. Keep my eye on you."

"I do like the sound of that, Mark. I'll see you in the morning."

"Oh, I thought maybe you would—"

"Good night, Mark." She stood and grabbed her

handbag from the coffee table.

"Good night." Mark shook his head. *You don't like to be interrupted, but you have no problem interrupting me,* he thought.

****

Dr. Helmer looked around the room a third time and cleared his throat. They had just finished dinner and were waiting for coffee.

"Are you expecting someone? Or just admiring the décor?" Dr. Fleming asked with a half-smile.

Helmer grabbed his napkin from his lap and blotted his mouth. "I'm going to call it a night. I'm not feeling well."

"We still have things to go over. Can't you stay awhile longer?" Fleming asked.

"We can talk over breakfast. I'll see you then."

When Helmer walked out onto the sidewalk, he wasn't thinking about which way to go. On top of everything currently crowding his mind, a mixture of anxiety from being in such a large city and an undeniably terrible sense of direction made him turn the wrong way. He wasn't even sure how many blocks he had walked before he realized he was lost. With the darkness of night starting to set in, a low thrumming of fear started in his core. He stopped a young lady and asked her if she was familiar with his hotel.

She reminded him of one of his students. She looked in her early twenties, with black hair cut above her ears. She wore black pants and a short black top that exposed her waistline. Various piercings lined both ears, her nose, and her belly button. When she spoke, he could see her tongue hadn't been spared either. She looked him up and down in a way that did nothing to settle his nerves.

"I know where it's at. Maybe if I help you, you can help me with some cash." He let out a frustrated sigh and handed her a ten-dollar bill. She studied it carefully and put it in her pocket. "That'll work. You're about six blocks from your hotel. The easiest way to get there would be to go two blocks that way. Before you get to the traffic light, you'll see an alley on your right. Go down the alley, and you'll wind up on 23rd Street. Go left two blocks, and you'll see your hotel."

"I have to go down an alley? I don't know about that," he mumbled.

"It's a lot quicker. Don't worry, there's a lot of apartments that back up to it. No one's gonna mess with you."

Following her instructions, he soon found himself at the mouth of the alley. It looked to him about two blocks long, and several trash dumpsters lined both sides. As she had explained, there were several small balconies on either side and an occasional fire escape ladder. The sky had cleared and given way to a full moon, and the glow from the apartment windows contributed to the moonlight that lit the alley. But it also cast deep shadows, and he couldn't help imagining all sorts of dangers hiding in them.

Don't be a coward, he thought. Girding himself, he plunged into the alley's embrace, suppressing the urge to jog. About a third of the way through, he stopped and quickly turned around. *Were those footsteps?*"Probably just someone else taking the shortcut," he told himself, but he only half believed it. The guilt that had been weighing on the back of his mind started to force itself to the forefront, tossing gasoline onto the low-burning fire of his fear.

There was no turning back now, so he forged on. Immediately, the following steps started up again. Looking over his shoulder, he spotted a dark figure in the shadows.

"Is that you? Why are you following me?" he called out.

There was no reply.

He increased his pace, and noticed that the person behind him did the same. He stopped and turned. "Uh…Hello? To be honest, you're scaring me a little."

Again, there was no response.

"I have very little money on me. I-I can give you what I have."

Still no response. He calculated that they were at least one hundred feet apart. *Is it the girl who gave me directions? Or have they come for me?*

"Please," he pleaded, "I did what you asked me to. Can't you just let me go?" He was now a little more than halfway through the alley. He thought about running, but knew that anyone younger could run faster than he could at his age. The dark figure looked up to the apartments lining the alley. When he'd begun the trek through the alley, there had seemed to be so many brightly lit windows. Now there were only a few with lights on.

"Get yourself together," he told himself. He turned and continued. The footsteps came faster. He began to run, the mouth of the alley getting closer. *Almost there.* His eyes scanned side to side. *There must be something around here I can use to defend myself.* His panic reached fever pitch, and as he continued to look back, he crashed into a grouping of trash cans. Garbage and metal clattered across the pavement, and as he stumbled through it he grabbed one of the steel lids, brandishing it like a shield. The dark figure surged forward. He cried out and braced himself for what he knew was surely coming.

But nothing came. He opened his eyes, and the figure had disappeared. He spun around when he heard a familiar voice.

"Dr. Helmer, is that you?"

Lee, Fleming, and Berber approached from the street. "Why are you running?" Fleming asked.

"You look like you've seen a ghost," Lee added.

Gasping for air, Helmer bent over, clasping his knees. "Someone was chasing me."

Dr. Fleming glanced down the alley. "There's no one there."

"There was," he insisted.

"I called your room to make sure you made it back to the hotel all right. When you didn't answer, we got worried."

"I know, I know. I went in the wrong direction when I left the restaurant."

Dr. Fleming spoke up. "You said someone was chasing you?"

"It was probably just my imagination. Let's go, please." He tossed the garbage can lid back down and pushed past his mystified colleagues, unable to stop his hands from shaking.

Chapter 20

September 16th — New York City

Steve grinned as he watched Jenn staring out the cab window. Although she had repeatedly stated her exhaustion to him during the flight, the thrill of being in the Big Apple seemed to have freshened her senses. She stared out the cab window in wonderment, like a child visiting a theme park. It reminded him of Rebecca's reaction to seeing Paris on their honeymoon, and for the first time in a while the memory didn't sting quite as much. As they crossed the Queensboro Bridge, Steve watched her excitement grow.

"Oh my God, look at all those skyscrapers. And all those people. I've always wanted to come here. I hope we have some time for sightseeing."

"I don't know about that. I thought you were tired?" Steve replied.

Jenn yawned and stretched. "I'm tired but not sleepy. What time is it anyway?"

Steve glanced at his watch. "It's almost seven."

She yawned again. "Don't be a party pooper. We're here. I don't see why we couldn't at least go to the Empire State Building. And Times Square, and…why are you staring at me?"

"Sorry," he chuckled. "I guess it's just the way you can cast troubles aside and live in the moment.

Probably good to remind an old grump like me that there's still things to get excited about," Steve said. Jenn fell back into the seat, pondered a few moments in silence, and smiled.

The Belvedere was the only hotel he had been able to find a vacancy at on short notice that wouldn't break the bank. It sat on West 48th Street, just a few blocks off Times Square, which was nice, but it was six blocks from the hotel where Randall's team was staying. Thankfully, he'd been able to secure rooms across the hall from each other.

"What time is it now? My stupid watch needs a new battery," Jenn asked while unlocking her door.

Steve looked down at his own wrist. "It'll be eight o'clock in about…twenty seconds. You want to go eat?"

Jenn nodded. "Yes. After I freshen up. Give me ten minutes."

"That's fine. I'm going to set up a meeting for tomorrow morning. See you downstairs in fifteen?"

"Works for me. I can't wait to get out there and explore."

Once in the solitude of his room, he threw his bags on the bed and shook his head as he thought about the cost of the trip. *Maybe I should have just conducted the interview over the phone.* He had planned his semi-retirement out carefully, and last-minute trips to New York were not a part of the plan. He drew open the curtains and stared out at the unfamiliar busy streets below. Cars were backed up as far as he could see, and the intersections were full of people either crossing the street, or waiting to. *How could anyone live like this*? he wondered. He felt like such a fish out of water.

As he gazed, almost in wonderment, at the crowded streets, he thought he caught a glimpse of a familiar face leaning against a light post across the street, but when his eyes darted back to where he thought he'd seen the man, he was gone. He was tempted to dismiss it as more paranoia, but the stranger had followed them to Texas, and he didn't think his eyes were deceiving him now. "I saw you, you son-of-a-gun," he murmured as he leaned closer to the window and gave the street another careful look.

He made a quick call to Dr. Berber, and they agreed to meet for breakfast the following day in the Stanley Hotel restaurant. By the time he'd cleaned himself up and taken the elevator down, Jenn was already dressed and waiting for him in the hotel lobby.

She was wearing a pair of pleated jeans and a soft green knit top tucked into a wide black waist belt. On her feet, she wore brown lace-up boots. Steve was wearing his standard Wrangler jeans, a dark-blue long-sleeved button-down shirt, a leather belt, and a pair of black cowboy boots.

"How do I look? Is my makeup even?" Jenn asked.

"Uh, sure, looks fine, I guess. You ready?" Steve replied nonchalantly.

"Yep. Let's go see what's around here."

Steve tried to keep a cool composure, but he couldn't stop himself from casting furtive glances at their surroundings. The towering buildings, bustling sidewalk, and dull roar of city life provided too much cover for anyone who might be watching them. After a short walk, they found Maria's, a small mom-and-pop Italian restaurant two blocks down from the hotel. It was small, compared to the place Jenn had taken him to in California, and instead of booths it had small square tables, covered with black and white checkerboard pattern tablecloths that matched the floor tiling. The chairs were chrome-framed with burgundy seats and backs, and a vase filled with yellow flowers on every table. But even with the differences, it exuded the same familial charm. He scanned the room and saw the walls were filled with framed family pictures; some looked to date back to the war era, others were more recent. There were also pictures of famous people visiting the restaurant.

As soon as they sat, a younger man brought two glasses of water and set them on the table along with a basket of assorted bread wrapped loosely in a soft cloth. Steve took a sip of water and let out a sigh. They were face to face again, just the two of them, and yet Steve's eyes flicked to the front window every few moments. Jenn opened her mouth to speak but was interrupted by the waiter, who was smartly dressed in black pants and an open-collar, white button-down shirt.

"Welcome to Maria's. My name is Tito, and I'll be your server today. Our special this evening is spaghetti with meatballs. It comes with a house salad topped with our homemade dressing."

"That sounds good to me. What about you, Jenn?" Steve asked.

"Yes, I'll have that and a glass of wine too. The house red, please."

"And I'll have a beer. Surprise me."

"Very good," Tito said with a polite smile. "I'll have your drinks and salads right out."

Jenn picked her napkin up and unfolded it into her lap. "We've been eating a lot of Italian lately. We need to try something different next time," she said, quietly.

Steve let out a nervous chuckle. "Agreed."

"So, are you gonna tell me what's up, or do I just have to sit in the dark?"

"What do you mean?" Steve asked, trying his best to look innocent. Jenn huffed impatiently.

"Cut the crap, Steve. You've been all jumpy since we left the hotel. What's going on?"

Steve leaned his head back and exhaled before clearing his throat. "Listen, Jenn. We just have to keep our guard up, that's all." He studied her and waited for a reaction, which only seemed to aggravate her.

"Stop looking at me that way, like you're analyzing me or something, and tell me."

He realized that he was being unfair. So far, she'd handled everything about as well as he had. *Maybe better*, he thought, wincing at the patchy memory of her putting him to bed at his farm. "Okay. You're right. Our, uh, new friend is here. Saw him outside the hotel."

Jenn's eyes darted around the room. "Are you serious?" Her tone was animated but low.

"Yep."

"So he followed us again. Who do you think that guy works for?"

"I have no idea. But he's consistent. I'll give him that."

"Do you think he killed Randall?" Jenn asked.

"Hard to say. If he did kill Randall, why wouldn't he just kill us too?"

"That's a good point."

Jenn shook her head. "Well, that's just great. What are we going to do?"

"For now, we'll stick with our plans, meet Uncle

Randall's colleagues in the morning, and go from there. In the meantime, we'll just have to be careful and keep an eye out."

****

September 17th

"There they are," Steve said, nodding toward the three scientists sitting in the hotel restaurant the next morning. Fleming, Berber, and Lee were sitting at a large table at the back of the dining room. The three were in the middle of a hushed conversation as he and Jenn approached. "Good morning, gentleman."

"Where's Dr. Helmer?" Jenn asked.

Berber's lips pulled into a flat line as he waved a small greeting. "Oh, he'll be here soon, I guess. He hasn't been very prompt of late," he replied, with a clear note of irritation in his voice.

"Thanks for agreeing to meet. I know you're busy, but I wanted to get you all together in one place to talk," Steve said.

"You do have us curious. We can start, and we'll catch him up when he comes down. Do either of you want coffee?"

"No, I'm fine," Steve replied as he sat at the table.

"I'm fine," Jenn followed, plunking Steve's camera down. She'd begged him to let her bring it for sightseeing that day, and he hadn't had the heart to refuse. Her rough handling of it, however, was making him wish he had. She caught his startled expression and raised her hands in meek apology. He rolled his eyes, which made her giggle, and then turned his attention back to the gathered scientists.

"First, did Uncle Randall mention any scientific papers he came into possession of when you were here the last time?"

The three traded glances, and Fleming spoke up. "What kind of papers?"

"He said someone left them outside his hotel room door."

All three shook their heads and again traded glances. Fleming replied, "He didn't mention it to me."

"Me either. You?" Berber asked, turning to look at Lee, who shrugged apologetically.

"No. Not that I can recall."

Steve gave a disappointed sigh, then leaned in to speak quietly. "I don't want to alarm you too much, but I think they may be tied to his death."

"In what way?" Berber asked, his forehead creasing with concern.

"I'll go over everything that's happened and why I think that, but since we have limited time this morning, I wanted to warn all four of you to be cautious. Jenn and I have been followed, and there may be other connected deaths. You four were the closest to Randall, professionally speaking. Someone wants these papers very badly. I'm trying to figure out who and why, but until I do, you may be in danger."

Silence draped over the group as Steve observed the three's reaction. Berber's eyes widened, and he looked over toward Fleming.

"What is it?" Steve asked, and Fleming spoke with growing urgency.

"Dr. Helmer has been...preoccupied lately, with something he hasn't been keen to discuss. Just like Randall before...well, you know. Yesterday evening, he got lost coming back to the hotel and wound up in an alley. When we found him, he'd been running, looked like he'd seen a ghost. He said someone was chasing him, but there was no one there. We figured that it was just the stress of the conference getting to him, but…"

"Has anyone seen him since?" Jenn asked. There were nervous glances all around.

"I'll call his room again," Lee said as he stood and made his way to the lobby to find the house phone. The rest of the group followed, gathering around as he picked it up and pressed the zero button. "Yes, Dr. Helmer in room 906, please." They waited anxiously as the soft ringing continued. "He's not answering."

"I'll go check on him," Dr. Fleming offered, pushing the elevator button. "I'll be right back."

The group stood awkwardly while Fleming rode up to the ninth floor, and Steve felt the need to keep everyone calm. "I'm sure he's fine, I didn't mean to cause a scene," he ventured.

Lee nodded with an unconvincing smile. "Helmer's the worst when it comes to being punctual. He is probably—" He stopped talking when his phone chirped. He pulled it out and answered. "Hello? Dr. Fleming? I-I can't understand you, slow down, all right, we'll be right there." He pushed the disconnect button. "That was Dr. Fleming. He's having trouble breathing. We need to go up there. He doesn't sound good."

The ride up felt agonizingly slow. When the elevator door opened on the ninth floor, Steve saw Dr. Fleming bent over in the hallway, his hands clasped to his knees, breathing erratically. They ran to him, and Steve took him by the arm. "What is it? Do you have chest pains?"

Fleming winced visibly. His face was pale, and he didn't respond. He was fighting to get his breathing

176

under control. When he gestured vaguely behind himself, Steve could see that his hands were covered in blood. Berber and Jenn stayed with Fleming, while Steve and Lee moved cautiously down the hall.

Helmer's door was open, as was the one across from it, where Steve heard someone speaking rapidly in Spanish. He followed the voice to find a cleaning lady on the room phone. She had a panicked look, and she had been crying.

"Mr. Blake. Come here. Now," Dr. Lee demanded. Steve's head swiveled between Lee's voice and the cleaning lady, who was frantically talking to someone on the phone in Spanish. He could pick out just enough to realize she was on the phone with nine-one-one. He exited the room and saw Dr. Lee standing outside. His face was flushed, and his eyes were wide.

"What is it? Where's Helmer?"

Lee didn't reply. He just pointed weakly into Helmer's room.

Steve looked inside, but couldn't make out much of anything because the blackout curtains were closed. He felt the wall for a light switch and flipped it, illuminating a gruesome scene.

Helmer's body lay in in the bed amidst a red sea of blood. His arms were resting close to his sides, with both wrists slashed open. A single razor blade peeked out from the edge of the blood. Swallowing his horror, Steve scanned the room and stopped when his eyes caught something odd. It almost looked like a drawing on a corner of the bedsheet. His mind couldn't compute the peculiar site. But he saw something that he could understand on the other side of the bed. A small piece of paper with a handwritten note. Something that made him wince.

I'm so sorry, Randall. They were going to ruin me.

He froze after reading it. *What?* he thought, his mind racing a hundred miles a minute. He stepped out of the room and saw both Jenn and Dr. Berber advancing down the hallway. "Jenn. Stay..." he stammered. She shot him an odd look and stopped a few doors down from Helmer's room. Behind her, he could see the elevator doors opening to reveal the hotel manager and two paramedics with a gurney. He gestured emphatically as he strode closer to her. "My camera, quickly. See if you can buy me half a minute," he said, nodding to the newcomers as she handed over the camera.

He dashed back into the room and snapped as many pictures as he could of the relevant details, while outside he could hear the hotel manager barking orders for everyone who wasn't directly involved to leave. Before anyone noticed, Steve was back out in the hall, discreetly keeping the camera out of sight. Jenn gave him another curious look as he pressed it into her hands and then made a show of directing the paramedics into the room.

Steve was in his element for the next half hour as the police arrived and took statements. The scene was rather quickly deemed a suicide, and by all external indicators that appeared to be the case. While he didn't share it with the authorities, Steve wasn't entirely convinced.

Chapter 21

A morose silence hung over the group as they sat in the hotel restaurant bar. Steve had pulled two tables together to accommodate all five of them. The dim lighting and dark oak paneling of the speakeasy-style space seemed to complement the morbid mood that had settled in since the discovery in room 906.

"Do you guys know his next of kin?" Steve asked the three grim-faced scientists.

"We do. His wife," Lee said.

"You need to call her. It's best to come from someone she knows," Steve said.

"Won't the police do that?" Berber responded.

Jenn snapped. "Seriously? You are friends and need to call her right away before the police do. Jesus..." Her voice peeled away, and she rubbed her forehead. "I'm sorry, I—"

"Don't worry," Lee interrupted, "we're all on edge." He paused a moment. "She's right, though. God, what do I even say?"

Steve leaned back and sighed. "There is no easy way to tell someone that a family member is deceased. You just tell her what happened, offer your condolences. That's all you can do right now."

Lee nodded grimly. "Excuse me. I'll go and call her now." He grabbed his phone and walked out to the lobby.

"Maybe we should have seen this coming. He'd been acting very strange since Randall passed. Almost like a different person," Fleming said.

Steve shot a glance at the two and leaned forward in his chair. "What do you mean?"

"Well, at the time, it didn't seem out of the ordinary. After all, he was the closest to Randall of all of us. They knew each other in college. We, the three of us, met him five or six years ago for the first time."

Steve leaned back and pondered for a moment. "I didn't know that."

A server approached, and they all ordered coffee. She returned a few minutes later with it and water for everyone. Lee returned a few minutes after that and took his seat at the table. He shook his head. His face had no expression.

"How'd she take it?" Fleming asked.

"Not well. I called their son, too. He lives close and said he would be at her house shortly."

"That was good thinking," Jenn offered. There was an awkward silence, and then Dr. Fleming turned toward Steve.

"So, Mr. Blake, you started to tell us you thought we may be in danger?"

"Uh. Yea. Listen, I need to get more information, but if you've told me all you can about Randall, then it doesn't seem to me like you three are involved. To be on the safe side, just watch your surroundings, and…" He looked over and made eye contact with Jenn, his mind clearly elsewhere.

"What's going on, Steve?" she asked.

"I'm fine, just a little shaken. I'm sorry, gentlemen, we have to go, but I'll be in touch. As I said, just watch your surroundings, let me know if anything out of the ordinary catches your attention."

He stood, took a sip of his coffee, and placed a twenty on the table.

"Steve, wait a minute. Don't you want to show them the papers?" Jenn asked, her eyes squinting in confusion.

Steve rubbed his neck, keenly aware that all eyes were on him. "We'll have to do it later. You men have plenty to worry about already. My sincerest condolences."

Steve made his way to the door with Jenn in tow, and once outside, she grabbed his arm and pulled. "What is going on?" she demanded.

Steve gave her a level look and told her about the note he had seen in Helmer's room. Jenn stared back incredulously, her jaw working open and closed as she processed the information.

"Wait a minute. Do you think…he killed Randall? No way."

"I think it's a real possibility. The note indicated that 'they' would have ruined him, so that could be a motivation, and with how close the two of them were, he definitely had access. If he felt guilty, it would explain both his odd behavior, and what we found today."

"What about what they said about someone chasing him?" Her eyes widened, and she continued in a hushed tone. "What if this is another setup, like with Randall?"

"Yeah, you could be right. But he'd only be a loose end that needed cleaning up if he'd done something to begin with. Even if he didn't pull the trigger, he must've felt responsible. The real question is who are 'they', and what do they want? Listen, I need you to hang out at Maria's for a while."

"The restaurant by the hotel? Wait a minute. Slow down. You're not just gonna dump me somewhere and go off on your own."

"Jenn, listen, I am responsible for your safety, and Maria's is a public place where I know you'll be okay. I don't want you coming with me. I have to talk to our stalker friend," Steve said.

"Where?"

"I reckon he'll be waiting in my room."

"In your room. Yeah, just bust in there guns a-blazin', cowboy. Do you not see how ridiculous that sounds?"

"Well, when you say it that way. But I have a feeling he just wants to talk. And I need answers."

"Jesus, I'll tell you this much, you're not a boring date." She shook her head in protest. "It's your world, Steve, and I'm just living in it."

Once Jenn was safely at Maria's, he headed back to their hotel and made his way to the front desk.

"Anything to report?"

The lady behind the hotel counter scanned the lobby, leaned forward, and spoke quietly. "About an hour after you left this morning, a man came in and said he was your friend. He matched the description you gave me. He wanted to know what room you were in."

"And you told him my room number?"

"Just as you instructed. He left, returned about ten minutes later, and took the elevator up."

"Here, thanks." He handed her a twenty-dollar bill. She gave him a flat look.

"Really? Gee, thanks, twenty whole dollars."

Steve arched an eyebrow. A twenty used to do the job just fine, but he guessed city living meant things were more expensive across the board. Reaching back into his pocket, he plunked another twenty on the counter, and turned toward the elevator. He took it to the second floor and the stairs to the third, where his room was. With the stairwell door open just enough to look down the hall, he couldn't see anyone, so he made his way toward his room. He used his key card to unlock the door and threw it open with his Glock in hand.

The intruder was sitting in a side chair next to the window. Steve aimed his gun at him as he reached back and closed the door. The man gave a wry smile. "Hi, Steve, I was beginning to wonder if you would show up. And please, don't tell me you gave the lady at the front desk any money. I've made my presence pretty clear. You knew I'd be right here, waiting. Now, I know this is getting a little old, but where ar—"

"I'll ask the questions now," Steve interrupted. "You want the papers, and yet you say you can't tell me who you are or who you work for."

"That's correct. And no, I don't know what they are. And no, I had nothing to do with your uncle's murder."

"But you know it was murder and not suicide?"

"No. But you do. You're a fine P.I., Steve, but this is above your paygrade. Listen. I've been instructed to call someone who wants to talk to you." Without waiting for Steve's reply, he pulled his mobile phone from his shirt pocket and punched in a number. "Mr. Blake is here." He tossed the phone on the bed. Steve hesitated before putting the phone to his ear.

"Steve Blake, who is this?"

"Mr. Blake. I'm with the Federal Government. I'm the one who sent the man standing next to you. It is a matter of national security. If you don't give them to us, the FBI will soon knock at your door. And you don't want that to happen."

"And why is that? I don't take threats very well."

"As of right now, the FBI doesn't know anything about this. I sent the man there with you to retrieve the papers quietly. To…ask you to do the right thing. If you say no, I report that to my superior, and my superior goes with his plan B. The FBI. And we wash our hands of it."

"So, we have it narrowed down at least. Thirteen more national security agencies to eliminate."

"I'm just being as straight as I can be with you. Give him the papers, and all of this will go away. Haven't enough people gotten hurt already? We will be in touch soon. I hope you make the right decision."

The phone went dead, and Steve tossed it back onto the bed. The intruder stood up and retrieved it. He took a step toward the door and stopped when his phone buzzed.

"Yes?"

Steve watched him intently and listened.

"Really? Okay, I guess. I'll be there tomorrow for the brief."

With raised eyebrows, he pressed the disconnect button on his phone and said, "Good luck with this. I've been removed. I don't know what they're going to do now. You need to be careful, my friend."

Steve clasped his hands over his head and turned toward the window. He stared out over the city and let out an enormous sigh. "Is there anything you can tell me that helps make sense of any of this?"

The intruder slipped his phone into his pocket. "I was sent here to convince you to give up the papers. But between you and me, it feels like I'm just here to clean up someone else's mess. There are a lot of wheels in motion with stuff like this."

"Stuff like what? Who do you work for? Who was that man?"

"Listen, Blake; there's a landslide hanging over your head you can't see. But it's there. If this goes on much longer, it will come down on you. Hard. That's not meant to be a threat. I'm just trying to help you *make sense of it all*. As you asked."

Steve was still gazing out the window. After another minute, the intruder turned and opened the door. "I'm leaving. Good luck with—"

"Tell them I'll hand them over tomorrow," Steve interrupted.

"Okay, wise choice. I'll let them know. Wait for a call."

"What's your name?"

"You can call me Jack."

Chapter 22

September 18th — Texas

The morning sun peeked through the clouds as Steve made his way to the barn to ensure everything was secure. The wind was already howling from the west as a precursor to the stormy day that had been forecast. The death of Dr. Helmer had made him rethink the whole situation. He had taken responsibility for Jenn's safety, and now that Tony had been dragged into it, it was time to be rid of the papers and let everyone go back to their lives. If the suicide note was to be believed, then it appeared that Helmer had killed his uncle. The question of who put him up to it still nagged at his mind, but the case he'd signed up to solve looked to be closed. Jack was right. This was above his paygrade. They had stopped at Sally's on their way home from the airport to get the papers. After tonight, he'd be done with them for good.

He swung open the barn door, and the empty silence draped over him like a wet blanket. He stood in the middle of the structure and let his senses take everything in: the dusty scent of hay, and the familiar creaking of the wooden planks guarding the interior from the gusty winds. The barn without the horses felt just as wrong as the house without Rebecca. Satisfied that all was well, he returned to the house to find Jenn pouring a cup of coffee in the kitchen.

"You're up early," he said.

"I can't believe our flight was delayed like that. When we finally got in the air, I went right to sleep, so now I'm up at the crack of dawn."

"I know. You were snoring when I woke you up at the gate." Steve grinned when she shot him a curt glance.

"I don't snore...anyway...Between sleeping on the plane and the time change, my internal clock is all askew. And then I was tossing and turning all night long, thinking about all this stuff. Have you seen the weather report?" Jenn asked, pointing at the television.

"Yeah, it's going to get ugly today...listen, this will all be over soon. And you'll be back to your everyday life."

"You want a cup?" she asked as she pulled a mug from the cabinet.

"Just reuse my one from earlier. It's sitting in the sink."

"That's dirty, good grief. You need to use a fresh cup," Jenn growled, pouring him a fresh coffee and handing it over.

Steve raised an eyebrow. "You're in a testy mood."

"Honestly? I'm just not too happy you've called it quits."

Steve's eyes widened at the remark. He studied her and took a sip of coffee. "Where did that come from?"

"Come on, Steve. Let's discuss the elephant in the room. Do you really think Helmer killed Randall? And if so, why?"

"It's gone on long enough, Jenn. What I think is those damned papers killed him. If Helmer didn't kill

Uncle Randall, he was somehow involved. It's getting to be…uh…" He stopped talking when something on the TV screen caught his attention.

"Steve? What is it?"

"That's it," Steve said, his gaze fixed on the TV screen.

"What are you talking about?"

"Project Green. That was a TV ad for Project Green."

"Okay?" Jenn's tone was inquisitive.

"In Helmer's room, there was something drawn in blood on the sheet. I thought it might be nothing, but the logo on that ad looked just like it."

"Are you sure?"

"Hold on, I've got the prints hanging in the darkroom." Steve jogged down the hall and scanned the drying photos until he found one that showed the symbol without revealing too much else, then brought it back to show Jenn. "Positive. I mean, it's not perfect, but that's definitely it."

"So, there's our first clue?" Jenn asked.

Steve waited a moment to reply. He shook his head. "It could be, but I'm not changing my mind. I have a lot of people to consider, and you and Tony top that list."

"But we have a clue. I mean, come on, Steve."

The two locked eyes, and the tension hung uncomfortably between them, when suddenly Steve's mobile phone chirped. He held it up and hesitated before pushing the green button.

"Steve Blake."

"Mr. Blake. I'm glad you came around." Steve recognized the voice from the call the previous day.

"Where do I send them?" Steve asked matter-of-factly.

"Do you know where Meacham Airfield is?"

"I do."

"There's a hangar on the south end of the field. Hangar fourteen. You can access it off Lincoln Road. Just tell the guard at the gate your name. I'll have a plane there to pick them up. They'll be waiting for you at seven thirty tonight."

"We'll be there."

He hung up the phone and turned to Jenn.

"Well?" she asked.

"They're sending a plane tonight. Clue or not, it's time to end this."

****

"I think this is it," Steve said, pointing to a narrow asphalt road that turned north off Lincoln Road between a furniture store and a small, abandoned building. About a quarter-mile up the drive, the hangar came into view. It was surrounded by a tall chain-link fence with concertina wire rolled along the top. When they approached, the gate stood wide open, and the guard shack was empty.

"Is anyone in there?" Jenn asked.

Steve slowed the car and looked inside. "There doesn't appear to be. I guess we'll go on in, since the gate's open."

They continued through the gate and stopped in a small parking area right behind the massive hangar. Cloudy skies hid the setting sun, drenching the scene in darkness, and the trees swayed ominously in the wind as a storm cell passed to the south of them.

"This place is spooky," Jenn said as the two got out

of the car.

"There's a door," Steve said, pointing to the back of the hangar. It was a single door with a small light mounted on the wall to its right. "Let's go see if anyone's home."

Once inside, they both stopped and took in the hangar. The bright white, pristine floors reflected the light beaming down from the ceiling. There were three small jets, and a helicopter squeezed in between them.

"This place is enormous," Jenn commented.

"Yeah, this is the first time I've been in one of these. The floor looks like you could eat off it," Steve added.

The large floor-to-ceiling doors were open at the far end of the hangar, creating a gap of at least fifty feet. Parked right outside was a Gulfstream 550 twin-engine corporate jet. Its white paint and blue striping shone like new.

"Where is everyone? This doesn't seem right," Jenn said in almost a whisper.

Steve scanned the hangar. "Let's see if anybody is in the office."

Their footsteps faintly echoed throughout the hangar as they approached the administrative area. They could see there were lights on inside.

"Hello," Steve called out.

Jenn grabbed Steve by the arm and whispered, "Let's get out of here. I'm telling you, something's not right."

"I think I hear a TV on in there," Steve said, nodding to a door with an "Office" plaque. He tapped on the door as he opened it, hoping not to surprise anyone.

"Oh God," Jenn exclaimed as soon as the room was visible. Steve immediately surmised that they were pilots by the uniforms on their lifeless bodies. They were each slumped back in their chair with a single dime-sized bullet hole in their forehead.

Steve grabbed his Glock from his waist belt and grabbed Jenn around her shoulders. "Don't look," he said, his head spinning as he scanned the area.

Jenn buried her face in Steve's chest. "Too late."

To their left, about ten feet away, was another door. Steve put his left hand under Jenn's chin and raised her head to make eye contact. "Stay behind me. Do as I say." She replied with a quick nod. With his Glock leading the way, he threw the door open and quickly scanned from side to side. "Shit."

He saw another body. The man was dressed in casual clothes, and was also slumped back in a chair, but the bullet had entered his head from the side. The white wall to his left was splattered with blood and brain matter. "We need to get out of here."

All Jenn could muster was a quick nod of the head and a death grip on Steve's shirt. The back door they had initially entered through was about forty feet away, and still open. "Okay, we'll make our way to the door. If anything happens, you do your best to get to the car and get away from here. Here are the keys; it's this one."

Jenn took the car keys from Steve. "What do you mean? I won't leave you here."

"Do as I say. Now come on."

As they approached the door, Steve stopped and signaled for Jenn to stay back using his left hand. With his back against the wall, his Glock still in hand, he turned just enough to look outside. Not seeing anyone, he signaled for Jenn to follow, and they made a mad dash for the car.

When they were ten feet from freedom, Steve heard the telltale click of a gun being cocked, and a voice called out, "That's far enough." They stopped and turned slowly to see a man with a scar running down his left cheek. "You must be Mr. Blake."

The two froze and Steve didn't reply.

"Now put the gun down, Mr. Blake. We don't want anybody to get hurt. Just give me the papers, and I'll be on my way."

Steve spun his head around to his right when he heard another voice. One he recognized.

"And leave all these witnesses?" He saw Jack stepping out from the tree line some twenty feet away, pointing a handgun toward the stranger. "Come on, Preston, that's not your style."

"What are you doing here, Jack?" Steve asked.

Preston laughed. "Yeah, *Jack*, what are you doing here?"

"Intuition," Jack replied.

"I just want the papers, Jack, and I'll leave. No one gets hurt," Preston offered.

"So, Preston, you found someone that pays better than the government?"

"You could say that. Now put your guns down and leave the papers."

Steve could sense Preston's demeanor had taken a dark turn. Even though the small parking lot was dimly lit, he could see well enough to make out his icy stare and clenched jaw. He had seen this look of desperation before and knew he had little time to defuse the situation before bullets started to fly. He raised his hands and spoke gently. "I'll get the papers out of the car. Look, I'm putting my gun down."

Steve bent to the ground, holding his gun loosely with his thumb and index finger. As he did so, he turned his head toward Jack, making pointed eye contact. Jack nodded very slightly, and Steve yelled out, "Now!"

Simultaneously, Steve grabbed Jenn's arm and pulled her to the ground, and Jack squeezed the trigger. Preston returned fire with a single shot and ran through the door into the hangar, holding his side.

"Jenn, get in the car, quick," Steve commanded.

She froze, her eyes wide as saucers. She pointed to where Jack had stood and cried out, "Steve. Is he…?"

"I'll check on him, and you start the car."

Jenn put her hand over her mouth and stared in Jack's direction. Steve placed his hands on her shoulders and said in a matter-of-fact tone, "Look at me. I need you to stay strong. Start the car. I'll be right back. Got it?"

She nodded quickly, took a deep breath, opened the car door, and jumped inside. Steve spun around and saw Jack lying on the ground, blood pooling around his head. Fearing the worst, he dashed over to find Jack's eyes fluttering open. Steve helped him sit up, and over the sound of the now-running car, they could hear the growing whine of a jet engine starting to spool up.

"That's him. He's leaving," Jack said as he stumbled to his feet.

"Are you okay?"

Jack took a handkerchief from his pocket and pressed it up against the side of his head. "It's just a graze. I'll be fine. Damned head wounds bleed like a sieve."

"I'm a little confused. Why are you here?"

"When they told me to stand down, I asked why and didn't like the answers I was getting. I got suspicious and decided to tail you for a while. Something just didn't feel right."

"Well, I owe you my gratitude. Is that guy from the same place you work?"

"He is…was, I guess. If I were you, I'd get those papers somewhere safe. Someone is clearly coming for them, and I don't know what resources they have at their disposal. Right now, you two need to get out of here. Someone will have heard those shots, so the police won't be long," Jack replied. He turned and started walking toward the hangar. Steve called out after him.

"Jack, I need to know what happened here. Tell me something."

"No time, Blake, I'll be in touch…now go."

Steve opened the driver's side door and gestured for Jenn to scoot over. Without hesitation, she moved over to the passenger side.

"Steve, where did that man go?"

"He's taking the jet."

"What about Jack ?"

"He'll be fine. It looked a lot worse than it was. The bullet just grazed his head."

"A bullet doesn't *just* graze your head. Jesus…" Jenn slowly shook her head. Steve didn't respond. He knew what she meant, and agreed. It was just a graze, but the word understated the seriousness of what had happened. Silence took over as Steve put the car in drive and steered toward the exit. After turning onto Lincoln Road, Jenn turned her head and stared out the side window, watching the Gulfstream take to the sky. "Now what?"

Steve slowly shook his head and kept his gaze on the road. "Turning the papers over isn't going to happen any time soon. If the government side of things is compromised, I don't know who we can trust. We're gonna need to figure out what's actually going on here. I guess it's good we have that lead after all; I'll call Charlie, see if he can help." He picked up his mobile phone and punched in the number. "Charlie. Steve here. I need a favor."

"Sure, but make it quick. We're on our way to a call."

"I need you to send me anything you can find about an organization called 'Project Green.' "

"Hold on, let me get a pen…Project Green. Got it."

"Thanks. I have to go."

"I'll see you later, I guess…hey, did you just turn onto Main from Lincoln?" Charlie asked.

"No, it couldn't have been me."

"Your doppelganger is driving a car just like yours, then."

Steve grimaced and replied, "Be safe, Charlie. I'll call you." He briefly glanced at Jenn and studied her for a moment. "You okay?"

"I'll be fine. Hell. It takes more than a few dead bodies and getting shot at to get me bothered," she replied sarcastically.

"I'm sorry I got you into this mess. I'll figure out something."

"We almost got killed back there, Steve. Why? Is

the government trying to kill us now?"

"I wish I knew, Jenn. I wish I knew."

Steve felt a need to put some distance between them and the hangar scene. They jumped onto Interstate 35 and headed south. Fifteen minutes later, they exited the highway and pulled into a gas station.

"We need to fill up. You want anything?" Steve asked Jenn after shutting off the motor.

"No, thanks. What time is it?" she asked, staring distractedly out the window. Steve's eyes flicked from her, to the console clock right in front of her, and then worriedly back. She wasn't taking this well.

"It's almost eight. It's been a long day, I know."

Jenn shook her head, her eyes slightly glazed. "Tell me about it."

Steve filled the tank, went inside to pay, and returned a few minutes later. "That was strange. None of my credit cards would work. Good thing I had some cash on me."

Before Jenn could reply, his mobile phone chirped. "Who is it?" Jenn asked, the look in her eye now sharp and focused, if a little wild.

"I don't know."

The two traded glances, he pressed the answer button, and put the phone to his ear. The now familiar voice of the government official came through clearly. "Mr. Blake. That was not supposed to happen. I still expect those papers to be delivered to me immediately...Mr. Blake?"

Steve's expression hardened. He pressed the disconnect button and started the car.

"Who was it?" Jenn asked nervously.

"He still wants the papers."

Jenn slumped in her seat and stared straight ahead. "Of course, he does. There's something we're not seeing here."

"Do me a favor, can you go in and try to buy something? I think I might know why my cards wouldn't work."

"You think…?"

"Yep."

Jenn went into the store a returned a few minutes later. "My credit card and my ATM card both wouldn't work. This is unbelievable. What the hell? We were going to give up the papers tonight, their guy tries to kill us, and now we're being treated like criminals?"

"They're trying to put pressure on us; they don't want us disappearing with the papers. I need to think," Steve replied as he started the car and pulled out of the gas station.

"Where are we going?"

"Back to the farm."

Chapter 23

Steve entered the house first and did a walk-through, gun drawn. "It's good. Come in," he called out to Jenn on the front porch. When she entered, Steve was walking out of the office holding an envelope. "I've got five hundred in here. It's my rainy-day fund. Grab some things. We need to get going…Jenn?"

She sat on the couch and rested her head against the cushion. "Did all this really just happen, or am I having a nightmare?"

Steve sat next to her and rested his arms on his knees. "We need to get going."

"But, you now know who killed Randall. Helmer. Why can't we just mail someone the papers and be done with it?"

"Because it wouldn't end there. I'm afraid we're loose ends. Whoever is in charge here clearly doesn't want this situation in the public eye, otherwise they would have already sent the FBI in, like he threatened to. But they haven't. They keep sending one guy, who either won't tell us shit, or isn't afraid to resort to violence. They're trying to hide something, and if we want to get our lives back, we need to figure out what it is." He noted Jenn's look of confusion. "I mean, we may be in a position where we already know too much. This thing goes way beyond Helmer. Only way to finish it is to make sure we have the upper hand before we play their game. They don't want us to disappear, so we've gotta do just that."

Jenn picked up her cell phone and dialed a number.

"Who are you calling?" asked Steve.

"Claudia."

"Hold off on that. I need time to think."

"Think about what? Five hundred dollars isn't going to last very long. We need to eat…need I say more?"

"Jenn, I'm just not comfortable taking her money."

With a softer tone, Jenn replied, "I don't like it either, but what else are we going to do?"

Steve laced his fingers over his head and blew out his cheeks. "All right. You call Claudia. I'm gonna call Kasandra."

"What for?"

"We can't be driving around with these papers on us, we need them somewhere safe."

"What about your lawyer friend that we left them with last time?"

"No good. She's on her way to Vegas for the week."

"Isn't it a bit risky to leave them with Kasandra?" Jenn asked with raised eyebrows.

"Maybe, but no one is gonna know she has them, and she's the only person I trust enough."

"Not Charlie?"

"Charlie's a good man. I trust him with my life. But he's still a cop, and he'll follow procedure. Right now, procedure might get us killed."

"Fair enough, but Jack followed us pretty easily. They know what you drive."

Steve gave a slanted smile. "I've got just the

thing."

****

"Are you sure they can't trace this car to you?" asked Jenn as they jumped onto Interstate 30 and headed east. It was approaching ten o'clock, and the sky was finally clear. The full moon lit the road ahead as the Camaro's V8 engine purred and carried them forward. She was a thing of beauty, and Steve was sorely tempted to open her up, see what she could still do. But there'd be no badge to save him this time if he got pulled over.

"We had to sell her when I was still in school, and times got tough. I only tracked her down a few months ago, sitting all lonely in some guy's storage shed. I got her fixed up by some friends, but she's still in the other guy's name. There's an issue with the title. So as far as the law is concerned, he's still the owner. Where'd you put our phones?"

"They're in the glove box. The batteries too. I took them out. We're getting new ones from Claudia anyway."

"Good thinking. I hope she's able to make it happen," Steve said.

"She will. Assigning us company phones was ingenious, really. We don't want to be using our own if we can help it. She said there'd be instructions on setting them up in the telegram."

They continued on, eventually checking into a Holiday Inn on the outskirts of Texarkana—a city named for its proximity to Texas, Arkansas, and Louisiana. At the desk, Jenn had waved off getting her own room. Steve hoped the scowl he gave the desk clerk's knowing look had set the record straight.

"Thanks for understanding, Steve," Jenn said as he opened the door to room three-eleven. I know it'll feel awkward sharing a room, but I don't want to be alone tonight."

"Don't mention it," he awkwardly mumbled, tossing his bag on one of the twin beds and changing the topic. "We should find a phone book, see if there's a library close by."

"Why?" Jenn asked.

"Some libraries have computers now that you can use to get on the internet. We can go first thing tomorrow. I'd like to see if we can find out anything about this 'Operation Green.' "

Jenn flopped down on her bed and closed her eyes. "Project Green," she corrected him. She rolled over on her back and put her hands over her eyes. "I'm exhausted, Steve. It's half past midnight, and we haven't stopped all day. Can't this wait until the morning?"

"You go to bed. I can do this."

"Just ask the concierge if the hotel has one. After all, it is nineteen ninety-seven," she responded, her hands still covering her eyes.

He called the front desk and was told the hotel had a new business center with a computer. "We're in luck. The hotel has one."

"Well, let's go," Jenn said as she threw her legs over the side of the bed and stood.

"I can do it. Go on to bed."

Jenn gave him a sardonic smirk. "No, you can't. You probably don't have a clue of how the internet works."

Steve chuckled. "You're probably right."

Once they found the business center, Jenn sat in front of the computer and started typing. "Okay, let's search for 'Project Green.' " She entered the name into the search box, and after approximately thirty seconds, the results were displayed. Steve was a little blown away. With a double click of the mouse, they were looking at the home page of Project Green. "There you go, it looks like a recruitment site. We'll click here, and it will probably display a form to print," Jenn said. She clicked on the button and a page popped up with instructions explaining how to print the form, and an address to mail it to.

"No phone number?" Steve asked.

"Let's go back to the home page. There it is." She pointed to an "800" number in the top left corner of the screen. Steve wrote it down.

Once they were back in their room, he dialed the number using the room phone. "I doubt if there'll be anyone there this late. I'm just curious."

After one ring, he was surprised when a lady answered.

"Thank you for calling Project Green. This is Emily. How can I help you?"

Emily sounded a little distant, and Steve wondered if he had reached an answering service. He made eye contact with Jenn and shrugged. "Uh…hi, Emily, I got your number off your internet site. I was just looking for information about your organization."

"What would you like to know?" she asked.

"Who founded the organization, and where is it based?"

"If you like, I can sign you up for an orientation. Where are you located?"

"No, that's all right, can you just tell m—"

"I'm sorry, sir," she cut him off. "You will need to attend an orientation. When would be a convenient time for you?"

"No. No, that's fine. I'll call you back. Thank you." He hung up, feeling a little deflated. "That was a dead end."

"Got shot down, huh?" Jenn quipped.

"No, I didn't get shot down. She said I need to attend an orientation."

"Can I try?" Jenn asked.

"You won't get anywhere either. We'll have to approach it differently."

"What? Are you scared I'll show you up?" Jenn grinned and arched an eyebrow.

"No, I'm not scared you'll show me up. Go ahead, but you won't get anything out of her either," Steve said with a bit of irritation in his voice.

"Okay." Jenn shrugged innocently, picked up the phone, put it on speaker, and punched in the number. Emily answered after two rings with the same distant tone. Jenn barreled in, her voice taking on a new confidence. "Hello, Emily, this is Darcy Flannigan with Green Elegance magazine. I see you're a night owl also. I'm sure you know who we are, so I won't bore you with the details." She continued without giving Emily a chance to respond. "Anyway, I'm pushing my editor to do a big story on your organization. I'm putting together a preliminary to present to him tomorrow morning, so I just need a few things from you."

"Uh, I don't…"

"Don't worry, honey. I only need a few things,"

Jenn interrupted, "You do read our magazine, don't you? Anyone who considers themselves to be a true environmentalist reads our magazine."

"Of course, I do," Emily replied, her tone matter of fact. Jenn shot Steve a smug smile.

"I'm sorry, dear, I shouldn't have even asked. Now, let's see, first, who founded Project Green?"

"Camilla Amores…what was the name of your magazine?"

Jenn ignored the question. "Is that Amores with an 's', or a 'z'? I'd be terribly embarrassed to get it wrong in print."

Emily sounded flustered. "Uh…an 's'."

"Thank you very much." Jenn motioned to Steve, who wrote the name down. "Okay, and what would you say the organization's major goals are?"

There was a pause. "Officially, to raise awareness of global warming."

"Emily, you're doing great. Now, where is the main office located? And how do I get in contact with Ms. Amores?" Steve gestured for her to slow down as he scribbled on the notepad. She made eye contact with him and cracked another smile.

In a low tone, Emily replied, "We don't have a main office, per se. She pays me to take calls here at home. We have several branches, but they're all run out of people's homes."

"How industrious, but she must have an office somewhere."

"Oh. *Her* office is in Alexandria, Virginia. Close to the airport. I was talking about the local branches."

"Do you have the address? So I can send her a copy for approval, of course."

"Sure. It's one-eleven Reaver Street, Suite twenty-three."

"Perfect. What can you tell me about Camilla?"

"Oh, she's great. And recently she got the backing of some bigwig ex-senator." Lowering her voice again, she continued, "Rumor is, they are romantically involved."

Steve looked up at Jenn. They again made eye contact and traded grins.

"Really?" Jenn replied, trying to sound shocked.

"Yes, his name is Mark Kensington. Have you heard of him?" Emily asked, clearly enjoying the gossip.

Steve wrote his name down as Jenn replied, "No, but that is very interesting. This will help a lot, Emily." There was a slight pause.

"Please don't tell anyone I told you any of this." Emily suddenly sounded nervous.

"Oh no, not a chance, Emily. Don't worry. I never give up my sources. I have to go now; I need to have this on my boss's desk first thing tomorrow morning."

"I can't wait to read it."

"Thank you, buh-bye now."

Jenn placed the receiver on its cradle and looked at Steve defiantly.

"Kensington?" Steve asked.

"Aren't you going to say 'good job,' Steve?"

He grinned despite himself. "You may have missed your calling. Good job. Kensington…Kensington. That name is familiar."

"Well, let's do a search."

The two made their way back to the business center. Jenn typed in his name and waited for the results to pop up. "There you are, Mark Kensington. This looks interesting." She clicked a link that said "*Kensington's Fall From Grace.*"

Steve leaned forward and began to read. "Geez. It says here that others who were implicated either went missing or were found dead. It never went to court, but he lost his leadership position in the Senate and was primaried the next year."

"Sounds like a real stand-up guy," Jenn commented.

"Yeah, but his rumored connection with Amores is worth looking into."

Jenn's face took on an amazed look. She slapped her forehead with her palm, and her eyes opened wide. "Oh shit. I know why Kensington's name sounds familiar. It just hit me. He was that tall man we saw at Claudia's house. She introduced him as Mark Kensington."

Steve leaned back in his chair and cocked his head. "Yep. Has to be him. Claudia said he's an ex-senator. Well done, Jenn. Didn't she say he was sniffing around for money for some new project?"

"You think it's connected to Project Green?"

"I think we'd better find out."

Chapter 24

A bullet in the side was all Preston had gained from his failed attempt to get the papers, and he was furious. His career with the agency was over; Jack showing up at the hangar made certain of that. Now, if he couldn't somehow get the papers, there would be no payday. He wasn't going to let that happen. He just needed to rethink the situation.

He'd taxied out and taken off without talking to ground control or the tower. A corporate jet on final approach had been forced to break off its approach when he lifted off, going in the wrong direction. He couldn't have cared less. The rich pricks already had everything; they could go around and reapproach. He climbed to one-thousand five hundred feet. Once at altitude, he made sure the transponder was off and flipped the autopilot on. He needed a minute to assess his wound. His destination wouldn't matter if he bled out on the way. He unstrapped from the seat and stumbled back to the galley, putting pressure on his side, though the blood was running over his fingers at an alarming rate. He rummaged through various compartments until he found a first aid kit.

He peeled back the layers of clothing to see what the damage was. The bullet had grazed him on the right side of his torso. Luckily, it hadn't penetrated too deeply or lodged inside him. But he was sure one of his ribs was cracked, and it had torn a dangerous-looking gash that was costing him too much blood with each heartbeat. Spilling the contents of the first aid kit out, he located gauze, tape, and antiseptic wipes. He quickly realized that the wipes would be useless, given his condition. He stuffed a wad of gauze onto the wound and put as much pressure on it as he could stand.

Gritting his teeth against the pain, he continued his desperate search until he found a mini-bar that had little bottles of vodka. He poured one into his mouth and then, bracing himself, poured another over the wound. A wave of nausea and lightheadedness washed over him, but he couldn't afford to lose consciousness. Punching the cabinet next to him to get through the initial pulse of pain, he tapped into his training to find his feet and return to his supplies. A few agonizing moments later, he had stuffed and wrapped the wound to the best of his current ability, using the last of the bandages to tie some ice packs on the wound to slow the bleeding. Grabbing bottled water and paper towels, he cleaned up the galley as best he could.

He flew north for several miles before turning east. In his condition, he knew he couldn't stay airborne long. He searched a map he found in the cockpit and decided the Sulphur Springs airport would be a good place to land. It was located outside the sleepy East Texas town on a small lake. Once on the ground, he called for a cab. Fortunately, the bleeding was still at bay. He asked the cab driver to take him to a motel and used an alias to check in. He made his way to the bathroom, intending to check on his wound. He set out some clean bandages and sat in the bathtub, not wanting to leave too much of a mess, but before he could unwrap his dressings, darkness took him.

He was awakened the following morning by a knock at the door. It took him a moment to gather his senses, but the events of the previous day quickly spiked into his foggy brain. With his Ruger in hand, he made his way to the door and looked out the peephole. "Who is it?"

"Maid service."

His side was throbbing, and when he pulled his shirt up, he saw that his bandages were soaked through. "Can you come back later?"

"Okay. No problem."

He relaxed, glad for the privacy, but when he took a closer look at his side, he quickly realized what a mistake that was. "I'm going to need some help with this," he said to himself. He picked up the phone and pressed zero for the front desk.

"Front desk, how may I assist you, Mr. Williams?"

"Yes, I just sent the housekeeper away, but I need some extra towels. Can you send her back, please?"

"Certainly, Mr. Williams. I will let her know."

A few minutes later there was another knock at his door. After gazing through the peephole to make sure it was the maid, he opened it. Ever since he'd checked in, he had used a Colombian accent, hoping it would help to guard his identity, and he was relieved to see that the maid was Hispanic as well. He pointed to the desk, obscuring himself behind the door, and spoke to her in Spanish. "*Just set them there.*"

Before she reached the desk, Preston had shut her in and thrown the deadbolt. She spun around to see him with the Ruger, shook her head, and raced toward the room phone. Preston blocked her path and held up his hands. "*I will not hurt you; I promise—I need your help. See? I'm putting my gun down.*" After setting his gun on the desk, he reached into his pocket and pulled out a wad of money. He counted out two one-hundred-dollar bills and laid them on the dresser.

"*All you have to do is bring me a few things to help with this cut.*" He motioned toward the bloody sight on his torso. He took one of the bills and handed it to her. "*When you return, the rest of the money will be yours.*" He'd intentionally called it a cut. A gunshot wound might have scared her more than she already was, and it would work well with the cover story he was constructing.

"*Mr. Williams, you should go to a hospital.*"

He put on his best pathetic face. "*I know, I know, but I can't. You see, I'm not a U.S. citizen. I'm from Colombia. I'm here seeking family and work. It's a long story.*"

"*How did you get cut?*"

"*Some gringos tried to take my money.*" He let his desperate look shift to pride. "*There were three of them but only one of me, and I still have my money, but without your help I won't last long.*" He could see that his ploy had reached her. She nodded sympathetically.

"Si, señor, *I will help you. I, too, came to seek work. I know the terrible things that can happen.*"

"*Good, thank you so much. Here is a list of the things I need. When you get back, I will give you the money.*"

She couldn't hide her smile. "*Thank you. I will be here later today. I still have two rooms to clean. Is that all right?*" He winced, thinking of how much blood he had already lost. He carefully peeled out another

210

hundred-dollar bill and laid it on the dresser.

"*Can you go now? It won't take you long.*" She looked at the money hungrily.

"*Yes, that will be fine.*"

After she left his room, he picked up his mobile phone and punched in a number. After three rings, the voice on the other end answered.

"It's me, and I have a little problem," he said, hesitantly.

"Really? You said it'd be a piece of cake. Your words."

"Calm down, Kensington. I'm lucky to be alive. I didn't get the papers, but I took a bullet in the side. I wasn't counting on the cavalry showing up."

"You told me he was going to be taken care of. You said he wouldn't interfere—"

"And he will be, so calm down," Preston interrupted.

"I'll calm down when this is over. Jesus. I put a lot on the line here. Do I have to take care of this myself?"

"Kensington, don't fuck this up. I'm going to handle this."

"Yeah, we'll see. How about you just do what you said you would. What's your plan now?"

"First, I have to patch myself up a little. Then, I've got a little errand to run for our...mutual associate. Then, I'm going to eliminate anyone in our way and find the fucking package."

Chapter 25

CIA Headquarters, Langley, Virginia

"Goddamn it!!" As if the missing Russian papers weren't bad enough, the rogue agent had caught CIA Director Randy Davis completely off guard. He smashed the receiver back down onto his phone, then picked it back up and slammed it down several more times in frustration. The vein in his forehead popped out dramatically as he paced back and forth. Over the last couple of hours, the situation had spun wildly out of control. *What the hell am I supposed to do now?* he thought.

Going back to the Hoover days, there'd always been a kind of cat-and-mouse game played between the CIA and Congress. He was quite aware that some were always looking for reasons to pry deeper into the agency, and if this debacle got out, they'd have just that. Now he was in survival mode; he could see his job and pension going up in proverbial flames.

Davis had attended Georgetown with the Secretary of State, Mark Edelson, and they belonged to the same country club. It would surprise no one that their friendship played a role in the way the two did business; even if the CIA was supposed to answer directly to the Director of National Intelligence, things in Washington sometimes got wound around the axle, and rules got thrown out the window. It didn't matter that everyone knew that was the way the game was played though, if their backchannels went public over this...

Edelson had asked Davis to find the papers quietly. He'd explained how he was leery of the FBI because of the history of leaks under the current director. It had seemed like the kind of political favor that would pay off. Davis understood that sending one of his CIA assets to harass a U.S. citizen was a considerable risk. Almost taboo. That is why it was supposed to be done quietly and delicately. Jack's lack of results had been disappointing, but Preston had just blown the whole operation out of the water.

Why would Preston do this? Secretary Edelson's lying to me. He has to be. Preston just shit-canned his career over those papers; they have to be far more important than Edelson let on. If this gets out, God only knows how many committee hearings they'll deem necessary. The ones on the other side of the aisle will ensure this stays alive through the November midterms. I have to squash this quickly and quietly.

His thoughts were interrupted when his secretary's voice came alive over the speaker. "Samantha Berry here to see you."

"Send her in."

He stood and watched her come in, closing the door behind her. She carried a black suitcase, and was wearing gray pants, a white button-down top, and a gray jacket. She had an olive complexion, large brown eyes, and a heart-shaped face framed by black hair running down to her shoulders.

"Director, what is the point of my top-secret

security clearances if I'm going to be forced to present my credentials not once, not twice, but three times whenever you call me to your office?" she said as she strode over to his desk.

"I know it's inconvenient, Sam, but your official title is still 'Field Analyst,' and it would raise too many questions if you could just march in here any old time. Now take a seat, please," he offered.

His office was large and airy. A dark walnut bookcase lined the entire left-hand wall when you entered. His mahogany desk sat in the middle of the room, facing the door. Behind the desk was a wall of windows that overlooked a courtyard lined with tall hedges, although tonight they merely reflected the office's interior. To the right was a wall covered in framed certificates, accolades, and news articles. Up against it was a brown leather sofa, where Sam now sat, forcing a smile as she pulled her briefcase onto her lap.

"Coffee?" Davis asked, walking over to a small table and picking up the coffee pot, copied by his ghostly mirror-image in the window.

"No, thank you. I already had my quota."

After pouring himself a cup, he stood staring into his reflection for a long moment. He took a sip of his coffee, turned toward Sam, and shook his head. "Where is he?"

"Where is who, sir?"

"Preston, my dear…Preston!"

"He got away in the Gulfstream."

"Well, can't they get his flight path from the FAA?"

"They're looking into it, but I doubt they'll find anything. He's most likely staying low, keeping his airspeed back under 200 knots. And I'm sure he turned his transponder off."

"They'll at least be able to find his initial course, won't they?"

"He's not an idiot. He most likely stayed VFR on an initial heading for a while, then turned toward his intended destination. The aircraft will show up eventually, but he'll be long gone by then," she replied.

"Do you realize how hard it will be to deal with Blake now? That was the only way to get my hands on the papers without stirring a hornet's nest. We've already gone as far as I'm willing to go for Edelson on this. God knows where those fucking papers are now."

"Sir, we've cut off their accounts and we're tracking their phones. We'll find them."

"You'd better. You see, I've been in this business for a long time. I've always put the interest of our country first. We do the things that need to be done. In our business, the end is supposed to justify the means. But I don't have a clue about the Secretary's missing papers, not a damned clue, and I'm not about to be burned for something I don't even understand."

Sam nodded her head and stayed quiet while he continued to rant.

"I've had just about enough of this. I need to know exactly what we are dealing with, or the Secretary can get his friends in the FBI to help him."

"Well, sir, we've picked up chatter that a large sum of money is being offered for some scientific papers, and a missing Russian asset. We're not one-hundred percent certain, but Blake's uncle was a scientist, and it looks like those are what we're dealing wi—"

Raising his voice, Davis interrupted, looking

almost apoplectic. "A fucking Russian asset? Did Edelson know about this?" Sam opened her mouth to say something, but he cut her off. "And now I have an agent who has gone off the deep end, and you're telling me there's money on the table? Well goddamn, I wonder if there's the answer to that fucking puzzle! You tell the Secretary I want a full briefing on those papers, and I want it now. Do we understand each other?"

"Is there anything else, sir?"

Davis planted his hands on his desk, shook his head, and replied, "I think that's enough for one day."

Sam set the briefcase down beside her and opened it. Reaching inside, she retrieved a large manila folder. "This is for you, sir," she said as she stood and handed it to him.

Davis looked at it, clearly blindsided by its appearance. "What is it?"

"The briefing you requested, sir," she replied.

After a long pause, he shook his head and said, almost under his breath, "Just put it on my desk. You could have told me when you entered, you know."

"No worries, sir. Is there anything else you want me to pass on to the Secretary?"

"Stay here. I'm going to look at this now."

Sam sat back down on the sofa. Davis sat at his desk and opened the folder. After a few minutes, Sam glanced at the coffee pot. "Maybe I'll have some coffee now."

Davis didn't look up. He gestured with a hand and said, "That's fine. The cups are on the shelf underneath."

She nearly spilled the coffee everywhere when

Davis suddenly slammed the folder down.

"Are you fucking serious?" he shouted.

"Sir?"

He glared at Sam. "Edelson's a real piece of work. I can't believe this. Did you know about any of this?"

"Any of what, sir?"

Davis shook his head and rubbed his forehead. "Oh my God. How could he be so stupid?"

"Sir?"

He slowly closed the folder and shoved it aside. "Just so we are clear here...I am not going to want my name associated with this. I want you to get rid of this file. Make it go away."

"Sir?"

"You heard me."

He took a pen from his pocket and started scribbling furiously on a notepad. When he was done, he folded it up and sealed it in an envelope. "Give this to the Secretary, then take this folder and shred it."

Sam stood, took the envelope, and paused.

"Something on your mind, Sam?"

"Sir, about our arrangement."

"What about it?"

"Well, sir, I'm an analyst. I speak seven languages, including Farsi, and I have five years of field experience. But I don't analyze anything. You've had me on loan for almost a year now, and I was wondering...well...how much longer will you and the Secretary need my services?"

Davis leaned back in his chair, made a steeple of his fingers, and rested them on his chin. "I'd say, as long as he's the Secretary of State. You being our liaison may not be one-hundred percent ethical in some eyes. But some of the things we discuss need to stay between him and me. Sam, your skillset may be underutilized here, but your discretion is not. If it helps, just look at all the free time you have while drawing a hefty salary."

"Yes, sir."

"Good. By the way, has Jack checked back in for debrief yet?"

"No, sir. Not yet. Why?"

"No matter. Go shred that file and take that envelope to the Secretary."

"Yes, sir. I'll take care of this right away."

After she left the office, he pulled a bottle of well-aged single malt from his desk drawer and poured a healthy glass. Just as he went to bask in its soothing flavor, his intercom came alive again. "Yes," he answered. He was already dreading whatever the new interruption was, but when his secretary's voice came through, he downed his entire glass in one swallow.

"Mark Kensington on line two, sir."

Chapter 26

September 19th — Holiday Inn, Texarkana

It took a moment for Steve's mind to catch up, seeing Jenn fast asleep on the other bed when he woke the next morning. He was still conflicted as to the best way to keep her safe. *Are you doing the right thing?* he wondered. On the one hand, he felt keeping Jenn by his side was the best thing, but he also knew he was now a target, and as long as she was with him, she was as well. But the alternative would be to send her away, and he would have no way of protecting her.

He had slept in his jeans, shirtless. He usually slept in his boxers, but things were awkward enough without him stripping down with her in the room. He shook off the thought and started a pot of coffee. He then quietly pulled the ironing board and iron from the closet. The smell of fresh coffee wafting through the room seemed to bring Jenn to life, and she smiled as Steve caught her eyes.

"Good morning," Steve said. Her smile faded, and she quickly pulled the sheet over her head. "What's wrong?"

"Uh, nothing," she replied.

"Then why are you hiding under the sheets?"

"For God's sake, Steve. Just look the other way. I don't want you to see me. My hair is a mess, I just woke up…just…turn around so I can get in the bathroom."

Steve chuckled. "All right, but I don't see why you're making such a big deal out of it."

"Because you are a man, that's why. Are you looking away?"

Steve turned his back to her. "Okay, I'm not looking."

She quickly stood, grabbed her bag, and darted to the bathroom. After she was washed and dressed, they made their way downstairs for breakfast. Once seated, Steve used his fork to examine the eggs on his plate.

"I don't think these are real eggs. Probably powdered."

"Well, it's free, so don't complain," Jenn mused.

"Fair enough. I hope we can learn something about Kensington when we interview Amores. After all, the rumor mill says there's a romantic connection there," Steve said, a little mockery in his tone.

"Do you still think that's the way to go?"

"Why wouldn't it be? Everything seems to be pointing us in that direction."

"Well, that's just it though. How can we be sure we aren't being deliberately pointed in the wrong direction?"

"I understand what you're saying. But this is more than just coincidence. Helmer made a last-minute decision to draw that picture. The Project Green logo."

"How do you know it was last minute?"

"He did it after he slit his wrist. It was drawn in blood. He could have been murdered, just like Randall, and the note could have been forced or faked. If that was our lead, I'd feel just like you do. But regardless of whether he pulled the trigger on my uncle, and regardless of if he took his own life or it was taken from him, that bloodstained symbol was the last thing he ever did. He must have had a last-minute regret or something."

"I didn't even think of that. You're good."

"Well, it pays the bills at least."

"How long is the drive to Washington?"

"Seventeen hours if the traffic's light, and we don't run into too much road construction. That's why I want to get going."

"I hope you're not planning on driving nonstop. My bladder won't take that."

"You won't have to worry about that, Jenn. I hate driving long distances, so we'll make quite a few stops. Did you get the address for the Western Union from Claudia?" Steve asked.

"Yes. It's in a Wal-Mart down the road. And I gave her the address to the hotel in Washington to send the phones."

"All right, I'm gonna make a quick call before we go. I'll meet you at the car." He watched Jenn leave, then found the payphones and dialed Charlie's number.

"Hey Charlie, it's Steve. Just wanted to check if anything came up on what I asked you about?"

"Steve, good to hear from you. Listen, I did some looking into Project Green like you asked me to do. The ringleader, Camilla Amores, it's the damndest thing, but she didn't exist until about twelve years ago."

"What do you mean?"

"I did the usual. Checked her social security, banking records, residency history, and credit history. I couldn't find anything on her before nineteen eighty-five. Nothing."

"You figure she took a new name at some point?"

"Seems that way."

"That is strange. I appreciate you looking. I've got to get going. I'll talk to you later, Charlie."

"Hold on a minute, Steve." The irritation in his voice gave Steve pause.

"Yes?"

"What do you want to tell me about a Detective Skinner?"

"Skinner?"

"Come on, Steve. Don't play games with me. Why didn't you tell me about what happened in California?"

Steve paused, unsure how to answer. "What'd he want?"

"He's investigating the murder he called you about. The one you failed to mention to me. He had some questions about you." Charlie's voice softened. "Listen, buddy, I know you don't like asking for help, but come on. We go way back. Sometimes, you gotta let people in."

Steve tried to steer the conversation. "He asked about me?"

"Yeah, Steve. He's investigating a murder. And you were recently at the murder scene. You know the game. And I got questions of my own, man. You're clearly holding out on me. You got home invaders with high-tech skills the likes of which I've never seen, you're being all secretive, and for God's sake," his voice got quiet over the line, "don't try and tell me that wasn't you coming away from the airfield. I got a bunch of dead bodies over here and no explanations. I'm not about to make life difficult for you, but you gotta tell me what's goin' on."

Silence dominated the line for a full ten seconds, until Steve finally spoke up. "Charlie, I don't know what to say. I need you to trust me on this one. Here's what I can tell you: Uncle Randall didn't kill himself. He was murdered. You should probably tell Skinner to link up with the NYPD. Looks like they got the perp there; a doctor Randall worked with by the name of Helmer, but he's dead now too."

"Christ Almighty, what did you get yourself mixed up in?" Steve didn't answer, so Charlie continued. "I'll pass along your message to Skinner. He also asked me to run some prints through our database. And a few other things. I'll be working with him on this end. Anything else you can tell me would be a help. I assume this Camilla lady may be a part of the puzzle?"

"She's got something to do with it all, but I need you to give me more time. I really don't have anything for you on the killing at the marina that I haven't already told Skinner. I wish I could tell you more, I really do, but I have to go. We'll talk soon."

****

The rain was so heavy that, at times, Steve could barely see beyond the car's hood as the two headed northeast through Arkansas on Interstate 30.

"I hope we don't get blown off the road. Or hit by lightning. Thunderstorms make me nervous," Jenn said. The car rocked slightly as a gust of wind danced across the road, and Steve watched her wince.

"My mom used to say that unless there's a tornado nearby, the car is one of the safer places to be in a storm," Steve replied, hoping to ease her fear.

She seemed to relax slightly at that, and the two sat

quietly as the rhythmic sound of pouring rain filled the vehicle. A few minutes later, Jenn shifted in her seat toward Steve. "You mentioned your mother. Are your parents still alive?"

"No. They're both gone."

"I'm sorry."

Steve kept his eyes forward and didn't respond.

"Never mind, I'm sorry. We can change the subject."

They continued down the highway, and an awkward cloud of silence filled the air. Over the next several miles, Steve would see her occasionally glance at him in his peripheral view. After a while of this, he broke the silence. "Dad died in prison, back when I was in high school." There was a long pause. "Soon after that, Mom's health fell off a cliff, and she passed six months later."

"I'm sorry. That's…that's so sad."

"Yeah, well, that's life."

Jenn shifted back straight in her seat and stared forward. After a couple of aborted attempts to respond, she turned back to Steve.

"Cancer," she said quietly. Steve was caught off guard.

"Pardon?"

"My mom, so early I barely remember her. My dad when I was seventeen. Cancer took them both. Randall was practically all I had left and…Look, you don't have to share your life story with me. That's just fine. I won't pry. But it's not just you, you know. You don't have to be alone in it. I guess you're right though. That's life."

Outside, the storm raged on, buffeting the car with

wind and rain. Inside, Steve was buffeted by the winds of time. He hadn't spoken about his father in so long, but here he sat, in a physical representation of their time together. He could almost feel him sitting in Jenn's seat, and her vulnerability pulled him into a stillness he hadn't expected. He looked over and caught Jenn's eye.

"Dad was a dirty cop. He got caught in a sting operation with five other cops. He and another one died before the trial, but eventually the rest of them were convicted of extortion, conspiracy to commit murder, and corruption."

"That's terrible. What happened to him?"

Steve's face hardened. "Cops don't do well on the inside. Soon after he was arrested, some of the other inmates...As I see it, if you lie with snakes, don't be surprised if you get bit."

"That's really tough. Thank you for sharing. Did that have anything to do with you becoming a cop?"

"Maybe. I get asked that a lot. It didn't make it easy for me, that's for sure. I was the son of a dirty cop. I always had to do better than the other guy. Once I got accepted into the academy, they did everything they could to get me to quit."

"But you didn't. Did you?"

"Let's talk about something else."

"That's fine."

The two rode quietly until reaching Knoxville, where they stopped for dinner at a Denny's by the highway. Afterward, as they pulled out of the parking lot, Steve noticed Jenn yawning. "Why don't you get some rest, and I'll drive until I get sleepy," he offered.

"I am tired. I think I'll take you up on that. How much longer do we have?"

"About seven hours. We should be there by midnight."

She shifted in her seat, laid her head back, and shut her eyes. Rain enveloped the car, and the cadence of the windshield wipers slapping back and forth created a kind of white noise that called to Steve and made his eyes weary. Three hours after they left Knoxville, he felt the need to pull over somewhere. He saw a rest stop ahead and changed lanes to exit. The slowing of the car made Jenn wake up. "Where are we?"

"We have about three and a half hours to go. I need to stretch my legs and go to the restroom."

"Me too."

The low skies had begun to scatter, and the moon occasionally made its presence known. Steve parked the car, and they both made their way to the restrooms, which were on opposite ends of the building. The rest area was well lit, and only one other car was parked at the far end of the lot. When he was done with his business, he was almost back to the car when he heard a muffled scream. He stopped and surveyed the area—his antenna suddenly on full alert.

"Steve!"

This time it was more apparent. "Oh shit. Jenn, I'm coming!" he yelled out. He bolted to the lady's restroom and blasted through the door. Jenn was sitting on a toilet, a man standing over her holding a four-inch knife. The guy turned his head when he heard the door burst open, and Jenn kicked him in the groin with all her might.

The force of her kick sent him out of the stall, where Steve grabbed his hand and forced it down onto the sink, knocking the knife loose. Then, holding him by his hair, Steve slammed his head onto the porcelain sink. His legs buckled, and he slumped toward the floor. Steve's breathing was heavy as he released the man, allowing his limp body to drop.

He glanced at Jenn, seeing the terror on her face start to subside. He pushed his hair back with one hand and reached for Jenn with the other.

"Look out," Jean said, fear in her voice.

The man had opened his eyes and was making a mad scramble for his knife. Steve grabbed him by his shirt, pulled him to his feet, and delivered a striking blow to his stomach, making him double over in pain and fall back to the floor. He bent over him and struck his jaw. Blow after blow, blood splattering the white tile floor with every strike.

Jenn's face contorted, her eyes widened, and she screamed, "Steve. Steve! Stop! You're killing him!" Steve threw his head back, breathing hard and sweating. Blood ran down his cheeks like cheap mascara in a rainstorm. "What are you doing?" Jenn barked. She scowled at him angrily, though also with compassion in her eyes. He let go of the guy, leaving him in a pool of blood. He straightened up and clutched his right hand with his left, rubbing his knuckles. Jenn slowly shook her head. She started to say something but couldn't find the words.

Steve's breathing slowed back to normal. He grabbed the sink faucet and turned on the water. "I'll...I'll clean up." He washed the blood from his face and arms while Jenn watched in horror. Her mouth was half-open, and her eyes were homed in on him.

"I'll get your bag so you can change. Are you going to call the cops?"

"We can call anonymously from a payphone."

A few minutes later, she returned with his travel bag. She handed it to him and looked him up and down. "Do you need any help?"

"No."

Her eyes flicked to the man lying motionless on the floor. "Is he…?"

Steve followed her gaze, and watched the man's chest rise and fall. "He's alive."

"Okay…I'll wait for you in the car."

After he was free from the blood, he changed into fresh clothes, used paper towels to pick the knife up, and threw it onto the roof of the building. Jenn was leaning against the hood of the car with her arms crossed. She stared intently at him as he approached.

"Let's get out of here before he comes to," Steve said as he opened the car door.

Suddenly, she flung her arms around his neck, hugged him tightly, then pulled her head back and gazed into his eyes.

"What?" Steve asked.

"You are a complicated man, Steve Blake."

Steve took her hands into his, separated her arms from his neck, and gently pulled away.

"Thank you for saving me," Jenn said softly.

One corner of Steve's lips twitched slightly upward, and he shrugged. "From where I stood, it didn't look like you needed much help. You're a little scrapper."

Jenn forced a half-laugh. "Yeah, I was gonna kick his ass."

They got back in the car, and once they were on the road again, Jenn was quiet for the first few miles. Steve knew he owed her an explanation. "You're wondering why I let loose on that guy."

"Well, yeah. It wasn't much of a fight. You already had the guy down."

"I spent over ten years dealing with scumbags like that. They operate on fear. But all I could do was handcuff them and take them to the station, where they would lawyer up, some judge would give them bail, and they would be back on the streets."

"I can see where that would be frustrating. But that's how the law works, right?"

"Yeah, that's the law. I don't know. All those frustrating years caught up with me. Seeing it happen to someone I care about." He could feel Jenn's eyes boring into him from across the car, but he couldn't bring himself to meet them.

Chapter 27

Washington, D.C.

What a mess, Jack thought as he sat on the park bench outside Samantha Berry's apartment complex. He was wearing a black wig, dirty jeans with holes in the knees, a torn plaid shirt, and a weathered brown jacket. He'd been tracking Preston ever since the night at the hangar. Every lead had turned up empty until, out of the blue, the agency had received intel that Preston was in Seattle. God knows why he would run to such a wet, miserable port town. But it was moot anyway. When he'd followed the intel, he'd been ambushed by the docks. Preston and a band of thugs had clearly known he was coming, and he'd barely escaped with his life. He'd been set up, and it had to be by someone in the agency.

Could he trust Sam? There was a time he'd been certain he could. But with all that had happened, he needed to be extra careful. It was approaching noon, and he knew she would be home for lunch soon. It was a Friday, and she'd once told him she liked to relax at home and finish whatever reports she had outstanding.

He saw her coming up the sidewalk from his right. He scanned the area to make sure she was alone. He stood as she approached, bumping into her. "Sorry," he said under his breath.

She gave him a curt look and used her hands to brush her jacket off.

"You dropped something," he said, gesturing with his head. After a few steps, Jack looked back and saw Sam bending over and picking up the paper he had dropped. Her mouth hung open when she looked up and made eye contact. He shot her a quick grin and watched her read. *21:00, Jason Street Bar.* She rolled her eyes and pursed her lips, but then nodded surreptitiously.

The Jason Street Bar had once been both a neighborhood and an agency favorite. Good food and cheap drinks. The bartender had owned the place for over forty years. He'd worked himself into financial freedom, and unfortunately, to an early grave. His wife had promptly sold the business after his death, and it was never the same. Eventually, all the regulars found a new place to meet, and the old crowd was gone. That's why Jack had picked the bar for his meeting with Sam. He knew she would know it, and he also knew no one else from the agency would be there. Of course, he would still be cautious, but he was confident it was a good place for the meeting.

From half a block away, Jack watched her enter the bar at nine o'clock sharp. He waited for a few minutes and then proceeded to the front door. The place was as he remembered it—small, dark, and smoky. Three older men were sitting at the twenty-one-foot-long oak bar, sitting two bar stools apart from each other, all nursing a drink, and all doing their part to fill the bar with a combination of cigar and cigarette smoke. The old twenty-seven-inch TV was still in the same place as Jack remembered, hanging from a bracket attached to the ceiling at the end of the bar. The floors were cheap linoleum. Once upon a time they'd been an off-white, but now were a dark beige from the years of dirt dragged in off the streets and spilled drinks that never seem to clean up thoroughly. Other than the trio at the bar, the place was empty.

Sam had taken a seat next to the rear door. The booth was made of solid oak with rust-colored vinyl bench seats. Jack slid into the seat opposite her and craned his head to scan the room. The bartender took his cigar from between his stained teeth and looked their way.

"What are you havin', buddy?"

"Jack and coke," he answered, "and red wine for my friend."

Sam looked him up and down. "Why are you dressed like that?"

"It's a long story."

"You'll have to fill me in."

Jack started to respond but stopped when the bartender walked over with their drinks.

"That'll be eight fifty."

Jack pulled some folded bills from his pants pocket and handed him a ten. "Keep the change."

The bartender gave him a suspicious look, took the money, and returned to the TV without a word. Jack took a sip of his drink. He set the glass down and studied Sam. She was the first to break the silence.

"Where the hell have you been? Davis has been losing his mind looking for you."

"I'll bet," he replied coolly. "I was set up, Sam. Someone in the agency is working against me."

"What are you talking about?" she asked. Her face told him that her surprise was genuine, so he switched tactics.

"What's with Preston?"

"Obviously, he went bat shit crazy, but I assure you the agency is not after you. Davis said he would personally meet you anywhere you wanted. This whole Preston thing has got him more than a little ticked off, and he wants him contained."

"What do you know about those papers? The ones Blake has and the government wants?"

Sam took a sip of her wine. "I don't know a lot yet. There have been some feelers put out. The Secretary of State is the one who put Davis onto this, but don't ask me what the connection is. One thing is for sure; Blake doesn't know what they are or what they represent."

"Maybe. He's determined to find who's responsible for his uncle's death. None of this adds up. A lot of people are dead," Jack replied.

Sam took another sip of her wine and didn't reply. After a minute of silence, she took another sip. Jack studied her face and waited for her to talk. "Preston would have been my first guess for who's doing the killing, but I know where he was when Blake's uncle died. That's when all this started."

"And you're sure you don't know what those papers represent?" Jack asked in a suspicious tone.

Sam scanned the room with her eyes and leaned forward. "Okay, this is what I know. It all has to do with the polar ice pack. A Russian explosive expert is running loose, and the Russians are after him."

"Really? A Russian explosive expert? The polar ice pack? That sounds awfully vague, Sam," Jack rebutted.

"There was a name floating around, Kolya Zaytsev. We know he's on the run, and there is a lot of chatter being picked up from Moscow about him."

"What does that have to do with any of this?"

"Nothing, other than the fact that right after Blake's uncle wound up with the papers, the guy goes missing, and the chatter from Moscow went through the roof."

"Do you think Blake's uncle was a Russian asset?"

"We haven't heard or seen anything that would take us in that direction."

Jack surveyed the room again. "I don't know what the Secretary thinks Davis can do now. He's going to have to hand this over to the FBI. And why is he involved anyway? Isn't this a DNI matter?"

"I know, but he's tied up in this somehow. And Davis is in full damage control. They're already spinning the incident at the hangar. The Fort Worth locals don't know that Preston or you were there. They just know there was a gun battle, and a lot of people died," Sam said.

"I guess that means Preston took out the security cameras."

Sam nodded. "He grabbed the tapes from the VCR. The hangar sits in a remote area with a very long taxiway connecting it to the rest of the airport. So, there were no other cameras. But the locals have their suspicions. They know who the hangar belongs to, and it's someone with close ties to the Secretary."

"So, I'm assuming Preston's on the take. Why else would he do this?" Jack observed.

"Afraid so. Preston has apparently been offered a lot of money to deliver the papers to someone. We're still working on that end of it," Sam replied.

Jack took a sip of his drink as he scanned the room

again. "Preston's a crafty SOB. He got to Seattle pretty quick."

"Seattle?"

Jack tilted his head. "You didn't know?"

"Didn't know what?" Sam replied, confusion on her face.

"You didn't know that Davis sent me to Seattle?"

"First I've heard of it. Why?"

"Davis sent me on a wild goose chase. Preston was there with some shady characters, and I was lucky to get out alive. That's why I'm dressed like this."

Sam's brow furrowed as she took another sip of her wine. "So, are you saying Davis and Preston are still somehow working together?"

"How else would Preston know I was there? Preston told me that Blake and I are all that stand in his way. He wants those papers Blake is holding, obviously. And after the thing at the hangar, he sees me as an impediment to getting to Blake. He thinks we're working together."

"Are you?"

"We may have to now."

He went on to tell Sam what had taken place in Seattle. He wanted to gauge her reaction, her facial expressions. He was desperate to trust her, but he could feel she was holding back.

Sam called out to the bartender for another round when he was finished. After he brought the drinks, she took a sip and stared into the glass. "I swear, I didn't know. But I'll keep my ears open."

After scanning the room one final time, Jack downed his drink. "Tell Davis I'll be in touch."

Sam nodded. "If you want to find Preston, I say

you keep Blake and his lady friend in sight. I'll feel around a little and see what I can dig up."

Chapter 28

September 20th — Washington, D.C.

Yesterday had been another long day for Steve and Jenn, so they had both agreed to not set their alarms and sleep in. Steve was up at six anyway, though, full of anxiety about the coming day. He waited until nine for Jenn to wake up. Having driven as far as they had, they decided to walk to Camilla's office. Twenty-two minutes after leaving the Holiday Inn, they stood in front of the building that housed Camilla's office.

Project Green's office in Alexandria was in a red brick three-story building. It was just minutes from the capital, but one would never guess it by looking at the area. The streets were narrow, lined with mature trees and a mix of apartment buildings and businesses.

"Let's go see what we can learn," Steve said to Jenn.

"Hold on. Don't we need a plan or something?"

"A plan? Not really. This is just a fishing expedition. That's why I wanted to show up unannounced. It gives her no time to prepare."

"Well, you're the pro. I'll follow your lead."

Colonial style was the best way to describe the building's exterior. But inside, it had been gutted and rebuilt. The small foyer had a granite tile floor, and a staircase rose neatly at the far end. There were two doors, one on either side of the room, but the one on the left had a small metal sign that had "Amores Enterprises" engraved on it. As Steve reached for the doorknob, Jenn spoke up.

"Wait, who are we?"

"What do you mean?"

Speaking in a near whisper, Jenn replied, "You know…our cover."

Steve chuckled, "I'm Steve Blake, and you're Jenn Murphy."

Still speaking quietly, Jenn said, "I guess I'm a little nervous."

"Don't worry, Jenn, just follow my lead."

Steve opened the door, and the two entered the small reception area. A handsome young man in his early twenties was sitting behind a black desk with a glass top, talking on the phone. To the left was a small sofa with two end tables, on which sat small crystal lamps and some magazines. Steve saw that the entire place had furnishings that those magazines might describe as "modern contemporary"—clean lines and simplicity, with aspects of art deco adding a touch of boldness to the minimalist design. But Steve considered the style to be loud and silly looking.

The young man looked up at the two and held up a finger as if to say "one moment" as he finished with his call. "Oh, okay, great, thank you. I will see she calls you as soon as she walks in the door." He hung up the phone and looked the pair up and down. "And what can I do for you today?"

"Hello, is Camilla available?"

"And who wants to see her today?"

"My name is Steve Blake, and this is my colleague,

Jenn Murphy."

"And do we have an appointment?"

"No, we do not."

"And why do we need to see Ms. Amores?"

Steve caught himself getting aggravated but continued to keep a civil tone. He stepped right up to the young man's desk, leaning in conspiratorially. "Now, I could go over everything with you, but I would have to repeat it when I see her. I'm a private investigator looking into something that may interest her."

"You'll have to make an appointment. Ms. Amores a very busy lady."

"Is she in town?"

"I'm afraid I'm not at liberty to divulge Ms. Amores' schedule, Mr....uh, Blake, I believe you said?"

Steve pulled out a small notepad and pen from his pocket and started to write. "Here is my name and the hotel we are staying at. And here is my card. Can you have her call me, please?"

"I will give it to her, but as I mentioned, she is a very busy lady. She won't be back until late."

Steve nodded curtly, and they turned to exit the room. Just then, the door opened, and a women entered from the foyer. She was wearing a low-cut red blouse tucked into a tight black skirt, medium heels, and a wide black belt that held it all together.

"Jimmy, I forgot to take my phone. I was halfway there before I realized, can you..." She trailed off as she took in the newcomers.

"Ms. Amores, these two were here to see you. I told them you are busy," Jimmy explained.

Camilla looked them up and down and politely smiled. She held out a hand to Steve. "Hello. Camilla Amores. To whom do I owe the pleasure?"

Steve shook her hand. "I'm Steve Blake. And this is my associate, Jenn Murphy."

Jenn stayed quiet. Camilla considered for a moment, then cast a polite grin and gestured to a door at the back. "Come into my office. It's not every day a tall, handsome man drops in to see me." After Camilla turned to walk into her office, Steve cocked his head and shot the secretary a wry grin with a wink.

The three walked through the door, and Camilla turned back. "Hold my calls, Jimmy."

"Will do, Ms. Amores."

Her office décor was also contemporary and airy. Steve's reaction to it was the same. "Please, sit down," Camilla offered, pointing to a seating group comprised of a leather sofa and two high back leather chairs, all set around a maple coffee table in the middle. The carpet was a mix of soft grayscale tones.

"Can I get you anything to drink?" she asked.

Steve smiled. "No, thank you."

"And you?" she directed toward Jenn, slightly less enthusiastically.

"No, thank you," Jenn replied.

Steve sat without leaning back, resting his forearms on his legs with his hands clasped together. Jenn leaned forward and mimicked him.

Steve spoke first. "Ms. Amores—"

"Camilla," she interrupted. "Please call me Camilla."

Steve smiled. "Camilla. I'm investigating my uncle's death."

"My goodness, I'm so sorry. How did he die?"

"He was murdered."

The mood of the conversation took a sudden, serious turn. "Well now, that's interesting. I don't know how I could help you, Mr. Blake."

"It seems as though one of his colleagues, who may have been involved, just committed suicide. A note was found at the scene with a reference to your company. Now, obviously, I'm not accusing you of anything, I'm just trying to get a clear picture."

She fiddled with her bracelet. "What was in the note?"

"I'm afraid I'm not at liberty to say."

"I see. So, you are looking for the man that killed your uncle, a colleague of his committed suicide, and he said something about my company in his suicide note. Do I have it right?"

"Close enough. Do you have any climate or ocean scientists in your organization? Anyone who works in the field."

"No, not formally. We have quite a few associates, though."

"Did any of them recently attend a conference at the United Nations?"

Camilla's lips smiled broadly, but the smile didn't extend to her eyes.

"As a matter of fact, I was personally in attendance at that very conference. It proved quite fruitful for our endeavors. I'd heard that there was some…commotion with one of the scientist groups, I hope that's not connected to your case."

"I'm afraid it is, Ms. Amores."

"Call me Camilla, please. I'm so sorry, how

terribly tragic."

"Thank you for your concern...Camilla. What about Danny Jennings?" Steve asked.

Camilla's smile faded ever so slightly. She glanced down, but recovered quickly, her smile plastered back as convincingly as before. "Where did you get that name?"

Steve's face bunched in thought. "I don't remember, exactly. Seems my uncle may have mentioned him."

Camilla smoothed the front of her blouse. "Now that you mention it, yes. Danny Jennings. He signed up and attended an orientation a while back. But I don't recall seeing him in New York."

"How well do you know him?" Steve asked.

"Not that well. I met him in L.A. while attending another global warming conference. He mentioned he was a consultant on climate studies."

"Have you talked to him lately?"

"No, as I said, I met him once and have not had contact with him since."

"I see. And what is your relationship with Mark Kensington?"

Her face almost imperceptibly flushed, and she inspected her fingernails before answering. "Mr. Kensington is a powerful man. A good one to have on your side. We are collaborating on some things. Why?"

"Oh, no reason, really. I hear he's been making waves in the global warming world, though."

"Indeed," Camilla answered, with a tight smile.

Steve stood, reached into his pocket, and pulled out a business card. "Thank you for your time. Here's my card. That is my mobile phone number written on it. If you think of anyone else that I may want to talk with, please give me a call."

Camilla stood and took the card from him. "Of course. Where are you from, Steve?"

"Excuse me?"

"Your accent, it's so endearing, so I asked where you are from?"

"I live in Texas."

"Oh, I love Texas. I should have guessed by your dashing cowboy boots. What part?"

"In a small town just south of Fort Worth."

"I've been there, Fort Worth. It is a different world. Such a ruggedness to it. Wouldn't you say?"

"No place like Texas."

Camilla showed them out, her eyes lingering on Steve. While walking back to the hotel, Jenn turned and asked, "What was that?"

Steve didn't reply, looking instead toward the sky. The wind had picked up as the clouds overhead formed a dark shade of gray. "Looks like rain."

"You're ignoring me again. Are you thinking about taking her out to see if you can extract some information? She seemed to like you."

Steve cocked his head. "What? No. Of course not. I was just being polite."

Jenn laughed. "You looked all…googly eyed. She *is* beautiful. And about your age too. I think she'd probably go out with you, if you asked." Steve gave her a dismissive look. "I'm just kidding. Don't look at me like that."

"Did you catch her reaction when I asked about Kensington?" Steve asked.

"It did look like you struck a nerve. Who's Danny

Jennings? For some reason, that name rings a bell."

"Really?" Steve asked.

"Yeah. Maybe it'll come to me. Where'd you come up with that name, anyway?"

"Here's the real question. Why was she so quick to dismiss his name when she obviously knows him?"

Jenn gave him a puzzled look. "What do you mean?"

"I was fishing. I'd never seen his name before I saw it written in red ink on the secretary's desk. 'Get Danny Jennings on the phone today.' Circled, with an exclamation mark, and a phone number written underneath. She probably gave me more information than she would have liked. But just throwing it out there as I did, she had no time to think of an airtight answer."

Jenn stopped walking and grabbed Steve's arm. "I remember now. Six months ago, or so, Randall told me not to take calls from him. He said he had a bad feeling about him. Something about the way the guy was always asking questions or something."

"Really? We need to talk to him," Steve said.

A loud clap of thunder roared across the sky as the clouds opened and the cool rain began to fall. Jenn smiled, looked up to the heavens, and raised her arms. "I love the rain."

Steve shook his head and smiled at her. "You are crazy. We better get going."

"Can we go shopping now?" Jenn asked. "I am in desperate need of some clean clothes."

"Yeah, sure, but I want to take a cab. The traffic here is horrible, and I did my time behind the wheel yesterday." They raced the rain back to the hotel, and

Steve called a cab. While they waited for it to arrive, Steve pulled out the new cellphone that Claudia had sent along. "I need to call Charlie, Kasandra, and Tony and give them my new number." He dialed Charlie, and while it was ringing, the cab arrived. As they dashed through the downpour to get in, Charlie picked up.

"Hey, Charlie. Steve here. I'm just calling to give you my new number. I'll explain later. It's—"

"Thank God you called," Charlie interrupted. "I've been trying to reach you all morning. Steve, I don't know how to tell you this, but…there was an incident at Kasandra's house this morning."

Steve wiped the rain from his face, closing the cab door behind him. He thought that maybe he'd misheard. "Incident? What do you mean?"

"I'm really sorry. She was shot, Steve. Kasandra's dead."

It took Steve a moment to process what he'd just heard. "Oh, Jesus. Is Tony okay?"

"He was at school. He's fine, given the situation. They took him to his aunt and uncle's house. You'd be proud. Kasandra didn't give up without a fight. She unloaded on them."

Jenn gave Steve a concerned look. The color had left his face. He squeezed his eyes shut and massaged between his eyebrows.

Jenn put her hand on his shoulder. "What is it? What happened?"

Before the cab could pull away, Steve pulled a twenty-dollar bill from his wallet and handed it to the driver, opened the door, and exited the cab.

Jenn quickly scampered out of the cab and followed him back into the hotel, hurrying to keep up.

"Steve. Tell me what's going on. What is it?"

Steve pulled his phone out of his back pocket. "I have to call Tony."

"Steve, please, tell me what's going on."

He stood and paced in the lobby, slowly shaking his head. His eyes locked on the floor.

"Kasandra's dead."

"What?"

He stopped, placed a hand on the wall to brace himself, and fell against it. Jenn approached him and put her hand on his back.

"Charlie said there was an incident. I don't know. He…"

Jenn covered her mouth with her hand. Her eyes fixated on Steve. "Oh my God…is Tony all right?"

"Charlie said he's fine. He's at his uncle and aunt's house. I need to call him." He lifted his phone and punched in the number, waiting until a groggy voice answered. "Tony. It's Steve. I just got off the phone with Charlie. Are you okay?" Steve's face started to contort. He tilted his head back and fought not to lose his emotions.

"I guess," Tony replied, his tone somber.

"Listen, we're going to leave right away and come back home, all right? Tony? Are you still there?" Steve's heart wrenched. He could hear constant sniffling on the line.

"Yeah. I'm here."

"I'm coming, Tony, okay? Can I talk to your Uncle Ben?"

"Yeah. Hold on." There was a rumble as the phone changed hands, then Ben came on the line.

"Ben, this is Steve. I just got a call from an old

friend on the force. He said there was an incident. What happened? Have you talked to anyone or been to the house?"

"Yes, Erika next door called the police when she heard the gunshots, and she called me next. I went right over. It's a mess. Maybe a home invasion."

"How's Tony holding up?"

"You know Tony. He's always trying to be the adult in the room. I'm a little worried he needs to talk to someone, Steve. He hasn't said much."

"We're in D.C. but we are leaving right away. Please watch him closely, and I'll be there as soon as possible."

"Thank you, Steve. Drive carefully."

After pressing the disconnect button, Steve pushed off the wall and started walking despondently toward the hotel lounge. "I need a drink."

"What?" Jenn asked, her forehead wrinkled.

"I'll be at the bar. As I said. I need a drink. Just one."

Jenn stepped in front of him and placed a hand firmly on his chest. "No, sir. You...you need to get your ass to Texas and take care of your friend, not drown yourself in drink. I'm not going to let you do that. No, sir."

They made eye contact, and he noted her frozen, ferocious stare and raised eyebrows. When he met her gaze again, his eyes were wet, and he watched her demeanor reverse course. Her breathing was heavy, as if she'd just run a few miles. He collapsed ever so slightly onto her hand, hanging his head and sighing heavily.

"Steve, I'm sorry, I just—"

"You're right," he interrupted, his face hardening into resolve. "It's okay, you're right. Let's pack up and get going. We can stop at a Wal-Mart on the way. I'm…I'm sorry you haven't been able to go shopping."

Jenn's face melted into a puddle of sympathy. "I'll be fine, Steve. That's the least of our worries. I'll be ready in ten minutes."

Chapter 29

September 22nd — Texas

The funeral was held at Kasandra's church, where she'd been a member since she was a girl. It was a melancholy affair, but Steve thought that they did her proud. After the service, family and friends gathered at Tony's uncle and aunt's house. It was a modest frame house just a few blocks from where Tony and his mother had lived. The white siding contrasted with the black wrought iron burglar bars installed on the windows, a reminder of how dangerous the neighborhood could be.

"Here we are," Steve said as he parked the car on the street.

"Why do people live like this? Look at the iron bars on their windows," Jenn asked as she surveyed the area.

"It's not like they were living in the suburbs and decided they wanted to move here one day. They struggle more than most, but this neighborhood is full of God-fearing people who work as hard as you and I."

"I know, but—"

"When you look around here, you see poverty," Steve interrupted. "I see a neighborhood trying to be better. It's a different world than you're accustomed to, I get that. But I have a lot of friends here, and they are no different than us. I have people here who would do anything for me. All I have to do is ask."

"You're right, I'm sorry. I'm in no position to judge. Well, let's get in and see how he's doing," Jenn said as she opened the car door.

There were several people arriving at the same time, friends and family wanting to show their respects, being greeted by a short, plump Black woman in her late fifties. Steve nodded respectfully as they approached.

"Hi, I'm Steve Blake. We are—"

"I know who you are," she interrupted. "What other white folks would come to this neighborhood?" She let out a big laugh. "Come on in. I'm Dotty Jenkins, Reverend Jenkins' wife."

"Dotty, it is a pleasure. This is Jenn Murphy."

"Nice to meet you, Jenn. Please, come on in."

The house was small. The front door opened into the living room, where two walls were lined with antique sofas that displayed flowery patterns. There was also a small roll-top desk and a low bookcase that held a twenty-inch television.

Jenn gazed at the sofas. "Did they have those restored? They're beautiful."

"Oh, yeah," Dotty replied. "You can't keep her out of those thrift stores."

"Where's Tony?" Steve asked.

"He's in the kitchen, I think. Go on back there. I'm sure he's looking for you."

"Thank you, Dotty."

Steve and Jenn made their way to the back of the house, where the kitchen was located. They passed through a dining room with an oversized table that almost blocked the way, and had to descend one step into the kitchen. Tony was talking to a guy that looked to be his age. His eyes lit up when he saw Steve. A pang of guilt clutched at Steve's heart. *Did I cause this? Did those papers get Kasandra killed?* He had to shut down that line of thought. This was a place for grieving; his personal guilt, deserved or not, didn't belong.

"Hey, Tony. How are you holding up?" Steve asked.

"Hanging in there," he replied.

"I'm so sorry," Jenn added.

"Thanks." He held up a finger. "Hang on a sec."

He turned his attention back to his friend. "Thanks for stopping by, Alex."

"No problem. I'll catch you later, man."

His friend turned and walked out of the kitchen in the direction from which Steve and Jenn had just come. Steve studied Tony, searching for clues as to his state of mind, and glanced at Jenn for support. He saw her raise her eyebrows and tilt her head, gesturing. He reached out, and the two briefly embraced. "I'm so sorry. I don't know what to say. You know you're welcome at my house."

"Thanks, man. I'm going to just chill here for now. I don't know what I'm going to do." His eyes started to water. He wiped his eyes and tried to smile. "She gave 'em hell, man. I bet they wished they'd chosen another house."

"That's what Charlie said. Uh, well, I'm here for you." Steve had never known how to handle these situations. When Rebecca had passed, he'd started to resent the unending overt showings of emotion from everyone, and he didn't want to make Tony uncomfortable. He gave a manly but heartfelt squeeze to Tony's shoulder and handed him a slip of paper. "This is my new mobile number. If you need anything, let me know. You hear me?"

Tony rubbed the back of his neck. "I will, man. Thanks."

Before things got too awkward, Steve turned and walked back through the house with Jenn in tow. He said his goodbyes on the way out, but just before they reached the front door, Tony's aunt stopped them. "This is for you, Steve. It was with her will." She handed him a sealed envelope with his name written on the front. He took it and slid it into his jacket pocket, thanking her as he did so.

"Why are we leaving so soon?" Jenn asked once they were outside.

"This is a time for family. I don't want to overstay my welcome. I paid my respects, now it's best I let them mourn. Besides, something just dawned on me that I want to check out." When they returned to the car, Steve pulled out his mobile phone and punched in a number. "Charlie. It's me. I need a favor."

****

"What are we doing here?" Jenn asked when they pulled up in front of Kasandra's house. Charlie was already there, waiting for them in front.

"I want to have a look around."

"What are you looking for?"

"As much as I want to be done with them, we have to see if those damn papers are still here. And the way Charlie described the scene…Something's off."

Steve and Jenn followed Charlie under the yellow

police tape and stopped at the front door. The squeaking of the screen door seemed to play into the dreadful scene that lay ahead. Charlie slid the key into the lock and pushed open the door.

"Five minutes, Steve. I won't be able to explain this if someone comes, and we're expecting the cleanup crew soon."

"I'll be in and out in no time, thanks."

Steve briefly paused and stared through the door into the living room. The house was silent, and the faint smell of gunpowder hung in the air.

"I've never been here when it wasn't a cheerful place. You can wait here if you want. I won't be long."

"No, you have me curious."

"Are you sure? It won't be a pleasant sight."

"I doubt it could be worse than finding Randall."

"All right, fair enough. Follow me, and don't touch anything." He proceeded to walk through the living room toward Kasandra's bedroom. In the doorway, he stopped and pointed to the nightstand. "That's where she kept her HK. We used to do drills on grabbing it and being ready to defend herself if something happened. Look around and tell me what you see."

He watched as Jenn looked around the room with her arms folded, pointedly trying to avoid the large bloodstain on the bed. "The bedroom door is busted at the lock. The drawer is open, and there are bullet holes everywhere. So, looks like a home invasion. Someone broke in, got surprised by Kasandra, they both opened fire, but the intruder must have been quicker. Right?"

"Not quite." Steve walked over to the wall opposite the bed and examined the tagged bullet holes. "There's only a couple of shots from the intruder, marked over there with yellow, and they mostly hit their mark. But see the bullet holes marked with blue sticky papers? Those are the ones from her gun, and they spread out everywhere. No, the scene was made to look like something it wasn't. She would have never fired indiscriminately like that. She was good. She usually hit what she was aiming at."

Charlie was standing in the bedroom doorway. "You see what I mean, Charlie?"

Charlie cocked his head and moved closer to Steve. "You're right. I don't know why I didn't catch that."

Jenn cocked her head. "Have you seen something like that before? Someone using a gun to stage a scene like that?"

Steve nodded. "I've seen some variations of it. One guy tried to stage a shooter scene to cover up the fact he shot his wife. But more than that, if this was a home invasion, why is the door to the *bedroom* broken open?" He stepped back into the living area. "All the quick-grab valuables are out here; this is where any thief would start. Do you know yet if anything is missing?" Steve asked.

"Not yet, but as you can see, they rifled through all her drawers."

"Junkies are jumpy. They don't tend to stick around after a gunfight, searching for hidden things, not if they're cogent enough to shoot the way they did. The intruder, whoever they were, wanted to make it look like Kasandra was scared and just started pulling the trigger."

"Well damn, Steve," Charlie breathed, guiding them back to the front door. "Guess I should call a halt on that cleaning crew. We're gonna need to take another look at this place. You two hold tight. I'm gonna put the call in."

As Charlie jogged back to his car, Steve whispered in Jenn's ear. "Keep an eye out for me. Let me know when he's on his way back." Jenn gave him an inquisitive look, but he just held a finger to his lips and quickly made his way back to the bedroom. It took him a moment to locate the loose floorboard where he knew Kasandra hid specialty items, but once he pried it back he breathed a huge sigh of relief. The papers were safely tucked inside. He heard Jenn call out for him, so he stuffed the papers under his shirt, tucking them into his waistband, placed the board back, and hustled back to the entryway just as Charlie rejoined them.

"You two finished here?" he asked. Steve gave him a nod and exited the house.

"Yeah, thanks, Charlie. I've seen enough. Talk to you soon." For a moment, it strongly looked like Charlie was going to say something else, his brow creased with what could have been worry, but might have been suspicion. Eventually, though, he nodded back, and they went their separate ways.

Once they were back in the car, Steve's shoulders drooped, and he rested his forehead on the steering wheel. When he didn't move for an awkwardly long time, Jenn started getting concerned.

"Steve?"

"It's my fault," he said without raising his head.

"What is?"

"Kasandra. I got her killed."

"What are you talking about?" Jenn asked, taken aback.

"Whoever did…that…they weren't robbing her

255

randomly. They were looking for something specific. They were looking for these." He took the papers out and smacked them onto the dashboard more forcefully than necessary. "I can't believe I was so stupid."

Jenn eyed him sternly. "Steve, look at me." He remained still, so she smacked his shoulder with the back of her hand. "Look at me, damnit!" He was so stunned that he met her gaze, rubbing the light sting in his arm. "That's better. Now listen—no one knew that you gave those to her, and even if they had somehow miraculously figured it out, that still wouldn't make this your fault. You got that?"

"Yeah, geez, I got it, I got it."

"Good, 'cause right now I need you focused. We're being hunted by God-knows-who, and we need to make a plan. So, where to, the farm?"

Steve shook his head and sighed. "Farm's no good, they'll be expecting us to go there. The funeral was already too public. We should find a motel, somewhere low-key that'll take cash."

"Okay then. Another thrilling evening together in a rented room," she mused sarcastically.

Steve winced. "Actually, I…well, I talked to Camilla this morning."

"You did?"

"Yeah, she just called me out of the blue. I wanted to push her more on Jennings anyway, so I'm glad she called."

"Jennings?"

"Yeah. It's probably nothing but the fact that Camilla tried to hide that she knows him, and with what you said about him and Uncle Randall, we definitely need to talk to him. I'd say that puts him at the top of the list."

"Okay…and?"

"Well, turns out she's in town, flew in this morning. So, we're having dinner tonight."

"You're not serious, are you? When we left her office, I asked you if you were going to take her out, and you said no. Remember?"

"You were joking. Besides, I had no idea she was coming here. Things change."

"They sure do. What time are we meeting her? And where?" Steve didn't respond. After a short while, Jenn asked suspiciously, "I'm going with you, right?"

"It'd be better if I went alone. Maybe she'll open up more if it's just her and I."

Jenn shook her head slowly. Her eyes narrowed, almost closed. "Really?" She shrugged her shoulders and changed her tone to dismissive. "Well…I don't care. Do what you want. I'll just hang out and watch TV or something."

"I just think it—"

"I said I don't care." she interrupted. "If you feel that's the way to go, then I'm fine with it. Really."

"Thanks for understanding."

****

Jenn stayed busy the rest of the afternoon, folding and packing the recently purchased clothes and organizing their belongings. She hadn't planned on being so obvious, but Steve clearly picked up on her foul mood and decided it'd be best to leave her be. He spent the afternoon outside, tinkering with the car. When he returned, she was meticulously cleaning his camera and polishing his lenses.

"Come on, Jenn. You don't have to do that."

257

She didn't look up and kept scrubbing. "Just trying to earn my keep."

"Suit yourself. I have to get ready to go." He shook his head and continued to the bathroom.

When he emerged, Jenn begrudgingly admitted that he was well put together. He was wearing pressed jeans, rattlesnake boots, and a red-striped shirt. His beige sports coat brought it all together. "You look nice. What restaurant are you going to?"

"Cattlemen's Steak House. Do you want me to bring you something?"

"Nah. I guess I'll see you later. I ordered something in. Be careful."

"You still mad? I hope you understand. I just think—"

"No. I'm fine," she interrupted. "I'll be here when you get back." He turned to leave, and she mumbled, "Where would I go anyway."

He paused and let out a slight laugh. "I heard that, you know."

Just then, a knock sounded at the door. Steve looked toward her, his eyes sharp. "Think that's your food?"

Jenn's worry was plain on her face. "If so, they're lightning fast, I only called a couple of minutes ago."

Steve edged carefully toward the door and looked out the peephole, and Jenn saw his whole body relax. He undid the chain and opened the door to reveal Charlie standing there.

"Hope I'm not, uh, interrupting?" he said, eying the room nonchalantly.

"Charlie, what the hell are you doing here?" Steve asked.

"I could ask the two of you the same thing."

Steve looked at his watch, sighed, and then ushered Charlie inside. "Get in here. How'd you even find us?"

Charlie gave him a sardonic look. "That fancy-pants car out there isn't terribly subtle, you know. It honestly didn't take me long."

Jenn laughed. "Well, so much for flying under the radar, eh, Steve?"

Charlie clocked the remark. "And why, exactly, are you trying to stay under the radar?" Steve gave Jenn a pointed look, took a deep breath, and opened his mouth to speak when Charlie cut him off. "Spare me the bullshit, Steve. I could always see your bluffing face from a hundred paces. Now look, I got an LA detective asking questions, mysterious dead bodies at an airfield, a staged shooting, and as far as I can tell the one linking factor is you, and you're acting shifty as hell. So cut the crap and tell me what's going on."

Steve's face fell. He looked like a kid caught with his hand in the cookie jar. "Charlie, I promise I'll fill you in, but now's not a great time. I'm following up on a lead and I'm gonna be late for the meeting if I don't head out."

"I'll do it," said Jenn, suddenly. She watched shock ripple through Steve, his eyes flicking between the two of them with his mouth hanging open. "Steve, it's fine. I'll be safer with him here anyway. You run along on your little date, and I'll bring Charlie up to speed."

"It…it's not a date," he stammered.

"Well," Charlie piped in, smirking, "you're dressed nice and pretty for an interview, partner." He and Jenn shared a look, trying not to laugh as Steve spluttered. Eventually he found his voice.

"Well, all right then. But, Charlie, this is strictly off the record, you hear me? I guess I'll see you two later." He stood there uncomfortably for a moment, then left.

Jenn gestured to Charlie to sit on one of the beds, twining her fingers together.

"Charlie," she started, "before we get into everything, can I ask you something?"

"Sure."

"I'm just really curious about Steve. He told me how Rebecca died. But what I don't understand is, why did he leave the police force?"

Charlie blew air into his cheeks and rested his arms on his knees. "That's a complicated question."

"There's that word again. Everyone uses it when they talk about him."

Charlie hesitated a moment. "I don't know if I should tell you. It's personal; maybe you should ask him."

"I'm just trying to understand him, Charlie. Please?"

"Okay. I'll tell you the short version. About a year after Rebecca died, he and I were sent to investigate a call from a woman in distress. We were investigating this lady's boyfriend already. That's why they didn't send a uniform. We found the lady sitting on her porch step crying. The boyfriend was long gone, and she had a busted lip. I still remember her name. Sadie. She was a thirty-one-year-old Black single mother of two."

"That has to be hard," Jenn commented.

"The next thing I know, Steve is helping her get a restraining order. She couldn't afford an attorney. I tried to tell him not to get involved and let family services handle it, but once something gets into his head. Well. You know."

"I'm beginning to," Jenn replied.

"It made things worse, the restraining order. One night, she called Steve in hysterics because the ex-boyfriend called her to say he was angry about it and was coming to her apartment. Steve was on the phone with her when he arrived. He heard the door being kicked open, her screaming in the background, and two shots fired."

Jenn cupped her hand over her mouth. "Oh my God."

"By the time we arrived, she was dead, and the ex was nowhere to be found. After they took her body, Steve suggested I take a cab back to the station."

"Why?"

"I think that's when he decided to call it quits. And he didn't want to involve me. Gave me that same damn look he's been giving me recently with regards to whatever you two are mixed up in."

"So, what did he do?"

"He found the guy and damned near beat him to death that very night."

"Did he get in trouble?"

"He was reprimanded, but he kept his job. A week later, the ex-boyfriend came up missing and hasn't been seen since. The week after that, Steve put in for early retirement and left the force."

Silence hung between them for a good thirty seconds before Jenn spoke.

"Thanks, Charlie…I…wow."

"You wanted to know."

"You know, he's suffering, don't you?

Charlie looked down briefly. "Steve carries a lot on

his shoulders. More than he should. More than anyone should. But—"

"You know he drinks sometimes," she interrupted.

"Yeah. I know. He went to rehab once but left after a couple of days. The funny thing is, though, it helped. If you'd seen him before, well, at the time, I'd feared he was gone. But hey, maybe having someone around has been good for him."

Jenn frowned uncertainly. "Maybe. I hope so."

"Now, Ms. Murphy, I've answered your questions, I think it's high time you answered mine."

Chapter 30

The Cattlemen's Steak House was a Fort Worth landmark established in 1947. Before crossing the street, Steve took a minute to admire the restaurant's façade. The outside of the building had a strong western theme. It was covered in vertical brown wood planking, and there was an awning on the front of the building, held up with six-by-six cedar posts and beams. There was a sign attached featuring a life-sized statue of a Hereford cow standing tall, overlooking the street.

He had agreed to meet Camilla at the bar inside the restaurant at seven o'clock for a drink before dinner. Their reservation was for seven thirty. When he entered, he had to work his way through a crowd of people who had not made reservations and were waiting for a table. The bar area had a large, ornate oak bar with a mural on one wall depicting a scene from an era when cattle were herded down Main Street on their way to the nearby slaughterhouse. Halfway there, he heard his name being called out. He looked up to see Camilla waving at him.

"You look handsome," she commented as he reached her.

"Thank you. You look nice too," Steve replied as he pulled out a stool next to her and sat. Camilla wore a low-cut little red dress that flowed down her petite body. Her hair was wavy, and she was wearing bright red lipstick. The bartender approached from behind the bar and tossed down a paper coaster.

"Can I get you anything?"

"I'll have the house draft. Camilla, are you ready for another?"

"Yes. I'll have what he's drinking."

After the bartender left, Steve turned to Camilla. "So, what brings you to Fort Worth?"

"What else? Business." As she was speaking, the bartender returned with two pints and set them down. "And I remembered you said you lived here, so I didn't see any harm in mixing business with a little pleasure." She made eye contact with Steve as she took a drink of her beer.

Steve grinned and started to say something when a hostess approached. "Ms. Amores, your table is ready. I know it's early, but I can seat you now if you like."

"Steve?"

"Yes. Let's go."

Once they were seated, a server came over and handed them each a menu. "Would you order for me, please, Steve?" Camilla handed the menu back to the server.

He eyed her casually. She was setting an interesting tone for the evening. He needed to throw her off a bit if he was going to get anywhere. "We'll start with calf fries. And let's have the Texas rib eye." He lowered the menu. "How would you like yours cooked?"

"Medium, please."

"Both medium," he conveyed to the server.

"Very good, sir. I'll have the appetizer right out."

After the server walked away, Steve took a drink

from his beer and studied Camilla for a moment. She returned the look in kind.

"I assume your business came up after we talked yesterday," he ventured.

"Yes. Having a private jet does pay off," Camilla replied.

"So, what is Project Green? What do you do?"

"Our mission is to bring the threat of global warming to the forefront. We, and I mean everyone on the planet, need to start addressing the problem before it's too late. If it's not addressed with real solutions, the polar ice packs will melt, and that will cause sea levels to rise, which will cause massive loss of land. Millions will be displaced. That's just one of the catastrophes that will happen."

"You seem dedicated."

"Very. But I didn't come here to talk shop." She offered a coy smile.

"Fair enough. I was just curious."

Camilla took another drink of her beer and raised her chin to make eye contact. "But you must tell me why you think someone in our organization would be involved in your uncle's death."

"I can't. Not at this time. I have friends in the know, and it's a confidential thing."

Steve saw Camilla's smile fade. "Or someone is attempting to fool you. There are a lot of people who wish we'd go away. You don't feel that way, do you?"

Before he could answer, the waiter appeared with their calf fries. Steve divided them evenly onto two small plates the waiter had brought and handed one of the plates to Camilla. He then speared one with his fork, put it in his mouth, and began to chew. "I'll warn you;

they are a bit chewy. But you'll like them."

She pushed the calf fries on her plate around with her fork. "What are they?"

"Calf testicles. A Texas delicacy."

She forced a half-smile and pushed the plate away. "I'll wait for my steak…I was asking about your opinion on Project Green."

"Sorry. I shouldn't have assumed. I can order you something else."

"No. But thank you. You know, global warming is a real threat."

"I've heard." Steve could see he'd unnerved her. If she was going to let anything slip, now would be the time. "Can I ask you something about your organization?"

"Certainly."

"Is there a militant wing? I mean, we did an internet search. I saw when you guys held a rally downtown, and it got pretty ugly."

Camilla waved off the question. "People in my organization can get carried away at times. They are very passionate about the cause. It's people like you who sit on the sidelines…" She stopped and took a drink of her beer. Steve waited for her to finish, his eyebrows raised. He knew he was getting somewhere, but didn't want to push too hard and make her shut down. She cleared her throat. "What I meant was, we could use people like you. You are intelligent, and I can tell you are a good communicator."

"I'm just attempting to find my uncle's killer, Camilla. That's the cause I'm passionate about. In fact, we were thinking of making a trip to talk to Jennings."

"Really? I don't think he can help."

"Didn't you say he did expeditions like my uncle?"

"Well. Yes. But I hate for you to waste your time. That's all. We've just secured final funding for a new expedition, and Jennings will be leaving on the ship very shortly."

Steve could tell by the way her eyes had hardened that he wasn't likely to get anything else useful out of her. A few minutes later, their food arrived, and they traded small talk while they ate. When they were done eating, the waiter took their plates and brought the check. Camilla snatched it from the tray and pulled out a credit card.

"You don't have to pay." Camilla leaned forward with her eyes homed in on Steve's. "I find you fascinating, Steve. I'd like to get to know you better. I am only here today; I have business elsewhere in the morning. Come to my hotel. My driver can bring you back after breakfast tomorrow."

Steve chuckled. "You don't waste any time, do you?"

"I usually get what I want."

Steve stared a moment into her eyes. "I'm sure you do."

"Well?"

Steve rubbed his hands together and blew out his cheeks. "You are beautiful. But as tempting as it is, I'm sorry, I'll have to pass. Come on; I'll walk you to your car."

****

It was approaching ten o'clock when he walked in the door to their motel room. Jenn was cuddled up on the bed, watching a movie. She grabbed the remote and pushed the mute button.

"You're back early."

Steve took off his sports coat and boots, set them down in the side chair, and then sat on his own bed. He glanced at his watch. "It's almost ten. That's late for me. Charlie didn't stay?"

"He left an hour or so ago."

"How did he take everything?"

"Pretty well, actually. He promised to keep it all under his hat until we've followed up on our lead. So, did you learn anything?"

"She's an interesting lady. That's for sure. But when I asked what exactly Project Green does, it sounded like a canned answer. Like an elevator pitch."

"What's an elevator pitch?"

"It's something salespeople use to explain what they do. If they run into someone in an elevator and the subject comes up, it's short and concise enough that they can get it out before the elevator door opens back up."

"I've never heard of that." She shifted her body so she was facing Steve. "Hey, listen. I'm sorry I acted like that earlier. I guess I *was* a little jealous, if we're being honest here."

"For the record, you are more my kind of people than she is."

Jenn smiled. "Thank you."

"And I'll tell you what, for some reason she definitely doesn't want us talking to Jennings."

"That's interesting. What do you expect to find out from him?"

"Who knows? We just need to dig and see what comes up."

"Do you think Camilla had something to do with

it? She doesn't come across as someone who would be capable of murder to me," Jenn said.

"I agree. But if we want a shot at finding out, we'll have to get to Jennings quickly. Camilla said he's leaving soon on a research expedition they're funding."

"Hmm. On that note, we looked up that number you got from Camilla's office. It was a California area code, somewhere in L.A. Charlie was very helpful, put in a call to Detective Skinner and got an address for Jennings."

"Oh, fantastic. Probably for the best. With Preston after us we don't want to stay in one place too long. Charlie's right about the car, though. It's not the subtlest ride."

"Well, even if Preston knows we're getting on a private jet, he won't know where we're going," Jenn said with a shy smirk.

"Wait, private jet?"

"Yeah, well, I called Claudia to fill her in on everything."

"What'd she say?"

"She was glad to hear from me and glad we're all right. She wanted to send more funding."

Steve winced, and he shook his head. "I hate this. Taking money from her."

"I know. But she really wants to help. Anyway, when I told her that our lead was pointing back to California, she insisted on sending her private plane to get us. Wouldn't take no for an answer. She brought up the fact that paying cash for one-way tickets could raise a red flag. She also said, and I agreed, we *really* need to stay under the radar on this move."

"It sure will save us a lot of time. We'll be able to

get to him before he leaves on that ship. When do we head out?" Steve asked.

"In the morning."

"We should get some rest then."

"Okay. I'm going to bed. Good night, Steve Blake."

Steve flashed another smile. "Good night, Jenn Murphy."

Chapter 31

September 23rd — Los Angeles

"How long of a drive is it going to be?" Steve asked Jenn as the two descended the jet's stairs onto the Hudson Air Service ramp at Los Angeles International Airport.

"Forty-five minutes to an hour. Depends on traffic. Claudia said the lady in the office would direct us to the rental."

The traffic was lighter than normal and they arrived exactly forty minutes after pulling out of the lot. The afternoon sun peeped through the clouds, but was quickly being overtaken by dark skies. The apartment complex was comprised of six buildings, each three floors tall. The wind was gently blowing from the west, and Steve glanced up at the sky to see a storm forming almost on top of them.

"Great," he said softly. "Seems that stormy skies have followed us lately." Steve pulled the piece of paper from his pocket with the address. He pointed to the farthest building to the left. "That must be it."

The apartment was on the first floor, and as they approached, they could see the door was wide open. Steve put a hand out and gestured for Jenn to get behind him, then rapped his knuckles on the door jamb and called out.

"Hello, anyone home?"

From the stillness inside, a gunshot rang out, followed by the telltale sound of running feet. They heard a door slam. Steve reached behind his waist and grabbed his Glock. "Jenn, stay here." Holding his gun with both hands, he slowly entered the apartment, his eyes never resting in one place. Halfway into the living room, he saw a man on the kitchen floor, blood flowing from his chest. That side of the apartment was clear, so he called out to Jenn as he continued his search. Jenn froze mid-step as she entered the kitchen. "See if he has a pulse." She didn't respond. "Jenn. I need you to do this. Now, please."

She dropped to her knees as he cleared the rest of the apartment. "Okay. Okay. I got it, oh God." She checked the man's wrist and neck and shook her head. "No, he's gone, Steve."

Steve darted toward the back door.

"Where are you going?"

"Call nine-one-one, I'll be right back."

The back door opened onto a small concrete patio with a gas grill, table, and chairs. A small retention pond separated the apartment complex from a busy tree-lined street. Steve made his way around the pond and searched the immediate area. Not seeing anyone, he decided to cross the street. After waiting what seemed like a lifetime for a hole in the traffic, he crossed and stopped on the other side.

It surprised him how quickly he went from what looked like a nice, safe neighborhood to a not-so-good-looking area. He glanced to his right and glimpsed someone turning down an alley between a liquor store and a payday loan operation, both with heavy iron bars guarding the windows. He sprinted toward the alley, stopped before exposing himself, and looked around the corner. Seeing it was clear, he dashed down the alley, passing overfilled trash cans and a mean-looking barking dog on a chain.

Several tracks with train cars waiting to be put together were before him. Being extra cautious of his surroundings, he made his way between the train cars, constantly looking left and right and dropping to his knees to look underneath for any signs of the person he had glimpsed. He kept moving, and when he cleared the next track, he saw a train slowly moving toward the edge of the yard.

One of the railcar doors was open, and he spotted someone inside. The train had just started rolling, and he ran toward the open door. Realizing the train's speed was increasing, he grabbed hold of the next railcar in line.

Light rain began to fall as he maneuvered up the ladder to the top. The train's speed was slow but showed no sign of stopping. He tested his footing on the wet metal surface and was concerned with how slippery it felt. The intensity of the rain grew, and an occasional clap of thunder shook the sky. He took four steps back and hesitated before he broke out in a full run.

Here we go. Fixating on his targeted landing spot, he flung himself forward. His left foot slipped just as he leapt, and he didn't make it all the way across. He found himself hanging, clinging to the other railcar's roof with both hands. He looked up, shifted his grip, and strained to pull himself up. Once safely on top, he collapsed onto his back and took a moment to catch his breath.

He then moved to the edge and threw his feet over the side, planting them on the ladder's third step. From the ladder, he reached around the corner, grabbed the top of the door opening with both hands, and flung himself in. A lightning bolt danced across the stormy sky, followed closely by a clap of thunder.

His aim was off, and he rammed his head into the thick metal door frame, causing him to twist mid-air and drop onto the railcar's wooden planked floor. He landed on his back, knocking the wind out of him. As he fought to regain his breath, an image of a person began to come into focus. He shook his head, trying to dispel the stars swimming in his vision, and blood began to run into his eyes from a gash at his hairline.

"Steve. Why did you have to interfere? I liked you."

Steve pushed up with his left hand while holding up his right hand in a stopping gesture. "Camilla? What are you doing?"

Camilla shook her head. "What needs to be done, Steve."

"Take your finger off the trigger. I can help you, but you have to put the gun down first."

"I don't want to kill you. So, if you have another solution, tell me."

Steve tilted his head as her accent took on a Russian influence. His gaze went from her stoic face to her steady grip on the gun. He couldn't think of anything to say.

"*Izvini*, Steve. That's sorry in Russian."

As she squeezed the trigger, the train abruptly came to a stop, and they were both thrown off balance.

The gun discharged wildly, sending a bullet through the roof. Inside the metal car, the reverberating explosion of sound was deafening.

Before Camilla could regain her balance, Steve saw his opportunity, lunged forward, and tackled her to the floor. He grabbed her gun hand and slammed it onto the wooden floor, freeing the weapon. He attempted to roll her over onto her back and gain control, but she rammed her knee into his groin with surgical precision and broke free. She sprang to her feet and lunged toward the gun. Steve swallowed the nauseating pain and leapt up a split-second behind her. He took her down again just as she grabbed the gun, and the two rolled toward the door, both fighting for control of the weapon.

They soon ran out of floor and flew out of the car into open air. The impact of the fall separated the two. They both lay on the ground, breathing heavily as sweat and blood washed away in the surging rain. Camilla was the first to move. She struggled to roll over and used her arms to pry herself up. She staggered to her feet and picked up the gun while fighting to steady herself. Her chest rose and fell rapidly as she leveled the weapon at his prone form.

Steve steadied his breathing and willed himself to his feet. He wiped the blood and rain from his face with his shirt sleeve and raised his eyes to meet hers. There was nowhere left to run. His mind emptied of everything but a single thought. *See you soon, Rebecca.*

"What are you waiting for?" he said defiantly.

He couldn't help wincing as a thundering gunshot echoed throughout the yard, but he felt no pain. After a moment, he opened his eyes. When he felt his chest, there was no gaping wound. He looked up, and Camilla's lifeless body collapsed onto the ground. His mind raced to process the situation, his head jerking around to find the source of the gunshot. A figure stood close by, lowering his service weapon.

"Detective Skinner?"

Steve watched in silence as Skinner walked over and checked her pulse. "This investigation just got even stranger."

Steve sputtered, but finally found his words. "What's going on?"

"Can you make it back to the apartment?" asked Skinner.

"I feel a little light on my feet, but I'll be fine," Steve replied.

"Good. Let's get back, and I'll explain."

When they returned to the apartment, Jenn appeared shaken, which was no surprise to him. She was standing, arms crossed, in the living room, speaking with an officer. She spun around when she heard Steve's voice. At first, her face lit up but veered the opposite direction upon seeing his condition.

"You found him. Thank God, what happened?"

"Camilla Amores," Steve said.

"What do you mean?"

"She did this."

Jenn's eyes opened wide. "No way."

"Yep."

Steve turned to Skinner. "So?"

"Do you remember when I called you and asked about the marina, and told you there was a body?"

"Yes."

"At first, it looked like a hit. The guy's gambling

debt had caught up with him. But a wealthy boat owner had surveillance cameras to protect his boat. It caught what happened. This guy's the one who killed the marina worker." He pointed to the body.

"How'd you track him here?" asked Steve.

"We dusted for prints, found several on your uncle's boat. And in the tackle shop. We ran the prints and got a hit in the database. Daniel Jennings. He did some time for grand larceny. I thought the name was familiar, and then I remembered looking up an address for your friend Charlie. And when I checked in with him, he told me you were on your way here. We show up, and what do we find but the guy who's on your suspect list shot dead on the floor, and you running. Doesn't look great for you. You wanna fill me in?"

"Hey, look, Jennings was killed by Camilla. The lady you just saved me from."

"That lady who also just happens to perfectly match the marina footage we got of the person you saw the day you were there. Which leads me to ask why she wanted to kill you?"

"I don't know. We were basically doing the same thing as you. Looking for answers."

Skinner pulled three pictures from his jacket pocket. "Take a look at these." Steve took them and shared them with Jenn. "I was able to get these from traffic cams by running his plates. If you walk outside, you'll see the same car parked out front. And as you can see there, that's him tailing you on Oakmont."

Steve and Jenn took a minute to study the pictures. "This guy's been tailing us from the beginning," Jenn said.

"Why?" Skinner asked.

"I can only assume it has to do with my uncle's killing," Steve said.

"I think you know more than you're letting on."

Steve didn't like the direction this was going. "What, exactly, are you investigating?"

"The marina murder, like I said," Skinner said innocently.

"And what about my uncle's death?"

"Oh, I got some interesting information once I got pointed toward that Dr. Helmer."

"You feel like sharing?" Steve asked.

"I suppose that depends. Do you?" Skinner countered. The two men stared at each other, clearly at an impasse. Eventually, Skinner broke. "Blake, I understand that you wanna do things your way. If I wanted to, I could drag you downtown right now and stick you in an interview room, but to be honest, I don't think that would do either of us any good. So why don't we go somewhere private, and off the record you tell me what's really going on here, and why bodies keep dropping like flies wherever you go."

****

It took a little while to extract themselves from the scene and get Steve's head wound bandaged, but later that evening he, Jenn, and Skinner sat in a booth in an otherwise empty diner. Steve offered a tight smile seeing the way the waitress looked him up and down. His shirt was ruined, so he'd taken it off and was wearing his bloody T-shirt. Skinner's expression was as empty as the drained coffee cups on the table, trying to process the tale he'd just been told. After a moment, he rubbed his temple and seemed to come back around.

"Damn, Blake, that's a hell of a story."

"Yeah, well, you feel like filling me in on your Helmer update now?"

"Okay, fair enough. We looked into his financials, and it looks like he had some irregularities. Huge deposits coming from offshore accounts going back a couple of years, adding up to over two million untraceable dollars. I spoke with Kathleen, Dr. Helmer's widow. Seems in going through her husband's safe, she found a bunch of strange documents she didn't recognize. Something to do with arctic seabeds, and a bunch of communiques written in Russian—which looks to make a lot more sense in light of what you just told me. There were also blueprints for a ship, *The Polar Star*, an icebreaker he'd worked on before. They were marked up, again in Russian. If I had my guess, the 'they' he referred to in his suicide note, that'd be the Ruskies. He must have been working with them for quite some time."

Jenn sighed. "The seabed maps. Helmer must have been the one supplying the Russians with the new data and keeping it out of the public eye. He couldn't let Randall expose the papers, or he'd be exposed too."

Steve nodded. "And then after Randall's death, he couldn't live with himself."

"That's all well and good," Skinner said. "But how does it all connect to Jennings?"

Jenn got a slightly guilty look on her face. "Well, actually, I think this might help clear that up a bit…" She reached under her shirt and pulled out a business-size envelope.

"What have you got there?" Steve asked.

"A notebook. And a lot of pictures. It was at Jennings' place. I started to flip through it, but the cops came."

Skinner looked taken aback. "You removed evidence from an active crime scene?"

Jenn held her hands up defensively. "Look, I'm sorry, but we've been getting by on our own. Someone from the government actively tried to murder us. It's not super clear whom we can trust. Steve, both our names are in here, and Kasandra's."

"Kasandra? Your friend with the potentially staged home invasion?" Skinner asked.

"That's the one," said Steve. "Jennings must be the one who killed her. Skinner, you run ballistics on any weapons you find in that apartment, my guess is you'll find a match, close the case for Charlie."

"And how exactly am I going to explain my sudden cross-departmental insight without the linking evidence?" he asked, gesturing at the envelope. "A random hunch?"

"Hey, hunches have solved a lot of murders. Isn't that what you told me?" Steve responded. Skinner didn't seem to like having his words thrown back at him, his eyes narrowing.

"Steve, I'm not going to get into trouble for taking this, am I?" Jenn asked tentatively.

"Don't worry, Jenn," Steve interjected. "I'm sure Detective Skinner understands...*right,* Detective Skinner?" Steve's insistent tone sent a clear message, but Skinner looked somewhat unconvinced.

"You two are just unbelieva—" He was cut off by his phone ringing. "Hold that thought." He lifted the phone and pressed the answer button. "Hello...I'm sorry, say that again...Really? Uh huh...uh huh...I see. Was it everything? Do me favor, run ballistics on those before you hand them over…I don't care. We'll tell them it was an oversight or something. Thanks, keep me informed." Skinner pressed the disconnect button and set the phone on the table. "Things just got weird. The feds have taken over the case."

"The feds?" Jenn asked.

"Apparently some guys in dark suits just barged in and took over the investigation. They grabbed everything—his computer, his file cabinets—just loaded them up into a box truck and left. My guys had already collected some firearms, so hopefully we'll get ballistics on them before they're taken."

Jenn flashed Skinner a smug look. "Well, looks like we might never know what's going on. If only someone had pulled some important evidence from the scene before the feds showed up…"

Skinner sighed and nodded in concession. "All right, let's see what's in there."

The three of them got another round of coffee and started poring over the contents of the envelope. The surveillance shots made it clear that Jennings had been tracking their movements and clearly depicted him searching for the papers. Jenn thumbed through the notebook.

"Steve, he has a daily log in here. He was watching Randall, and us, and Kasandra and Tony. It looks like he was after Randall's letter; he's got a flight to Texas logged here, right after his notes about us at the marina. That's the same night Tony was attacked. He's got a note here about Kasandra as well. He mentions that the papers would be there."

"How in the hell did he know that?" Steve wondered.

"I don't know," Jenn continued. "He mentions he needs to send reports a lot, to Camilla."

Skinner took a sip of his coffee. "The question is, who Camilla was reporting to?"

"Just before you took her out, she started speaking with a Russian accent," Steve remembered. "So that might be our answer."

"They must have sensed something wasn't right with her," Jenn said.

"Who?" Skinner asked.

"Randall's team. They didn't like her at all. I don't know if it's because they didn't take her seriously or what. But they looked at her as an opportunist. They didn't buy that she was serious about global warming. They just saw her as another rich person wanting to stand out."

"She did that well," Steve added.

"Science is supposed to be inquisitorial, not adversarial," Jenn mused.

Skinner perked up. "You had dinner with her, Steve, and you didn't get any inkling of what she was up to?"

"Nope. She seemed normal. Well, normal for a rich lady with a private jet. But there is something I didn't tell you, Jenn. And looking back on it, I—"

"Oh my God," Jenn interrupted. "Please tell me you didn't sleep with her."

"That's just it. I could have. She made that abundantly clear. But no. I didn't. She wanted me to stay the night with her at her hotel."

"You may have escaped one there, buddy," Skinner said.

"Holy crap, Steve," Jenn said.

"I know. I've given that a lot of thought. But I don't think she would have, well…We'll never know now, I guess."

"And that's a good thing." Skinner took a last sip of coffee, set the cup on the table, and stood. "I have to go. And I'll see if I can do something with those firearms. What will you two do?"

"There's more here than what meets the eye, and I have a feeling Preston may hold all the answers. But I don't think my brain can take anymore today. For now, I think we'll head home. I want to check in on Tony, and from there we can figure out our next move," Steve said, and Jenn nodded in agreement.

Skinner gave a mock salute. "Well, try and keep your heads down, and stay in touch," he muttered as he walked away, leaving Jenn and Steve alone in the booth.

After paying the waitress, the two left and were waiting outside to cross the street to where they'd parked the car. Jenn yawned and stretched her arms. "I still can't stop thinking about it. I've never known a cold-blooded killer. I mean, I didn't know her, but we met and stood in the same room."

"Rebecca used to ask me if I ever felt like I was becoming numb to it all. The violence and death. I didn't know how to answer. It was almost like I was being tugged in two different directions. I could have been a better communicator. I just wanted to insulate her from all of it."

"You must've really loved her."

He didn't acknowledge her comment and continued. "Maybe I just didn't want to face the truth. But it's like anything else. When you get accustomed to something, it doesn't seem so odd and out of place anymore."

"Like living alone?"

Steve felt her probing eyes on him. "Yes. Like living alone."

"You just need to find your ordinary world. There's a song by Duran-Duran, "An Ordinary World", which reminds me of you. The song talks about how he can't get the image of his love out of his day-to-day life. I'm not sure if it's a deceased love or just an ex-girlfriend. But what I get from the song is that there comes a time to move on. A time to find your ordinary world. Whatever that may be."

"So, you're a therapist now?" He paused to think about his response. "You may be right. Maybe it is time to…"

"To allow someone new in?" Jenn finished his sentence.

Steve leaned forward. "Maybe, or just accept the fact that being alone *is* my ordinary world now. Just me and my horses. If they die, I would be sad, but…"

"Not like losing a loved one," Jenn finished. "So, living alone the rest of your life is the plan? That's no plan. That's hiding from—"

"Okay! Okay," he interrupted.

"I'm sorry—none of my business."

He sighed heavily. "I admit it has crossed my mind. Having you around has made me start to think about it. I mean…you know."

"So, having me around hasn't been so bad after all?"

Steve felt her eyes probing for the answer she wanted.

"Listen. You've been a lot of help. I couldn't have figured out those papers without you. And look what you did today. You're a natural at this." Steve turned and saw her roll her eyes. "What?"

"Come here." She grabbed his arm, pulled him to her, and threw her arms around his neck. "I'm here if you ever want to talk about it, you big fuzzy bear."

At first, he resisted by just patting her on her back. After a short moment, he gave in and embraced her. "Thank you. I'm glad you're here."

Chapter 32

Evening had set in at Mark Kensington's Los Angeles estate. After a quiet dinner, he made his way into his office and sat down behind his oversized mahogany desk. He poured a glass of Rousseau Pinot Noir, pointed his remote toward the entertainment cabinet, and Mozart's Clarinet Concerto began softly filling the room.

The ringing of the phone shattered the tranquility of the moment. Glancing at the caller ID, he let out a sigh. *Relaxing will have to wait a few minutes*, he thought. "What is it, Preston?"

"Our lady friend is dead. And so is our deal, I guess. Jesus, what the hell was she doing there?"

Kensington stared into his drink glass and shook his head. "How? Where?"

"Blake and his friend walked in right after she paid a visit to someone named Danny Jennings, one of the little errand boys she had under her thumb. Blake chased her, then a cop showed up and shot her."

"And you weren't seen?"

"Not by anyone who'd recognize me. While Blake was indisposed, I chatted with the uniforms outside the apartment. I told 'em I lived in the building across the street and didn't see or hear anything. Looks like Camilla killed Jennings, and Blake caught her red-handed."

Kensington's face showed no emotion. He lifted his glass and took a drink. "That's a shame."

"You didn't answer my question. Why the hell was she there? I was close to getting the papers."

"Listen, Preston, she told me there would be some things she'd need to do in the peripheral. And she may disappear from time to time. She got all worked up when Blake visited her and asked about this Jennings fellow. Maybe he knew something she didn't want to get out. Or maybe she was just paranoid. I have no idea."

Preston said, "When I came to you with this plan, I told you we would have to watch her closely. And now my sources are telling me the KGB has sent a team to find the guy who stole the papers. This is starting to get crowded."

"I'm still confused about how you two knew each other. But maybe I don't want to know," Mark said.

"Mark, it was no coincidence we were both there at your conference that day. She had contacted me out of the blue and wanted to meet. She decided your conference would be a good place to talk. She said she was planning on attending anyway."

Mark chuckled. "The things getting a divorce will make you do."

"The divorce put me in a hole that my salary would never allow me to dig out of. A million would have allowed me to disappear and live the good life. So, hell yeah, I agreed. You said you could control her. But now she's dead, and so is our deal."

"Not exactly. You play checkers, Preston, I play chess, and I always hedge my bets." He winced at his mixed metaphor but pressed on. "What I mean is, I have another buyer lined up. For now, we need to keep going forward."

"Are you serious?"

"I know someone just as motivated as Camilla was to get the papers. I've already had a conversation with him."

"I hope you're right. But what do you intend to do about your very public ties to our dearly departed mutual acquaintance."

"I think my buyer will be motivated to help with that little snag as well. As I said Preston, chess."

"Fine. I'll stay on it. I'll have the papers soon, and I expect to get paid when I deliver them."

"You'll be paid when the job is done properly. To that note, I've been informed of another loose end we'll need you to tie up. I'll send you the details."

They hung up, and Kensington picked up his glass. Raising it to the light, he made a toast under his breath, "Here's to you, Camilla," and drank it down.

Chapter 33

Washington, D.C.

Jack sat silently in the darkness on Sam's couch. It was five a.m., and he'd slipped past her security system over an hour ago. He was still unsure who he could trust within the agency. He'd been tempted to arrange a meeting with Randy Davis, but he needed to know for certain whether Sam had been truthful with him about what she knew. He felt as if he were in the calm before the storm. *Instincts, always trust your instincts*, he thought. This time he hadn't bothered to alter his looks.

He watched from the shadows as she made her way to the kitchen. After pushing the brew button on the coffee maker, she stepped into the living room to open the curtains. He waited for her to pass before he stood.

"Good morning."

Her response was a spinning kick to the chest, knocking him back onto the couch. She crouched into a defensive position, then, seeing who it was, threw her arms up. "Goddammit! You scared the hell out of me! What are you doing here?"

Jack rubbed his chest and winced. "That's no way to welcome a friend."

"Seriously? How in the hell did you get in?"

"Your security system needs updating," Jack replied.

"Why didn't you call or something? Geez."

"I need some answers, Sam."

"Do you have any idea how bad you scared me? Damnit, I'm on edge as it is." Her lips trembled, and she wiped a tear from her cheek with her index finger. Jack was slightly thrown.

"What's going on? You don't scare that easy, Sam."

"I need coffee. I guess I'll pour you a cup too. Come sit in the kitchen," she said, somewhat begrudgingly. Sam poured two cups, handed Jack one, and took a sip from hers.

"Why are you so nervous, Sam? I know you. We've worked in the field together many times, and this isn't like you. What's going on?"

"This whole thing has gotten really strange lately, and I'm beginning to wonder who I can actually trust."

"Welcome to the party. But what exactly do you mean?"

Sam let out a nervous laugh. "It's no longer a diplomatic issue."

"A diplomatic issue?"

Sam took another sip of coffee. "Apparently, our Secretary of State, Edelson, was bamboozled by his Russian counterpart, Primakov. Edelson was made to look pretty stupid. And he's pissed, for lack of a better word."

"Bamboozled?"

"Yes. He was made to believe the papers Blake has concerned a mistress of Primakov trying to blackmail him with embarrassing nude photos," Sam responded.

"Blackmail who?" Jack asked.

"The Russian Minister of Foreign Affairs,

Primakov. Jesus, try to keep up with me. Edelson was being used. And he can't make a stink about it because he went way off the reservation in having his old college buddy, Randy Davis, get involved. You know? The CIA?"

"Wait a minute. You're telling me this whole mess, this shit show, was brought down on us because our Secretary of State was stupid enough to fall for Russian bullshit propaganda?"

"Afraid so. Edelson wants to be liked by everyone. He thinks if we're nice to our adversaries, they'll like us back and work with us. What an idiot. I shook my head in disbelief when the President appointed him. Everyone in Washington knew he would make a mess of things."

"I agree. Now he's got a mess waiting to be discovered by the press that'll end his career," Jack responded.

"Or leaked to them."

"Yeah. That too."

"That's part of what's worrying me. All I know is I now feel I am intentionally being left out of the loop. And my job is *being* the loop. I know you don't understand, but…Shit…"

"What?"

Her eyes had gone wide. She didn't respond to Jack, but picked up her purse and a packed overnight bag, and gestured for him to follow her out the front door. Once they were both outside, she closed the door behind them.

"They may be listening," she whispered.

"If you think you're being listened to, it's a little late to clue me in."

"The thought just entered my mind."

Jack studied her as she locked the door, her hands shaking as she inserted the key into the deadbolt. He'd never seen her so out of sorts. She tucked her keys into her purse and turned to him.

"I'm not staying here tonight. And I really don't want to be alone." She placed a hand on his chest and looked up into his eyes. The closeness of her was intoxicating, and it took all of his willpower to gently remove her hand and step back. He couldn't tell if she looked disappointed or relieved.

"Walk me to the lot?" she asked, stepping briskly off the front steps.

"You really think you're in danger?" he called after her.

"You mean more so than usual?" she responded, not bothering to turn around. "Are you coming?"

Jack hustled to catch up. A few steps later, he gently grabbed her arm, and they both stopped. "Wait a minute. How do you know all this? About Edelson?"

"It's complicated."

"I gotta say, you have me a little confused. What exactly is it you do these days?"

She took in a quick breath. "We can talk on the way. Come on." They continued down the sidewalk.

"I'm all ears."

"I act as a liaison between Randy Davis and Mark Edelson."

"Holy shit, Sam. The Director of the CIA and the Secretary of State?"

"I know, right? I'm the courier if one needs to talk to the other or send something. I relay messages. My official job title is still field analyst, but that's just for show. Only the two of them, and now you, know what I actually do. So, when you ask if I feel like I'm in danger...well..."

"They're using you. Why'd you agree to do it?"

"I had to do something, Jack. After my cover was blown, I couldn't work in the field anymore. This looked like the perfect cushy government job. I didn't think it through, I guess. Now, the whole thing with those papers, and Preston, may have put me in a place I'd rather not be."

"What do you mean?"

"Edelson was trying to keep the true contents of the papers from Davis, made it seem like he was just doing a simple favor for a friend. He asked Randy to send someone out—that was you—and appeal to Blake's patriotic side, get the papers back quietly. When Preston went rogue, Davis threw a fit, so Edelson had me bring over a file that contained the truth. A file Davis asked me to destroy. Which I did...but not before I read it."

"Jesus, Sam. What was in the file?"

"Edelson first admitted he was fooled into thinking the papers were about an ex of Primakov's like I said. And after he learned what the papers really were, he wanted to keep it to himself for obvious reasons. He said he apologized, he hadn't meant to be deceitful with an old friend, blah blah blah, that he'd panicked."

"So, what are the papers, really?"

"Some sort of top-secret data that the Russians were trying to keep under wraps. It talked about how the new frontier for natural resources will be in the Arctic region. As far as we can ascertain, the data set had to do with underwater volcanoes."

"Hold on, underwater what?"

"Here's where it gets interesting. The Russians have supposedly found underwater volcano vents near the Arctic circle. If they become active, it could melt enough on the ice pack that cheap resource extraction and new shipping lanes could get going in five to ten years."

"And the Russians don't want anyone else knowing about it, because every country with Arctic coastline will rush up there to lay claims," Jack said. "So *that's* what this is all about? Something that may or may not happen five to ten years from now?"

"Seems so."

"No. There's something else. Something more pressing. I need to figure out what the papers are myself. I'm going to talk to Blake," Jack said. They reached the parking lot entrance, and Sam stopped, looking down at her feet.

"There's something else. Until Blake went dark, Davis had us tracking his movements. I can't prove it, but I think Davis may have passed that information on to someone dangerous, and got an innocent woman killed. I overheard a conversation that I definitely wasn't supposed to. I don't think Davis saw me, but I'm not sure…What do you think? I should be nervous, right? Or am I just being paranoid for no reason?"

Jack shook his head slowly. "You definitely have reason to be nervous. Guess I won't be meeting with Davis any time soon. It appears they, whoever they are, are trying to clean up loose ends, Sam. With what happened in Seattle and now all this, maybe you should consider disappearing a while until I can figure it out."

Sam didn't respond. She held her key fob up and

pushed the alarm button at the fence opening to the parking lot. "I'm so tired I can't even remember where I parked."

"Did you hear me?"

"Yes! I heard you. I just need to get some sleep. I think I slept maybe thirty minutes last night," she replied, defeat in her voice.

Jack watched curiously as she franticly rummaged through her purse and pulled out a pack of cigarettes and a butane lighter. "I thought you quit."

"I did." She put one between her lips, lit it, and inhaled. After a long exhale, she kissed Jack on the cheek. "You could stay with me tonight."

Jack looked at her sadly. "We can't do that again. Go get some sleep. Here's my phone number. I bought a burner."

"I'll call you. I'm trying to reach someone that might be able to do something about all this. Once I talk to them, I might need your help."

She made her way across the parking lot toward her car, seven rows over. Halfway there, she turned, waved, flashed a timid smile, and continued. When she turned back around, she nearly bumped into a young woman carrying a cranky toddler. After a brief exchange, she continued.

As he watched her approach her car, Jack glimpsed a man standing next to the tree line fifty yards away. There was something unsettlingly familiar about him. A deep feeling of dread came over him when he realized who it was. "Oh God, no!" he said under his breath. He darted through the gate, running toward Sam. He desperately screamed to the young mother as he ran, waving his arms to tell them to get down, but he knew it was futile. It was already too late.

The blast threw Jack to the ground with such a force he momentarily blacked out. His ears were ringing when he came to. He rolled over on his hands and knees and tried to stand but collapsed back to the ground. He grunted and willed himself to his knees, the world spinning around him in slow motion. His breathing was labored, and his lungs caught fire from the smoke-filled air. The stench of burned flesh jolted his senses, and he quickly rolled over to empty his stomach onto the asphalt.

The symphony of car alarms was deafening as the blaze spread to three other vehicles. Shrapnel had shredded everything in a wide radius. His heart sank as he stared at what was left of Sam's car. After a few minutes, he was able to stand. The ringing in his ears let up and was replaced by the sound of sirens. Sweat poured from his forehead and blurred his vision. He used his shirttail to wipe his eyes clean, then looked to the tree line. The man was gone.

A crowd began to gather as he surveyed the area for anyone injured. His thoughts turned to the young mother with the toddler. Not far from him was all he could see that remained—a tiny, smoking, charred child's shoe. He had seen and experienced many horrific things, but this was different. This one hit close to home. He could feel the blood pumping through him like a machine.

His grief turned to primal rage, and he looked toward the row of trees where he had spotted the man. He raised a clenched fist and yelled out, "Preston!"

Chapter 34

September 24th — Texas

Stop Six, as a neighborhood, was finally beginning to show signs of recovery after longstanding neglect. It had been plagued with crime and poverty for years, but Aretha's Diner was one of its few success stories. It had a seventies-era feel. Each table had the standard napkin holder and salt and pepper shakers. The floor was tiled in a red and white checkerboard pattern, and the seat cushions were a bright red. The old television hanging from the ceiling at the end of the counter lent to the nostalgic atmosphere.

Steve, Jenn, and Tony's moods lifted as they walked through the door. Jenn took in the welcoming environment. "I just love these little hole in the floor places."

Tony and Steve shared a tickled look. "That's...hole in the *wall*, Jenn," Steve offered.

"Whatever. You know what I mean." It didn't seem that anything could dampen the elevated mood the trio bore. The little things in life tended to rise above overarching issues.

"Oh, sweet Jesus! Look who the cat dragged in." Aretha Moore, the proud owner of the establishment, lifted the hinged section of the long lunch counter and slowly squeezed her way through the opening, opening her arms to Steve. "Come, give me a hug, sugar. I thought you forgot about me." The two hugged, and the old gal almost lifted him off his feet.

"Forget about you? Never. And you're still strong as an ox."

She patted her enormous belly and chuckled. "Yep, it's all this good cookin', sugar."

Her focus turned to Tony with the look of a proud mother. "My, my, look at you, Tony Clayton. You are all grown up. You have become quite a handsome young man. Get over here and give Auntie Aretha a hug."

Tony hesitated, glancing at the pretty young girl behind the counter.

Aretha prodded him. "Don't worry, none of your friends are around and I won't tell anybody, I promise. Now get over here."

Tony hesitated, but he soon acquiesced. Aretha squeezed hard and said softly, "I'm sorry about your mama, baby. You have a lot of friends and family who love you." She released him, took a cleaning rag from her apron, and dabbed her eyes.

Her attention shifted to Jenn. After giving her a once over, she looked at Steve suspiciously and nodded her way. "And who is this?"

"Aretha, this is a friend, Jenn Murphy. Jenn, I'd like you to meet a legend in the food business."

Jenn offered a hand. "Nice to meet you."

Aretha's suspicion gave way to curiosity, and she gave Steve a sly smile. "It's a pleasure. You all just have a seat, and we'll get you taken care of." She showed them to a booth. Jenn sat next to Steve and Tony slid in across from them. "You all figure out what you want, and we'll be right back to take your order."

Steve watched her walk away. "Don't get the wrong impression, Jenn. She's like a mother hen."

Jenn smiled and glanced at Steve. "Oh, I think she's great. Always good to see a strong, successful lady like her."

There was a lull in the conversation, and Steve and Jenn traded glances.

"How are you doing, Tony?" Jenn asked.

"I'm okay, I guess. Uncle Ben says I can stay there as long as I need to."

"That's good to hear. We'll figure things out in due time," Steve added. The awkward lull resumed, and Steve's discomfort showed, his eyes wandering restlessly. Jenn gave him a kick under the table, and he sat up straighter. He cleared his throat and looked across to Tony. "So, uh, how's school treating you?"

Tony couldn't help but smile at the dynamic he witnessed across from him. "It's fine. They said I could take some time off, but I'll probably go back soon. I don't wanna fall behind."

"Good, that's…good," Steve said, nodding intently. He'd never been very good at this sort of thing, but thankfully at that moment Aretha returned to take their orders, and Steve sighed in relief. After making their requests, Jenn noticed that Steve was staring into the distance.

"Steve?" she prompted.

Following his line of sight, she saw that he was focused on the television. "Oh, sorry. That's D.C., right? Not far from where we were."

Jenn turned to see the television better and watched with Steve.

"I'm standing a half block away from the residential parking lot of the Windermere Condominiums here in D.C. at the corner of 6th and Ferguson. If you look behind me, they are still cleaning up debris from this morning's explosion. Now, the police have yet to make an official statement, so we don't know what caused the accident, but the damage has been widespread. Let me get my cameraman to pan out across the parking lot." The camera looked out across a scene of total devastation. Over the visual, the news anchor spoke to the reporter.

"That's certainly a lot of damage. Have you learned anything new?"

"We're still searching for witnesses. One person told me he saw a man running through the parking lot seconds before the explosion, yelling at people to get down. We'd like to find this man, but we were also told he disappeared right after the explosion. Just walked off the scene. It has been confirmed that there are at least two casualties, one of whom is, tragically, a young child. We'll continue probing for answers and get back to you if we learn anything new."

The screen jumped back to the news anchor. They transitioned out of the segment, and a commercial started playing.

Jenn shook her head slowly. "That's so sad. You never know what could happen. One minute everything is fine, and then *pow*, your life's over." Steve and Tony traded glances. Jenn covered her mouth with a hand and squeezed her eyes shut. "Oh, I'm so sorry, I—"

"It's okay, Jenn," Steve interrupted. "We know what you meant. And it's true."

Ten minutes later, a young waitress brought their

food and set their plates on the table. The uneasy quiet returned, covering the table like an unwanted blanket. They all began to eat, occasionally sharing small talk. Steve caught a glimpse of Aretha wiping down a table while watching Tony with a concerned look. He traded a somber glance with her. The kid had just lost his mom. The one person who had been there to ensure he didn't stray too far from the nest until he could fly on his own. Where would he find that guidance now? When they were all done eating, Steve paid the check. They said their goodbyes and proceeded out the door to take Tony back to his uncle and aunt's house.

After dropping Tony off, they were about halfway to a motel when he spotted a car following close behind them. The high beams were turned on, obscuring the view of the driver. The hair on the back of Steve's neck rose up. "Looks like we have company. That may be Preston."

Jenn craned her neck back to look. "Oh shit."

"I'll take a few random turns to make sure."

"You really think it's Preston?" Jenn asked, anxiety creeping into her voice.

"Maybe. Are you buckled in tight?"

Jenn tugged on her seatbelt. "Yes, why?"

Steve jerked the wheel and turned to the left just before the traffic light turned red. The Camaro hugged the pavement, and the turn put them on the surface road that paralleled the highway. "Okay, my friend, I know this neighborhood better than you. Jenn, look in the glove box for a brown piece of paper with a number on it. The first three numbers are five-three-six."

The mystery car was still following, closing in fast. Its high beams were flashing on and off, occasionally blinding Steve until he adjusted his rearview mirror.

"Here it is."

"Dial it and hand me the phone, please."

He braked and made a sudden right turn off the surface road onto a side street. Jenn was caught off guard and had to brace herself on his shoulder.

"Damnit! Tell me before you do that."

"Pay attention!"

"I was trying to dial the number. Here, it's ringing." Her hands shook as she handed it to him. He made a tight left turn onto a two-lane highway and continued south, taking the phone from Jenn. The area they were now in was run down, with bars and wrecking yards lining the old two-lane highway.

After three rings, a voice on the other end answered with a simple "Yeah."

"T-Bone, this is Blake. I need a favor…"

After discussing a few details, Steve sped up, the Camaro's V8 roaring to life, and made a hard right turn onto a narrow side street. The following car barely made the turn, swerving wildly across the asphalt as its horn blared over and over.

"What are you doing?" Jenn barked while clutching the dashboard with both hands.

"Just hold on."

After a couple of blocks, he braked hard and made a skidding left turn into a gravel lot. The weathered sign on the decaying metal building read "JJ's Garage". The double door opened, and he sped inside, stopping just short of the rear exit.

The following sedan entered the lot and stopped one hundred feet from the door, revving its engine.

"Who's that big guy with all the tattoos?" Jenn

asked nervously.

"That's T-Bone. Stay in the car." She nodded her head and checked her door to see it was locked. Steve opened the car door and stood.

"It would have helped if you lost him before you got here," T-Bone offered dryly.

T-Bone came in at a good three hundred pounds. He was well over six feet tall, and his muscle mass would have put most prizefighters to shame. He was wearing stained blue jeans and a red tank top. The metal hanging around his neck would weigh down most people of lesser stature. The tattoos that covered his body ranged from fire-wreathed skulls to puppy dogs. His face was hardened, and other than his size, his crooked nose was the first thing most people noticed about him. The right nostril sat a good half-inch lower than the left, as if no one had bothered to reset it the last time it was broken.

Steve didn't respond to T-Bone's quip. He remained next to his car, staring out toward the sedan. T-Bone grabbed a nearby pipe and gestured to a group of equally mean-looking men playing cards nearby.

"Come on, let's go say hi."

Three of them followed T-Bone out the double door, and the group made their way toward the car. Two were clutching their waistlines.

Steve opened the car door, bent over, and made eye contact with Jenn. "Get down on the floor." She slipped down as low as she could. She'd be safer there, but more than that, Steve wasn't sure what was about to happen, and he didn't think Jenn needed to see it.

Luckily, as the menacing foursome approached the sedan, it turned and sped off. T-Bone and his friends walked back to the garage. A satisfied smile lifted from the big man's face, showing his two gold teeth. "Damn, dude. That her husband or something?" He let out a big chuckle, and his crew laughed along with him.

Steve grinned. "No, nothing like that. How you been?"

"I'm hangin' in there. Neighborhood's like it was when you left, though. I heard you're a PI now. That true?"

"Yeah. Couple of years now. Listen, we have to get going. Thanks, man. Stay safe."

"Hey, man. Don't be such a stranger. You kinda disappeared after you helped me bring justice to that piece of shit who killed my sister."

Steve glanced at Jenn. His mind drifted to the image of the man he'd delivered in the trunk of his car, and he didn't want Jenn thinking of him that way. He'd left that behind along with his career on the force. At least, he hoped so.

"Trying to live the quiet life, T-Bone. We gotta go, my friend."

T-Bone let out a quiet laugh. "Yeah. How's that working out for you?"

"Until recently, pretty good."

"Well, I don't even want to know what that was, brother. But he's probably waitin' down the road. You still know how to get out the back way?"

"Yeah. I remember."

Two men opened the double door on the backside of the building and the Camaro set out through the back of the lot. After they had cleared a maze of sharp turns and driven through a densely wooded area, they were back on the highway, heading south.

"I don't see him following us," Jenn offered, looking into the rearview mirror. Her mood was somber. "Those guys back there were scary. How did you know them?"

"From my time as a cop."

"What was all that back there?" Jenn asked.

"I told you I have friends in the neighborhood. T-Bone's just one of them. And he's one of the more mellow ones."

"Steve…what he said, about his sister—"

"It's nothing," he interrupted. "Don't worry about it." He could feel her staring at him, and when he saw the expression on her face, realization set in. "Shit…Charlie told you?"

She nodded meekly, and he took a deep breath, trying to figure out how to explain himself. As he opened his mouth, she laid a hand on his shoulder. "It's fine. You don't need to say anything. I understand…I think."

He stared intently at the road ahead, unsure how to continue. He decided it was best to change the topic. "You still have my phone?"

Jenn dug through her purse. "Here it is. It looks like you have a voicemail. You actually have two."

"Call it and see who it is."

Jenn punched in the voice mail number and hit call. She listened to the first message and punched in nine to save. "You're not gonna believe this. Here, I'll put it on speaker."

A thick Russian accent played in the car. "*Hello. My name is Kolya Zaytsev. I am the one who gave uncle papers.*"

"Did he say he gave Uncle Randall the papers?

Play it again. I could barely understand what he said."

"Okay," Jenn replied.

"Hello. My name is Kolya Zaytsev. I am the one who gave uncle papers. Please call me here, quickly."

"This is bullshit. Someone is just messing with us," Jenn said dismissively.

"I'm not sure what to make of it. What was the other message?"

Jenn keyed in the number to check the voicemail again and held it to her ear. As she listened to the message, her face turned pale.

Steve gave her a quick glance. "What is it?"

Jenn shook her head slowly and didn't respond at first. Her hands trembled as she gave Steve the phone. "Here, press one to listen. That was Jack."

"Steve, this is Jack. If you saw the car explosion on the news today, it was not an accident. It was a bomb, and Preston was behind it. Call me."

He tossed the phone onto the dash, shook his head, and squeezed the steering wheel, taking a deep breath and exhaling forcefully. "You okay?"

Jenn chewed her lip and fidgeted in her seat. "Now we have bombs. Great."

Steve wasn't sure what her tone implied. For some reason he couldn't read her, which was unusual for him. "I'm afraid we just crossed the Rubicon."

Jenn shook her head slowly and stared out the side window. "I'm tired. Where are we going to stay tonight? No one's following us now." Jenn's voice had a defeated tone.

"We'll get a room for the night, get some rest, and approach it with a fresh mind tomorrow."

Chapter 35

They continued another twenty miles and found a motel in a rural area south of Fort Worth that had a single room vacant. He parked the car behind the building to shield it from the highway. In their room there was only one queen bed with squeaky bedsprings. Jenn sat on it, staring at the wall. Her eyes were empty. Steve sat down next to her and draped his arm around her shoulder. They sat silently, each deep in thought. The only sound in the room was the loud air conditioner.

Steve whispered, "Hey. We're safe here. And we'll figure this out, I promise."

"Are you going to call the Russian-sounding guy? And Jack?"

"Yeah."

Jenn straightened her posture, wiped her eyes, and pushed her hair back with her fingers. "I'm good. Really. I'm going to go freshen up."

As Jenn made her way to the bathroom, Steve picked up his mobile phone and punched in the number to call the man with the Russian accent.

"This is Steve Blake. You left a—"

"Yes. Yes. Mr. Blake," he interrupted. "You have papers?"

His accent was heavy. Steve ignored the question. "How did you get my phone number?"

"Not important. Do you have papers?"

Steve pulled the phone from his face and took a deep breath before answering. "First, tell me what this is about."

"We should not talk over phone. I try to catch you in car earlier, but you drive like madman! Big thugs scare me away. Please, meet me, do not run again. Is very important. I will explain. And maybe you help me."

So that's what all that was about. Decision time. Is this guy legit? Or is he with Preston? Or the Feds? he thought. A long pause followed. "Okay, but we meet under my terms. And if I get a whiff of anything out of place, I won't show. Do you understand?"

"Yes. Is good. You tell me where and the time. I will be there."

After telling the man where to meet, and what time, he took a deep breath and pushed the disconnect button. While he was putting on his jacket, Jenn came back into the room and sat down on the bed.

"Now, before you say anything—"

"I heard you. Hell no," she cut him off. "Why after dark? I don't want to go back out. I'm done."

"You're not going."

"What do you mean I'm not going? I'm not staying here by myself."

"You'll be fine. No one knows we're here. And that wasn't Preston chasing us. It was him. The Russian sounding guy."

Jenn shook her head and rummaged through her purse for her hairbrush. She started brushing her hair like she was up against the clock. "Well, that's a relief, I guess. As I said before. It's your world—"

"I know, I know," he interrupted, "you're just living in it."

She put on a nervous smile. "Ha-ha," she said sarcastically. "Okay. But you call me when you get there and call me as soon as you're heading back. Promise me you'll do that."

"I will, I promise."

"How long of a drive is it?"

"Twenty minutes."

"I still don't like this."

"I don't either. But listen. I wouldn't leave you here if I didn't think it was safe."

****

Twenty minutes later, Steve arrived at the meeting point. He drove another mile to obscure the car, parked, then called Jenn to tell her he had arrived. The landscape around him was fairly desolate except for some cattle huddled together in a field. He proceeded on foot back to the meeting point and waited behind a large oak. From here, he'd be able to see anyone coming up the dirt road.

A flash of lightning danced across the distant sky, and an occasional gust of wind would throw pebbles and dirt against the trunk of the tree, creating a chorus with the branches rustling in the wind. As the storm drew closer, his anxiety grew. He didn't mind storms but didn't want this meeting to occur in blinding rain.

The road was lined on both sides with a shallow ditch and a barbed-wire fence, spotted with an occasional oak tree. It wasn't maintained by the county, but all things considered was in decent shape, with only an occasional pothole. It was mainly used for ranchers accessing their pastureland.

After thirty minutes had passed, headlights appeared, and the driver stopped his car fifty feet from where Steve was waiting. He recognized it as the sedan that had been chasing him earlier, verifying Kolya's story. A clap of thunder roared across the dark sky. To Steve's dismay, the storm was now overhead, and heavy rain began to fall.

Just as Steve had instructed, the man exited the vehicle, opened the trunk, and with his hands up he backed away twenty feet. Satisfied the man was alone, he stepped out from behind the tree carrying his flashlight in his left hand and his Glock in his right. He approached slowly, checking the vehicle's front and back seats, floorboards, and trunk. After double checking the man was alone, he instructed him to get back in his car. The man didn't respond. The rain was now coming down in sheets. Steve had to raise his voice.

"Get in the car."

Before they got in, they both swiveled their heads, looking for any signs of unwanted company. Once inside, Steve kept his gun trained on the man. The guy didn't seem to care and pulled a pack of cigarettes from the console. His hands shook as he fumbled to retrieve one. He lit it and inhaled heavily and exhaled, not bothering to crack a window.

"All right. First, who are you?" Steve asked.

"I am underwater explosive expert. Best in all Russia." His tone was boastful and angry at the same time.

"Why are you here?"

"I must stop them. They plan something disastrous."

310

"What, exactly? And who?"

"Hard to explain. Here, take." He handed Steve a sealed plastic folder. There were business-size papers inside, and seven plastic squares. He studied it briefly and placed it on the dashboard in front of him.

"What are they?"

"I go now. You talk to government. No, President. Say I want protected." He took another long drag from his cigarette and lightly coughed when he exhaled.

"Wait. You have to give me more. Why did you choose my uncle?"

"I can tell you nothing more. I leave."

"Bullshit. I'm rapidly losing my patience. If you want my help, I need to know everything."

"No. I go. Get out!"

Steve looked at the package, then back to the Russian. "All right. I'll go."

He stepped out into the pouring rain and tucked the folder into his waistband, pulling his shirt overtop to protect it. He started to head back to his own car, when he heard the roar of an engine. Spinning around, he saw the headlights of a charging Humvee. He dove into the ditch beside the road a split second before impact.

With a terrible crunch, the car's rear two wheels lifted into the air, and it spun into the barbed wire fence. The force of the car snapped a wooden fence pole like a matchstick, sending a group of cows scampering. The car teetered overtop of Steve on its front end for a moment, and he scrambled in the watery ditch to get out of the way as gravity won, pulling the car down right where he was lying. Even as he slipped and slid, he knew he wasn't going to be fast enough, and the undercarriage of the falling car was the last thing he saw before everything went black.

Chapter 36

September 25th

When Steve finally came to, the storm had passed, and his surroundings were lit by the eastern sun. The soft, muddy bottom of the ditch had saved his life, giving way just enough as the car crashed down on him so as to stop him from being crushed. If the rain had continued, he surely would have drowned, but apparently lady luck had been with him.

He fought off the pain, dug out from beneath the Russian's car, and stumbled to his feet. He cautiously approached the car. The doors were opened, and the glove box contents were strewn out on the floor. The Russian was nowhere to be found.

He started limping back to his Camaro. When he wiped his face with his shirttail, he discovered that he still had the folder he'd been given, and miraculously, the seal seemed to have survived the night, though the plastic squares looked broken. Once back in the driver's seat, he grabbed his phone from the glove box and punched in Jenn's number.

"Steve? Oh, my God. Where are you? I've been calling all night." Her voice was panic-stricken.

"I'm fine. I'll be back soon."

"I wasn't sure what to do. I didn't know if I should call the police. I paid for another night." Her voice trailed off, and gut-wrenching sobs filled the line.

"Just hold tight. I'll be there soon."

The drive back was uneventful, but everywhere he looked he expected shadowy figures to come charging out at him. When he got back to the motel room, Jenn was frantically pacing the floor. She met him with an icy stare. Her eyes were bloodshot from a lack of sleep.

He didn't say anything, just stared emotionlessly at her. His face and arms were plastered with mud, and his ruined clothes were still wet from the rain the night before. Jenn turned away and marched to the window. She flung the curtain open, crossed her arms over her chest, and stared out into the parking lot. "You scared the hell out of me," she said in a hoarse whisper. "I didn't know if you were…were lying dead in a ditch somewhere or…or whatever. Jesus, Steve."

"Well, you weren't far off, actually. I'm sorry. We were sitting in his car talking, and when I got out, someone rammed the car, and I woke up lying in the ditch underneath it."

Still staring out the window, her tone went flat. "We need to put an end to this. We need to get him before he gets us. Those people who rammed the car must not have seen you. Or you'd be dead, or missing, or…" Jenn gathered herself and wiped her nose. "Give me a minute to wash my face, and then you can take a shower. I'm still shaking."

"Come look at this when you're done." Steve opened the folder and pulled out three papers and the stack of thin, broken plastic squares. Jenn returned from the bathroom and sat down on the bed next to them.

"What are these?" he asked.

"Let me see. Those are floppy disks. You put

314

information on them so you can transfer it to another computer. They look to be in bad shape, though," Jenn said.

"They won't work now?" Steve asked.

"I doubt it."

"And what do you make of these?" He was holding three papers. They were filled with small holes spread out in erratic patterns. Jenn studied them for a moment.

"I have no idea."

Steve held them up toward the light.

"You see anything?" Jenn asked.

Steve turned to her. His eyes widened, and a grin began to surface.

"Holy shit, Jenn."

"What?"

"Maybe these are the papers Uncle Randall was waiting for."

"Let me see them." She studied them for a short moment. "Maybe." She held them up with one hand for emphasis. "Yes, you're right, these must be keys. Shane said there would be keys to place on the paper with the grid on it. Holy crap, Steve."

"We need a safe place to go. There have been too many close calls here. How do you feel about one more flight?"

****

September 26th — Los Angeles

"When's your friend coming?" Claudia asked Steve.

The skies were clear, and a gentle breeze swept across her estate. The two were sitting on the veranda that faced the estate's rear, drinking iced tea. Steve looked across the lawn and saw Jenn walking down the path toward the garden gazebo. She used her left hand to shield the sun from her eyes. He took a sip of his tea and set the glass back down on the table next to his chair.

Appearing almost out of nowhere, Jack approached from the side and sat across from the two. Steve was startled by how easily the man had approached undetected. "Speak of the devil. Claudia, this is the guy I told you about. Seems we have some mutual interest now. Jack, this is Claudia," Steve offered.

Claudia flashed a half-smile and gave a polite nod. "Can I get you something to drink, Jack?"

"No, thank you. How's she doing?" Jack asked, nodding toward the gazebo.

"She's doing good. Who do you think has the Russian?" Steve asked.

"The KGB, I'm sure. The only person inside the agency I still trusted is gone now. But she had told me the Russians had a KGB team here looking for him."

"Is that who Preston got with the car bomb?" Steve asked.

"Yes. I'm afraid so."

"My condolences," Steve said earnestly.

"It's part of the job but thank you. What about the Russian? What'd he have to say?"

"He was pretty wound up. He mentioned something about a large catastrophe looming. Those keys may hold all the answers. I hope, anyway. These were also in the folder. They're damaged, but maybe you know someone who can do something with them," Steve said, handing Jack the keys and a paper bag holding the floppy disks.

"This is what Randall was referring to in that note

he left you?"

"That's what I'm thinking," Steve replied.

"I doubt if anyone can extract anything off these disks. I'll hold on to them. And you said something about a senator?"

"Claudia has a friend on the Senate Intel Committee," Steve said, then turned to Claudia. "Have you had a chance to talk to him yet?"

"I have a call in to his office. If he knows what's good for him, he'll call soon," Claudia replied, eyebrows raised over a wicked smile. Steve and Jack traded glances.

"Okay, let's get started. Show me the other papers." Jack said.

Jenn joined the group as Steve showed Jack the strange grid. Everyone watched as he placed the keys over it one at a time. They searched his face for clues, but he showed no emotion.

"Ah-ha."

"What?" Jenn asked.

"These are coordinates. They must be important. My guess is they correspond to the circles someone drew," Jack said, pointing to the seabed map.

"That's what I was thinking, too," Jenn said.

"These other two keys have me baffled though." He placed the second key over the grid again. "Wait a minute…look," Jack said while pointing to the paper. "7 9 9 1 0 2 0 1. That could be a date; it's just backward. October 2nd, 1997."

"That's less than a week away," Claudia chimed in. "What does it mean?"

"I'm not sure," Jack said, moving to the third key. "Let's see what we have here."

Steve and Jenn both stared at the paper as he wrote out the corresponding letters—v e h c a k l o t. Jack looked up at them with a glint in his eye.

"That's a Russian name. Tolkachev spelled backward. See?"

"And?" Steve asked.

"Tolkachev was executed as a spy by the Russians in 1986, but what was he known for?" Jack asked.

Steve and Jenn traded glances. "You tell us," Steve replied.

"He was a Russian electronic engineer who provided documents to the CIA. Maybe it's a code name we gave to verify your recently abducted informant," Jack replied.

"So, the Russian was doing the same thing as that Tolko guy?" asked Jenn.

"What do you think the date means?" Claudia asked.

"Could have been the date he was supposed to give them to someone else. Or the date coincides with the papers some other way," Jack said.

Steve held up a hand. "Hold on. There's something we're missing. Something else at play here. Let's recap what we know. Helmer helped the Russians secretly map out some undersea vents. Our new Tolkachev somehow got his hands on these papers and wanted to hand them over to someone here. An American. He decided to give them to a well-known climatologist, my uncle…but why? So it wouldn't get brushed under the rug?"

"That's possible. He double-crossed his government, and they followed him to your meeting," Jack said, gesturing toward Steve.

Steve pointed to Jenn. "Didn't those reports we went over at your house say the vents were already making the ice melt?"

Jenn nodded. "Yes, but at a very slow rate. But—"

"They want to blow them," Jack interrupted. "On October 2nd. And those are the coordinates where to place the explosives. The pencil marks. Those fools want to blow the vents hoping magma will spew out and melt a large area of ice so they can swoop up there and claim the resources."

Jenn slowly shook her head. "That would cause an unspeakable environmental disaster. Surely, they wouldn't do that. They would know it would be a disaster. Wouldn't they?"

"You would think so. But there is still something we're missing. Camilla's involvement," Steve said.

"Steve. Does the name Kensington ring a bell?" Jack asked.

"Yes. He was here that first day we dropped in on Claudia. And we later learned he and Camilla were dating, or something, when Jenn called to fish for information on Project Green."

Claudia broke in. "He is a tricky one, not to be trusted. Mark rarely comes out from the shadows unless it suits him. He wanted me to attend some conference he was hosting. He later called wanting backing for some cockamamie scheme he had. Something about an icebreaker to do research in the Arctic circle."

Jack, Steve, and Jenn's heads spun in unison to Claudia. "Did I hear you right?" Jenn asked.

"Oh yes, but I turned him down, of course."

Steve looked to Jenn. "The icebreaker. Helmer's wife said he had blueprints for a ship, *The*

Polar…something."

"*The Polar Star*," Jenn finished.

Jack stood up and started pacing. "That must be what Preston was doing in Seattle. He was right by the docks; I should have seen it! That's why they want the papers so badly, they need the coordinates to know where the vents are. They're going to use *The Polar Star* to deliver the explosives."

"Wait," Steve said. "Camilla used Kensington to get access to the icebreaker for the Russians. That makes sense. Russia wouldn't want their own vessel in the area. If anyone found out it would link back to them. But what was Preston doing there? How is he connected?"

Jack took a piece of paper from his shirt pocket, unfolded it, and placed it on the table.

"I went back to my friend Sam's apartment after the bombing to see if I could find anything before they swept it. I found this buried in a desk drawer."

It was handwritten in black ink.

To whom it may concern,

I have been working secretly as the liaison between the Director of the CIA and the Secretary of State. In doing so, I have been privy to conversations between the two. CIA assets have been used domestically, which goes against the Foreign Intelligence Surveillance Act of 1978.

Kensington. Preston

"She told me about this just before she was killed. She was going to reach out to somebody who could help. She was onto something. And it looks like she linked Kensington and Preston somehow. Steve? What do you want to do?"

All eyes drifted to Steve. He said nothing for a few seconds, his stoic features giving no hint of what he was thinking.

"First things first. We need to find out where *The Polar Star* is and warn someone. Camilla said Jennings was leaving on an expedition soon, so it might already be to sea."

Claudia stood. "I'll call my senator again. We'll find that ship."

Steve stood over the letter and placed a finger on it.

"We need to fill in the blanks. There's a missing link. Someone powerful wanted your friend dead, Jack. Preston was just the delivery man."

"I have a sneaking suspicion that the Director of the CIA may be pulling the strings here," Jack said.

"Then I say we flush him out," Steve replied.

"I do have a plan, but it will take a team effort...and some money," Jack responded.

"How much do you need?" Claudia asked with a determined look on her face

Chapter 37

September 27th

Steve and Jenn sat silently in their rental car roughly a quarter-mile from Kensington's L.A. estate. The community park was coming to life, with nannies pushing expensive baby strollers and locals being led by their purebred dogs.

"Here he comes," Jenn announced as a van pulled up beside them. They both got out of the car and made their way to the van's back door. Jack was waiting inside. An array of electronics was mounted on the van's side wall, including two small television monitors. Jack put a headset on, flipped a few switches, and the electronics came to life. After turning a few knobs, the two monitors fired up.

"This will do just fine," Jack said.

"Wow. This looks complicated," Jenn commented.

"Not really. I installed two small cameras last night. That's what the monitors are for. And you use this switch to toggle between the two. I was also able to bug the phone. That's what the headphones are for. You use this knob to adjust the volume."

"Jack, I assume you had no problem getting in and out last night," Steve asked.

"Nope. Took me two minutes to bypass his security system."

"What's that?" Steve asked, pointing to a black box.

"It's a top-of-the-line recording device, a bug, and I planted it under the table where the phone sits. Hopefully, if anyone detects it, they'll take apart the phone and find the bug I planted there, not the one under the table. It will record up to eight hours on a loop."

"Can you listen in too?" Steve asked.

"Yes."

"Are we in range for this to work, or do we need to be closer?"

"No, this is fine for now. I would say two to three blocks will be the limit," Jack replied, then he sat back, crossed his arms, and studied the surveillance equipment. "Okay. Everything seems to be working. All we need to do is take the magnetic signs off the van. We'll need to do either four or eight-hour shifts. Doesn't matter to me."

Jenn said, "Eight. If we do four, we won't get any sleep."

Jack turned to Steve. "Steve?"

"I agree. I'll take the graveyard shift."

"Sounds like a plan. I'll see you around midnight then."

****

September 29th

Steve stretched his arms over his head and checked his watch. His large body was not suited well for the cramped confines of the van. *Finally,* he thought when Jenn rapped on the door. He unlocked it and let her in.

"Anything exciting happen?"

Steve stretched his arms and yawned. "Nope. Two

days now, and absolutely nothing. Around two a.m., everything went dark for about fifteen minutes. Maybe it was just a power surge."

"That's weird."

"I'll ask Jack to look at the equipment. He should be awake by now. Maybe we're approaching this wrong."

"What do you mean?"

"I don't know. Maybe they're on to us. Or there's nothing here. I need to get some sleep to think with a clear head."

"How soon do I need to move?"

"I've only been here thirty minutes, so you have some time."

"I hope this chicken stays good until lunch. I forgot to bring more ice," Jenn said while glancing at the cooler.

"There's still some ice in there. It'll be fine. Remember to use different places for your bathroom breaks."

"I will. That's become the highlight of my day. This surveillance stuff is mind-numbing. Here are the car keys. I'll see you later." Jenn handed him the keys to the rental, and he was off.

When Steve returned to the hotel, he walked to the restaurant and saw Jack eating breakfast at a table.

"Good morning. Have a seat," Jack said, gesturing to the empty chair across the table. A waitress approached with a glass of water and a menu. "So, I'm assuming you have nothing to tell me," Jack said.

"It was a quiet night. Again."

"I say we give it a few more days," Jack said.

"You need to look at the equipment when you get a

chance."

"Why? Something not working?"

"Everything's fine now, but around two, everything stopped working for about ten or fifteen minutes. I started to call you, but it came back, and I didn't want to wake you up. This happens to me sometimes when I'm surveilling someone. Just a glitch of…"

Jack had been raising his egg-filled fork to his mouth but had stopped halfway. "Call Jenn and tell her to get out of there. Now."

"Why…oh shit." Steve frantically dialed her number and held the phone to his ear. "She's not answering."

They both stood and bolted to the door. Once outside, they ran and jumped into the rental car. "This is not good. Try her again," Jack said.

Steve threw him the keys and redialed her number. "Still not answering. Drive fast."

When they arrived where the van was parked, Jack brought the car to a skidding stop. They both jumped out and raced over to find the rear doors swung open.

"She's gone. Damnit!" Steve said as he spun his head around, searching the area.

"If he has her, he'll call soon," Jack said.

"We both know what he wants," Steve said as he jumped into the car's driver's side. "Give me the keys."

"Wait…What do you want to do?"

"We don't know where she is, but we know where Kensington is."

"Steve. Take a deep breath. What are you going to do? Bust in his door? That won't help us one bit. We wait for him to call. That's all we can do at this point."

Steve slammed his hands down on the steering wheel and screamed.

Chapter 38

Steve was pacing in their hotel room, clutching his mobile phone like a lifeline. "How long are we going to just sit here and do nothing?"

"Steve, he's not going to hurt her. He took her to trade for the papers. We have to be patient."

"I swear to God. If he hurts her..." he paused when his phone chimed. He studied it for a short moment. He felt the proverbial ton of bricks hanging over his head, and that his control over the situation was waning. "It's her phone."

"Keep him calm...try not to be aggressive. Preston's got a short fuse," Jack advised.

Steve gave Jack a glance and lifted the phone to his ear. "Steve Blake."

"I have a simple proposition. The papers...for the girl."

Steve looked at Jack and saw him motioning with his hands to stay calm.

"Let me speak to her."

"She's sleeping, sorry."

"How do I know she's alive?"

"You'll just have to trust me. Now listen very carefully. There's an abandoned factory at two-eleven Industrial. The east side has a large double door. You'll see the number above it. Be there tonight at ten p.m. If you call the authorities or if I think anything is off...I'll cut her throat."

The line went dead, and Steve slammed his fist onto the room's dresser.

"What'd he say?"

"Tonight, ten p.m., two-eleven Industrial."

"Let's figure out how to handle this," Jack said, his tone reserved.

Steve clasped his fingers together over his head and began to pace again. "There's nothing to figure out. We give him the papers and bring Jenn home."

"Steve, it's not that simple. And if you were thinking clearly, you would realize that. He has no intention of you or Jenn walking out of there alive. Preston isn't keen on leaving witnesses. Plus, he may or may not assume I'm working with you. We have to think this thing through."

Steve took in a deep breath and exhaled. "What do you suggest then?"

"We scope out the area. It'll give me an idea of his plan. The location will tell me a lot. Steve…Steve, are you listening?"

"Yeah…yeah…sorry…should we…?"

"What?"

"Talk to Kensington."

"Really? What, we knock on his door, and when he answers, we ask hey, Mr. Kensington, do you have our friend Jenn hidden somewhere? We'd really appreciate it if you would return her."

Steve shook his head. "Just a thought."

"You're just not thinking clearly. Too personal. Look at you. You can't sit still for a minute. That is the last thing we need to do. Things could go from bad to real bad, real fast."

"Okay. Okay, I get it. What is your suggestion."

"Like I said, we scope out the place—"

"And then?" Steve interrupted. Jack pulled out a metal case from under the bed.

"I find a spot where I can monitor the front of the building, from which I can get down fast."

"What for?" Steve demanded, continuing to pace.

"Why don't you sit down? You're starting to make me nervous," Jack said. He opened the case and started pulling out gun parts, which he proceeded to assemble. Steve stopped pacing and observed. Jack noted his interest. "It's a rifle. With a scope."

"Yeah, I can see that. Do you know how to handle it?"

Twisting the final piece into place, Jack looked up and grinned.

****

As Steve approached, a clap of thunder rumbled overhead, shaking the decrepit, old factory. What was once a sprawling manufacturing area was now an area of empty buildings with leaky roofs and empty narrow streets filled with potholes. The large metal doors swayed as the wind picked up from the impending storm.

As he approached the massive doorway, he saw Jenn tied to a wooden chair in the center of the rusted metal building. He stopped when he saw her face. Her mouth was covered with duct tape. Her eyes were wide open, and she tried to call out to him, but he couldn't understand what she was saying.

Steve scanned the catwalks forty feet above for any sign of Preston. A vehicle was parked twenty feet behind Jenn with its lights on bright. "Jenn, I'm here," he called out.

He scanned the catwalks again, still no sign of Preston.

"All right, Preston. I'm here. I have the papers. Let's get this done."

When Steve was within twenty feet of her, he stopped again and noted her actions becoming more animated. She nodded her head furiously. Steve, again, strained to make out what she was saying. His heart wrenched seeing the panic in her eyes.

Just as it dawned on him, he felt the cold barrel of Preston's gun on his head. Preston reached down, took Steve's Glock from its holster, and threw it to the side. Then he took the folder of papers from Steve's hand and dropped it gently to the ground.

"Now go stand by your lady friend."

Where's Jack? he thought. Preston followed closely as Steve followed the command.

"Now, get down."

Steve hesitated. *Jack...this would be a good time to show up.*

"Oh, if you're wondering where your friend is...well, he won't be showing up anytime soon." Steve heard him slip something off his shoulder, and a moment later Jack's rifle clattered to the floor, skidding away from them.

Jack's words rang loud in Steve's mind...*he has no intention of letting you or Jenn walk out alive.*

"Just calm down. Can I untie her?" Not waiting for an answer, he reached down to the chair.

"No!"

Preston stepped forward menacingly. As soon as he was in range, Steve lunged sideways, grabbing

Preston's gun hand and forcing it downward. The gun discharged, sending a deafening percussion throughout the decaying metal building.

With both hands clamping down on Preston's gun hand, he pushed hard, toppling them both onto the floor. He slammed Preston's hand against the concrete, forcing the gun loose, then spun around and put Preston in a choke hold, squeezing with everything he had. Preston's face turned red. His eyes bulged from the force. He grabbed Steve's arm, attempting to separate it from his neck.

After a few seconds, he gave up, reached around his waist, pulled a four-inch knife from its sheath, and swung wildly. Steve's shoulder caught fire. Blood ran onto the floor. His body shuddered, and that was all Preston needed to break free. His field knife had done its job.

Breathing hard…sweat covering his body, Preston stood, knife in hand. He massaged his throat with his free hand and swayed as he fought to regain his balance. "I told you I'd cut her throat."

Steve fought to stay alert. He used all the energy he could muster and crawled to Jenn's side. He pressed down on the wound to slow the bleeding.

"Don't hurt her. She's not a threat. Please."

Preston let out a morbid laugh. "It's just business, my friend. You understand."

Steve watched in horror as Preston grabbed Jenn's hair and pulled back, exposing her neck. Suddenly, one of the vehicle's headlights dimmed, and Jack rushed from the shadows, striking Preston across the back with a two-foot-long piece of steel rebar. Preston cried out and dropped to a knee, his knife flying off into the darkness.

Jack stood there, wobbling on his feet. He had a nasty head wound, and his face and body were covered in blood. He raised the rebar for another strike, but it was clear that he was weak, and Preston easily rolled out of the way and then staggered to his feet. The three men stood for a moment, assessing the situation. Steve was right beside Preston's abandoned gun, Jack was a few feet from his rifle, and Preston stood equidistant between the papers and Steve's Glock. Preston looked toward the Glock, then toward the papers. Looking back at the trio, his eyes hardened. Then, simultaneously, they each dove for a weapon.

Three shots rang out almost in tandem. At first, Steve wasn't sure of the outcome, but a second later the Glock dropped from Preston's hand, blood flowed from his mouth, and his body collapsed to the floor. Steve wasn't sure which one of them had hit him, and he was pretty sure he wanted to leave it that way. By some miracle, no one else seemed to have been shot. Jack rolled over onto his back, breathing heavily. Still reeling from the knife wound, Steve stood and walked to Jenn's side.

"You ready?"

She nodded frantically, and he ripped the tape from her face and untied her. Jenn pulled his shirt back, exposing his wound. Without a thought, she reached down, ripped a swath from her shirt, and pressed it against the wound.

"Hold this over it and push down. I'll check on Jack."

By now, Jack was sitting up, holding a rag over his wound.

"Are you okay? Let me look at that."

"It's a pretty good gash. But I'll make it. How's he?" Jack asked, nodding toward Steve.

"I'm fine. My left arm is useless right now. But I'll be okay," Steve replied.

"Bullshit," Jenn retorted. "Let's get him in the car." She pulled Jack to his feet and helped him hobble over to Steve. Jenn grabbed Steve's right arm and flung it over her shoulder.

"Where the hell were you?" Steve asked Jack.

"He got the jump on me," Jack said reluctantly. He walked unsteadily over to where Preston's body lay and picked up the folder of papers, as well as Steve's Glock. "We really need to get going."

"What do we tell the doctor?" Jenn asked.

"I'll make up a story. Got mugged or something. They'll look into it, then quickly file it away," Steve said.

Chapter 39

September 30th

In the early hours of the morning, the three arrived back at Claudia's house. Jenn rang the doorbell, and Claudia promptly answered. Steve took note of the horrified look on her face. He felt her heavy gaze as she took a moment to study the trio. Steve's left arm was in a sling, and Jack's head had a large bandage on the back.

"Oh, finally, thank goodness."

Her attention quickly turned to Jenn. "Come here, darling. I'm so glad you're all right."

Steve and Jack followed as she took Jenn's hand and led her into the parlor. "Sit here, dear. Can I get you anything?"

"No…no…I'm fine." Her voice was soft, her demeanor hard to read.

"Why don't you lie down and rest," Steve offered.

"I'd like that. You'll be here, right?"

"Yes, I'm not going anywhere. Go rest."

Claudia waited until she left the room, and her demeanor suddenly shifted. "Now, how did she get taken with you two there with her?"

"I know, Claudia," Steve said.

An uncomfortable silence filled the room. "Well, I talked to Senator Johnson from the Intel committee this morning." She turned to Jack. "The friend you lost in that car bombing? She had contacted him and wanted to meet."

"What about?"

"He said it had to do with the CIA, and she wanted whistleblower status. But they never met; she was killed the day before they were supposed to get together."

Steve sat down on the sofa and adjusted his arm in the sling.

"How long will you need that?" Claudia asked, pointing to the sling.

"Just until the stitches are out," Steve replied dismissively. He quickly changed the subject. "Is your senator able to do something about *The Polar Star*?"

"He knows whom to alert. I hope it hasn't departed yet. So, where do we go now?" Claudia asked.

"There are a lot of things hanging over our heads right now. The abandoned factory where we left Preston will make an interesting crime scene for the cops. I just wish Jenn could remember more," Jack said.

"I'm going to get some tea for everyone. With what that poor girl has gone through, it's no surprise she remembers nothing."

"I just need some ice water, please. And you're right; our minds do have a way of doing that," Steve said.

Jack, who was still standing, rested the tips of his steepled fingers against his lips. "I've got an idea."

****

When Steve opened the bedroom door several hours later, Jenn was in bed, lying on her side, facing away from the door. She flinched when he gently touched her shoulder to wake her up.

"What time is it?" she asked, turning to look at him.

"It's almost seven. You've been sleeping since two," Steve replied.

"Oh God, don't stare at me like that."

"Like what?"

"Like I'm a China doll that's about to break. I'm fine," she assured him.

"It's just…if anything had happened to you…I couldn't…I mean, I'm the reason that you—" She cut him off by pressing her fingers to his lips.

"Steve, this wasn't your fault. It was my choice to help you, the whole way along. Okay?"

He couldn't bring himself to look her in the eye.

"Hey, Steve, look at me. It's not your fault. Got it?" He took a deep breath and met her gaze. As he gave a slight nod, a smile crept over his face. "Why are you grinning?" she asked.

"No reason. I'm just glad you're safe, I guess. Now get dressed. We want to talk to you downstairs."

"What about?"

"Just get dressed and come downstairs, please."

Steve studied her as she threw back her covers and hastily sat up on the side of the bed. After a moment, she walked to the bathroom and stared into the mirror. She grimaced at her reflection. Her face was slightly swollen, and her eyes looked hollow. He watched her stare at her reflection for a few more moments.

"Don't take too long. I'll see you downstairs."

Ten minutes later, she came down to find everyone gathered in the parlor.

Steve stood when she entered the room. "We have

an idea to help your memory. Jack?"

"Jenn, one of the things I do in the agency is sometimes I use hypnosis to help people remember things."

Jenn stood up abruptly. "Oh, hell no…"

"It's perfectly safe," Jack said.

Jenn locked her eyes on Steve. "I don't know."

Steve held up a hand and said reassuringly, "It's okay, Jenn. You won't do *anything* you don't want to do. But it might be helpful. Who knows what may have been said while you were sedated?"

Jenn moved toward the passageway that led into the kitchen. "Can we talk? Just you and me?"

"Sure, let's go into the kitchen."

Once the two were alone, Jenn paced back and forth, shaking her head. She stopped and crossed her arms.

"I'm not comfortable with this…this…hypnosis thing." She began to pace again. Steve studied her and remained quiet. "Well? Aren't you going to try to talk me into it?"

"Nope. It's your decision. I told you that you won't be expected to do anything you don't want to do. It's that simple."

"God, I hate it when you do that."

"Do what?"

"That…that…thing you do when…hell, I don't know what I'm saying. That look on your face that says you're right and…"

"Jenn. It may help, and it may not. All he's going to do is help you remember something about when you were being held. I'll be right there by your side."

"I don't know, Steve. I'm not sure I want to

remember."

"I'll support you in whatever decision you make. Think about it and let us know what you decide."

Steve walked back to the parlor and poured a glass of water. All eyes were on him. He looked up and shrugged. "She's thinking about it. I told her—" Steve stopped talking when Jenn appeared from the hallway.

"Do you really think this will work?" Jenn asked Jack.

"I've had tremendous success, but it's not one-hundred percent. Some people suppress their memories in a lockbox that their inner self simply won't allow to be opened. But it's worth trying," Jack explained.

Jenn let out a heavy sigh. "I'll do it as long as Steve can be with me."

"That's no problem. Just sit right here on the sofa. Steve will be right there with you." Jack said, his tone reassuring.

Jenn gave Steve a concerned look. He smiled and said, "I'm not leaving. Go ahead."

She sat on the sofa, and Steve sat next to her.

"Okay, are you comfortable?" Jack asked.

"I guess."

"Close your eyes and relax. Picture your muscles becoming loose and limp, and you're feeling completely relaxed. And as you relax, imagine yourself drifting on a calm, beautiful river. Now, you will feel my touch on your shoulder, and that is your cue to go deeper and deeper into your relaxed world." Jenn stopped fidgeting, and her breathing slowed. Jack softly touched her left shoulder. "Smell the air and relax more deeply. It feels good to relax and let it all go. Good. Now, let's go back to the place you were held. They tied your hands behind you."

Her breathing escalated. Jack touched her left shoulder again. "Imagine you're in the room looking down on everyone. Do you see yourself?"

"Yes."

"Good. What else do you see?"

"There's a concrete wall with a small photograph...I can't quite make it out...I think it's an American flag." She jerked suddenly and her breathing became panicked. "Someone's coming."

"Can you see who it is?"

"It's blurry, they're talking...no, arguing."

"What are they arguing about?"

"There's a taller one. He's angry they brought me here because we're on his property. The other one doesn't want to move me. They're closer to me now."

"Whom do you see talking?"

"The tall man, he looks familiar. He's wearing a suit. Gray hair. And there's the shorter man. He's got short hair. He's...he's wearing jeans and a white T-shirt."

"Now, Jenn. Let's concentrate on the taller man. Can you describe him?"

"He's tanned. And...and his clothes are...perfect...I think it's...yes...yes, it's the man that was at Claudia's house when we...when we were there."

Jack looked up at Steve. Steve took out his notepad from his shirt pocket, wrote down "Mark Kensington", and showed him.

"You're doing good, Jenn. Now let's concentrate on the shorter man. Can you describe him more?"

"Yes. The shorter one, he has a scar on his left

cheek…It's Preston."

"Good…good…what are they saying? Stay relaxed."

"Something about…about money. Preston, he wants more. Wait…the ship, they're talking about *The Polar Star*. They're saying it's out of their hands. Since they don't have the papers, they're going to sink the ship at sea…I smell rubbing alcohol. Oh no…no. He's going to inject me again, more ketamine. No, please, I'll be quiet, I swear, please don't!"

Her pulse accelerated, and she began to cry. Jack touched her shoulder.

"I-I can't…wait…wait. Another man is here now."

Jack glanced up at Steve. This had to be it, the missing link.

"Do you recognize the third man?" Jack asked, trying to keep the excitement out of his voice.

"No…it looks like he's shaking hands…with…with them both. I don't want to do this anymore." Her pulse increased again, and her face was suddenly fearful.

"You're almost there, Jenn. Relax, we are almost there. Did you hear the third man's name?"

She began to cry again. "I can't hear them. I'm scared. It's getting darker."

"Almost there, Jenn." Jack put a hand on her shoulder. "Take in a deep breath and relax."

"He says, 'Call me as soon as you have possession of the package.' "

"Did you hear his name, Jenn. Almost done."

"Yes…yes, I did."

"What was it? What was the third man's name?

"Robby. No…something that starts

with…Randy…yes…they called him Randy…Preston called him David…wait…Davis. He called him Davis."

Steve looked at Jack. "We good?"

Jack pressed further. "Anything else, Jenn?"

"They're still talking. It's heavy in here. I can't breathe. Slush fund." She began crying.

"Bring her out," Steve said, his tone blunt. Jack nodded.

"You did well, Jenn. In a moment I will snap my fingers, and you will wake, safe and sound. You can come back now." He snapped.

Steve watched as she slowly opened her eyes.

"Steve?"

"I'm right here." Steve glanced at Jack for guidance.

"Take her hand. She's fine."

"How'd I do?" she asked.

Steve smiled and replied, "You did great."

"I feel so…rested."

"That's common; your trance was deep," Jack assured her.

"How accurate is this?" Steve asked.

"She saw what she saw," Jack replied.

"This explains a lot, but it doesn't surprise me," Steve responded.

"I remember now," Jenn said.

"What do you mean?" asked Steve.

"Before I blacked out, they questioned Davis about where the money was coming from. He said a special slush fund."

Steve looked at Jack. "Slush fund?"

"Oh yeah. The CIA's budget is huge. They have all sorts of ways to stash away funds. Have you ever read a novel where CIA agents in the field give large amounts of cash to warlords or corrupt heads of state to garner favor? It's not far from the truth."

Steve shook his head. "Taxpayers' money out the window. So, what do you think about the ship?" Steve asked.

"Just as I thought. They may be packing the ship with explosives intent on scuttling it. I hope that's not the case, but it makes sense. If they don't know where the vents are, they might as well just take out one of our only polar vessels. If they happen to hit one of the vents, all the better, but it's a win-win for them. Things are starting to fall into place. Are you sure you want to go any further, Steve? I mean, this could, or should I say, *will* get messy."

"Can't back down now. Charlie called me today. Jennings's fingerprints were found at Kasandra's. These guys need to be exposed," Steve replied.

"All right then. I'll touch base with Claudia's senator, and then arrange a meeting with Davis. If we do this right, we'll put an end to this once and for all."

Chapter 40

October 2nd — Washington, D.C.

"It's not going to fall in on us, is it?"

Steve and Jack were standing outside the abandoned Stuart Motor Company Warehouse in Washington, D.C. The building was once a beacon of its age. It now resembled something that had been through a war. The effects of time and modernization had not been kind to it.

"Hopefully we can get one more day from her," Jack replied.

Steve watched Jack rest his hand on the rusted door and studied it as if the hairline cracks and peeling paint had meaning. "Did you know the CIA developed film from U2 flights over Cuba here? Back during the Cuban Missile crisis. Right up there on the third floor."

Steve stuffed his hands into his pockets, not sure if he was interested in getting a history lesson right then. "You said he'd be on the second floor, right?"

"He'll be on the second floor. Let's go."

Davis was waiting when Jack and Steve exited the stairwell. He was wearing a gray custom-fit suit with black loafers and was holding a metal briefcase in his left hand.

"Still a snappy dresser, I see," Jack remarked.

Davis scanned the area and shifted his weight. "Are

those the papers?"

"They are. Why all the fuss, Randy?" Jack asked.

"They aren't what they appear to be. I'll leave it at that. Now, let me have them, take the money, and we're all good."

"Just like that?"

"Just like that. We already discussed this. You're being compensated for all your troubles, and I get the papers." Randy opened the case and held it so Steve and Jack could see inside. "A million dollars." He closed it and slid it to Jack's feet.

Jack nodded to Steve, who tossed the package over, letting it fall just shy. As Davis bent over to pick it up, Jack asked, "Did you know about the kidnapping beforehand?"

Davis glanced over at Steve and didn't answer.

"It would be a big fucking deal if it got out."

Again, Davis didn't respond and turned toward the stairwell.

"She saw you…with Preston and Kensington. You were wearing a dark jacket. Oh, and brown walking shoes."

Davis stopped and turned back toward Jack. "Yes, things tend to spiral out of control sometimes. It's part of the game. But the end often does justify the means."

Randy turned back toward the stairs, and suddenly four heavily armed agents jumped out of the stairwell while six more rappelled in from above, yelling commands.

"Federal agents, show your hands!"

With a smirk on his face, Randy did as commanded and raised his arms.

A man in a dark suit appeared from behind the four

agents and slapped handcuffs on Davis's wrists. Then he turned to Jack and gestured to the briefcase. "Good job. Can I see that?" Jack handed him the case, and he opened it. He whistled when he saw the money inside. "You guys can go now. And Jack, you can come back to work when you're ready. But I'll need to interview both of you soon."

"No problem. What's the status of the ship?" Jack asked.

"The Coast Guard boarded it an hour ago. You were right. The thing was packed with explosives. You got caught up in some crazy shit, I'll tell you. And Mr. Blake, your accounts have been restored."

With that, the man turned and walked away.

"Who was that?" asked Steve.

"Hal Lewis. Deputy Director, FBI."

Chapter 41

"You're back!" When he returned to the hotel, Jenn flung her arms around Steve's neck, and he grimaced. "I'm sorry...I'm just glad you're back."

Steve grinned, seeing her smile. He shut the door behind him as he entered the room.

"So, did they get him?"

"Yep. Handcuffed and dragged off to jail."

"Good. Is there anything else you have to do?"

"Not sure, to be honest. But it's time to get back to our lives. I'm sure my horses miss me."

"I'm sure they do," Jenn replied, trying not to make eye contact.

"Hey, why the tears?" Steve gently wiped a tear from her cheek with his thumb.

"Oh, good grief, you know me. I'm just glad it's over."

"We'll have to make it a point not to be strangers. Are you going to stay at UCLA?"

"Well, actually...I have something to tell you. I've accepted a job at UTA. I'm going to be working in the new climate sciences department. Or rather, I am going to be putting it together."

"No kidding? When do you start?"

"Not until next year. Shane told them about the work I had been doing with Randall, and I interviewed over the phone. They called yesterday and offered me the position."

"So, we're going to practically be neighbors. I'll take you to dinner to celebrate when you get moved."

Jenn smiled. "I'd like that, Steve. I really would." An awkward pause followed.

Steve cleared his throat and glanced at his watch. "Well, you have a flight to catch. I guess your cab will be here soon."

"I know. Call me to let me know you made it back to Texas. And I'll do the same when I land at LAX."

"Okay, but I won't be arriving until late. I don't depart for another six hours."

"I don't care. So, I guess this is goodbye." She wrapped her arms around his neck. "I'll miss you, Steve Blake."

"I'll miss you too, Jenn Murphy."

He walked her down and made sure she got her cab. As he watched her drive away, his phone chirped. He pressed the answer button and lifted it to his ear. "Steve Blake."

"It's Jack. I wanted to give you an update. I gave those floppy disks to a friend who's pretty good at those kinds of things. If there's anything there, he'll find it."

"Keep me posted."

"I will. And get this. I called my contact at the Journal and asked him if he'd like some info. He's been in a dry spell and was chomping at the bit for a juicy story."

"You're really gonna do that?"

"Hell yeah. This needs to be out there. Otherwise, it may get swept under the rug."

"Thanks. I'll keep an eye out for the news. So, that guy said you're free to return to work. That's good."

"I'll need to see how all this plays out. I've been notified I'll have to give testimony to the Senate Intel committee."

"That should be interesting. Do you think Davis was telling the truth that his intentions were for Preston to get the papers from me and bring them to him?" Steve asked.

"My gut tells me that night at the hangar is when it all went haywire for Davis. I think that was his intention, but Preston went rogue."

Steve shook his head. "What happens to Kensington now?"

"Not sure. But there are a lot of wheels turning. Couldn't have done this without you, Blake. You're one hell of a detective."

Epilogue

One month later…

"Good morning, ladies," Steve said as he entered the barn. He opened the feed room and made the rounds. After all the feeding troughs were filled, he stood back and watched them eat. He wondered if they were still upset with him for sending them off, but he'd been back for a month now, and they couldn't hold it against him forever. He brushed the thought off and said goodbye. He had places to be.

He took the Camaro into town. He'd grown quite fond of driving it when he wasn't working, and he had to admit he enjoyed the impressed looks he got from folks on the street. Aretha's Diner was his first stop of the day. When he walked in, Aretha's eyes lit up and her bright smile stretched right across her face.

"My, my, my, look who just walked through my door," she crooned, as jovial as ever. "Come, give me a hug, Steve. Where have you been? And where's that lady friend of yours?"

"Well, she's—"

"You just sit right here," Aretha interrupted, "I'll get your breakfast started, then you can tell me all about it. Johnny, make Steve's favorite breakfast," she yelled out. She turned back to Steve, eyebrows raised. "Well?"

Steve chuckled. "You have the wrong idea. We're

not involved that way."

"Lord, forgive me for this…are you that stupid, Steve? I could see it all over her face. That girl's in love with you, and—"

His phone chirped, and he gratefully held up his finger to cut her off. "Steve Blake."

"Steve, this is Jack. Are you in front of a TV?"

"Yes."

"Turn it to CNN. Hurry."

"Hold on." He lowered the phone. "Aretha, turn to CNN, please."

"Breaking just now. This is Jeremy Shaw in Washington. This is an exclusive CNN video of what happened this morning just before six. The FBI conducted a raid on the home of former Senator Mark Kensington. He was taken into custody.

"Our sources tell us this has to do with the scandal that landed CIA Director Davis in jail about a month ago. If you follow Washington politics, you'll remember Senator Kensington of New York was caught in an influence-peddling scheme about ten years ago. He was never charged but lost his seat in the Senate.

"And on another front, we don't yet know if this is linked to the raids, but we have learned from the same source that the Secretary of State has summoned the Russian ambassador. The President has announced a press conference to begin at two this afternoon in the Rose Garden. I will tell you this, Karen, this is the craziest thing I've seen in all my years covering the capital.

We will stay on this, and unless something happens beforehand, we will see you at the news conference. Jeremy Shaw reporting live from the White House."

"Good. They got him. I wonder on what charges," Steve said into the phone.

"It turns out a grand jury was summoned a few weeks ago. Do you remember I said if there was anything on those disks, my guy would find it?"

"I do."

"Well, there was. And he did. I also made someone at the FBI aware of the bug we left at Kensington's house, and they put some agents in place to monitor it."

"So, the bug is still active? They haven't discovered it yet?"

"No. They never found it. The FBI put agents on it twenty-four hours a day. I'm surprised they found a judge who would sign off on it, but apparently, they did."

"So, the bad guys are going to pay."

"Because of you, Steve."

"I don't know about that. Do you know what was on the floppy disks?"

"Now, this became classified right away, but I'm going to tell you anyway. I think you earned the privilege. It was their whole plan. The Russian government. It laid out how they were going to use a submersible with a robotic arm to place the explosives. It also had the explosive types and the amounts listed. They designed and built the submersible just for the operation."

"Really? So the ship was a back up plan I guess."

"Yep. It also laid out what they were going to do afterward. All sorts of coordinates where they would drill, the whole nine yards. And all sorts of bullshit propaganda to cover for themselves. The world would have assumed it happened naturally. A natural disaster."

"Jesus. We're lucky the Russian defector showed up when he did."

"Yeah. From what my guy told me, a very small circle of people was involved. He figured whoever designed and built the submersible didn't know what it was really being built for."

"I'm assuming Davis was mentioned?"

"Nope. I think what sunk his ship was the bug. Preston first made a deal with Camilla to get *her* the papers. And yes, she was KGB. Preston involved Kensington because he needed money to operate with. Hotels, food, plane tickets, and such. Camilla refused to front him any money. He approached Kensington with it and offered to split it fifty-fifty."

"How much?"

"Two million. A million each. After Camilla got shot, their deal died with her, so Kensington approached Davis, offering to get the papers for *him*."

"And Davis had no problem using Preston? After what he pulled at the hangar? And killing your friend with a car bomb?" Steve asked.

"I can't prove it, but I'm thinking Davis is the one who ordered it. The car bomb. I knew the guy sometimes drew outside the lines, but this magnitude surprises even me."

"Thanks for the call and keep me informed. I'm hoping our names stay out of it."

"I don't think you and Jenn have anything to worry about. The bureau took over the investigation into Preston's death. They won't be looking any further than the KGB on that. It was good working with you, Blake. But let's make it a one-time thing. See ya 'round."

Steve pressed the disconnect button and set his phone on the table.

"What was that all about?" asked Aretha.

"Washington politics."

Steve downed his breakfast; it was as good as ever. When Aretha offered him a coffee refill, he looked at his watch. "I have to get going. Jenn's flight lands in an hour."

"I think it's lovely she wanted to be here for this. I got a bottle of the good stuff in the back. You wanna have a toast?"

"Nope. I'm sober now. Leaving it behind."

"That's great, Steve. That's really great. I'm proud of you. I still think you two make a great couple, though."

Steve waved a hand and grinned at her statement. "Stop trying to get me married off, Aretha. We're just friends."

"Sugar, I know that's what you keep saying. But—"

"Aretha?" Steve interrupted.

"Okay, okay. I'll just mind my own business."

"You and I both know that ain't never gonna happen," Steve quipped.

Aretha let out a big laugh, slapped him with a cleaning rag, and roared, "Now you just go on and get out of here before I…"

"But seriously, Aretha, thank you for all your support. I'll see you soon."

****

Steve, Jenn, and Tony were all waiting in the hallway together outside the courtroom when Sally arrived.

"Here she is," Steve said, nodding in her direction.

"The gang's all here, I see. You guys ready to do this?" Sally asked in her thick Southern drawl. She was dressed in her usual style, one of her trademark skirts and a revealing blouse.

"As ready as ever," Tony replied.

Steve gestured between the two women. "Sally, you've never met Jenn. Jenn, Sally. Sally, Jenn."

Jenn smiled and shook her hand. "I've heard a lot about you. Nice to finally meet you."

"Nice to meet you too, sweetie. Maybe we can get together sometime and compare notes on this guy," Sally taunted.

"Sally!" Steve jokingly scolded her.

"I'm just kidding. Let's go get this done. I'm so excited!"

After the court proceedings, they all gathered around the judge's table for pictures. Steve was now officially Tony's father.

As everyone headed to the exit, he smiled, observing Jenn cut up with Tony. He looked at Sally in a different way. He thought of how she'd always been there and never hesitated to help when he needed her. *She has been a true friend.*

He thought of Rebecca and how she'd want him to be happy. She'd want him to move on. He looked at Jenn again, and a peaceful feeling settled over him.

Tony held the door open for Jenn and Sally to exit, then turned to Steve. "You coming?"

"Yeah. I'll be right there."

After Tony closed the door, he reached into his jacket pocket and pulled out the envelope Tony's aunt had given him at Tony's uncle and aunt's house. He held it up, looked up toward the ceiling, and spoke softly.

"I did what you asked of me. Rest in peace, Kasandra." He took in a deep breath, and grinned. *My new ordinary world?*

A word about the author…

Joe is an airline pilot approaching retirement, an entrepreneur, and a debut novelist. He grew up outside Fort Worth, Texas, and now lives in northern Kentucky with his wife of thirty years, and Mabel Ann, their rescue dog. They are world travelers with the goal of visiting all seven continents only needing two more to accomplish their goal.

Thank you for purchasing
this publication of The Wild Rose Press, Inc.

For questions or more information
contact us at
info@thewildrosepress.com.

The Wild Rose Press, Inc.
www.thewildrosepress.com